What people are saying about …

# SOLITARY

"A Y.A. novel for the hip, the savvy, the thinker-outside-the-box—and anybody else who wants a great read. And don't even try to predict this one. Just hang on and let it take you straight into the real world of the newest generation."

**Nancy Rue,** best-selling author of
tween and young adult fiction

"*Solitary* is a cautionary tale, startling and suspenseful. The characters are unforgettable, the prose stark, and the dialogue masterful. Travis Thrasher is a versatile storyteller who walks his readers through life's uncertainties while leading them toward glimmers of hope."

**Eric Wilson,** New York Times
best-selling author of *Valley of Bones*

What people are saying about …

# TRAVIS THRASHER

"Thrasher just keeps getting better."

***Publishers Weekly***

"Each time I read a novel by Travis Thrasher, I close the cover and tell myself that was his best. But I find it hard to imagine that Thrasher is going to be able to surpass *Broken* easily.... The story literally drove me to tears. The action is intense, the pace breakneck, the aura of mystery palpable, the sense of the supernatural mysterious. In the vein of *Isolation* and *Ghostwriter*, Thrasher gives us *Broken*, one of his best stories to date."

**Josh Olds,** author and book reviewer
at Christian-Critic.BlogSpot.com

"How does Christian horror actually work? I'm not really sure, but fiction writer Travis Thrasher has successfully figured out the formula. He's combined Christian faith with a Stephen King–esque setting to explore what happens to your psyche when you are in the midst of a spiritual attack."

**Rachel Laudiero,** author and book reviewer
at OldMustyBooks.com

"Not only will *Isolation* scare you, it will also challenge your faith and remind you of the all-encompassing power of the love of our Savior. [Travis] only gets better with each new offering, and this latest tale might just be his best yet."

**Jake Chism,** author and book reviewer
at TheChristianManifesto.com

# ALSO BY TRAVIS THRASHER

THE SOLITARY TALES

# SOLITARY

A NOVEL

# TRAVIS
THRASHER

David C Cook®
*transforming lives together*

SOLITARY
Published by David C. Cook
4050 Lee Vance View
Colorado Springs, CO 80918 U.S.A.

David C. Cook Distribution Canada
55 Woodslee Avenue, Paris, Ontario, Canada N3L 3E5

David C. Cook U.K., Kingsway Communications
Eastbourne, East Sussex BN23 6NT, England

David C. Cook and the graphic circle C logo
are registered trademarks of Cook Communications Ministries.

This story is a work of fiction. All characters and events are the product of the author's
imagination. Any resemblance to any person, living or dead, is coincidental.

LCCN 2010928035
ISBN 978-1-4347-6421-8
eISBN 978-1-4347-0252-4

© 2010 Travis Thrasher

The Team: Don Pape, LoraBeth Norton, Amy Kiechlin,
Sarah Shultz, Erin Prater, and Karen Athen
Cover Photo: iStockphoto, royalty-free

Printed in the United States of America
First Edition 2010

1 2 3 4 5 6 7 8 9 10

052710

FOR ACA

To die by your side

Well, the pleasure—the

privilege is mine.

—"There Is a Light That Never

Goes Out" by The Smiths

# PREFACE

I run through the dark woods.

And I see her smile.

A branch swats me in the face. A limb tears my coat and cuts my arm. My foot pounds against something hard on the forest floor. The wound in my side from the tree branch still throbs, wet with blood. I know my hands are stained with it—some my own and some not.

I hear her laugh.

I'm sprinting uphill, sucking in air, sweating. It doesn't feel like December. It doesn't feel like New Year's Eve.

Then again, nothing feels right. Nothing has felt right since coming to this godforsaken place.

*The Devil is strong here,* her voice tells me. *Don't doubt this.*

I feel her hand in mine, gripping, shaking.

She said this would happen, but I still find myself in disbelief, hoping I'll wake up, hoping the cold is just from the night air in my tiny cabin bedroom.

I want to look at my watch, but I don't dare.

Every moment is precious. Every second counts.

Endless trees seem to hover in the dead of night, guarding what is just beyond. Wind whips their skeletal limbs, whips my face.

Three months ago, I didn't know her.

Three months ago, I didn't know anyone like her even existed.

Three months ago, I didn't have the faintest idea what the word *love* meant.

But as I run, I know this: I'm willing to give my life for this girl.

I'm sixteen with what I hope will be a long life ahead of me, but I'm willing to give it up, to give anything to let her live, to let her make it through this night.

"Please, God," I call out.

But God is a stranger to this place. And to my heart.

I recall her words.

"I believe."

But I don't. I never wanted to—not then and not now.

A light cuts through the woods.

I'm close.

The gun is still lodged in my hand.

I know I'll use it again. I don't care.

All I care about is getting to her.

The wind howls in anger.

There are forces at work stronger than the darkness. Stronger than the wind. Stronger than the night.

I know this now: There is evil in the world.

And in this place.

The glow gets brighter, illuminating the towering trees around me.

I don't slow down.

I'm almost at the top.

I'm ready to kill.

I'm ready to die.

I'm ready to rescue her.

My searing legs finally reach the top of the hill where the fire rages, where the winds whip, where the night sky explodes above me.

And then I see Jocelyn.

# 1. Half a Person

She's beautiful.

She stands behind two other girls, one a goth coated in black and the other a blonde with wild hair and an even wilder smile. She's waiting, looking off the other way, but I've already memorized her face.

I've never seen such a gorgeous girl in my life.

"You really like them?"

The goth girl is the one talking; maybe she's the leader of their pack. I've noticed them twice already today because of *her*, the one standing behind. The beautiful girl from my second-period English class, the one with the short skirt and long legs and endless brown hair, the one I can't stop thinking about. She's hard not to notice.

"Yeah, they're one of my favorites," I say.

We're talking about my T-shirt. It's my first day at this school, and I'd be lying if I said I didn't think carefully about what I was going to wear. It's about making a statement. I would have bet that 99 percent of the seven hundred kids at this high school wouldn't know what *Strangeways, Here We Come* refers to.

Guess I found the other 1 percent.

I was killing time after lunch by wandering aimlessly when the threesome stopped me. Goth Girl didn't even say hi; she just pointed at the murky photograph of a face on my shirt and asked where I got it. She made it sound like I stole it.

In a way, I did.

"You're not from around here, are you?" Goth Girl asks. Her sparkling blue eyes are almost hidden by her dark eyeliner.

"Did the shirt give it away?"

"Nobody in this school listens to The Smiths."

I can tell her that I stole the shirt, or in a sense borrowed it, but then she'd ask me from where.

I don't want to tell her I found it in a drawer in the house we're staying at. A cabin that belongs to my uncle. A cabin that used to belong to my uncle when he was around.

"I just moved here from a suburb of Chicago."

"What suburb?" the blonde asks.

"Libertyville. Ever hear of it?"

"No."

I see the beauty shift her gaze around to see who's watching. Which is surprising, because most attractive girls don't have to do that. They *know* that they're being watched.

This is different. Her glance is more suspicious. Or anxious.

"What's your name?"

"Chris Buckley."

"Good taste in music, Chris," Goth Girl says. "I'm Poe. This is Rachel. And she's Jocelyn."

That's right. Her name's Jocelyn. I remember now from class.

"What else do you like?"

"I got a wide taste in music."

"Do you like country?" Poe asks.

"No, not really."

"Good. I can't stand it. Nobody who wears a T-shirt like that would ever like country."

"I like country," Rachel says.

"Don't admit it. So why'd you move here?"

"Parents got a divorce. My mom decided to move, and I came with her."

"Did you have a choice?"

"Not really. But if I had I would've chosen to move with her."

"Why here?"

"Some of our family lives in Solitary. Or used to. I have a couple relatives in the area." I choose not to say anything about Uncle Robert. "My mother grew up around here."

"That sucks," Poe says.

"Solitary is a strange town," Rachel says with a grin that doesn't seem to ever go away. "Anybody tell you that?"

I shake my head.

"Joss lives here; we don't," Poe says. "I'm in Groveton; Rach lives on the border to South Carolina. Joss tries to hide out at our places because Solitary fits its name."

Jocelyn looks like she's late for something, her body language screaming that she wants to leave this conversation she's not a part of. She still hasn't acknowledged me.

"What year are you guys?"

"Juniors. I'm from New York—can't you tell? Rachel is from Colorado, and Jocelyn grew up here, though she wants to get out as soon as she can. You can join our club if you like."

Part of me wonders if I'd have to wear eyeliner and lipstick.

"Club?"

"The misfits. The outcasts. Whatever you want to call it."

"Not sure if I want to join that."

"You think you fit in?"

"No," I say.

"Good. We'll take you. You fit with us. Plus … you're cute."

Poe and her friends walk away.

Jocelyn finally glances at me and smiles the saddest smile I've ever seen.

I'd be lying if I said I wasn't terrified.

I might look cool and nonchalant and act cool and nonchalant, but inside I'm quaking.

I spent the first sixteen years of my life around the same people, going to the same school, living in the same town with the same two parents.

Now everything is different.

The students who pass me are nameless, faceless, expressionless. We are part of a herd that jumps to life like Pavlov's dog at the sound of the bell, which really is a low drone that sounds like it comes from some really bad sci-fi movie. It's hard to keep the cool and nonchalant thing going while staring in confusion at my school map. I probably look pathetic.

I dig out the computer printout of my class list and look at it again. I swear there's not a room called C305.

I must be looking pathetic, because she comes up to me and asks if I'm lost.

Jocelyn can actually talk.

"Yeah, kinda."

"Where are you going?"

"Some room—C305. Does that even exist?"

"Of course it does. I'm actually heading there right now." There's an attitude in her voice, as if she's ready for a fight even if one's not coming.

"History?"

She nods.

"Second class together," I say, which elicits a polite and slightly annoyed smile.

She explains to me how the rooms are organized, with C stuck between A and B for some crazy reason. But I don't really hear the words she's saying. I look at her and wonder if she can see me blushing. Other kids are staring at me now for the first time today. They look at Jocelyn and look at me—curious, critical, cutting. I wonder if I'm imagining it.

After a minute of this, I stare off a kid who looks like I threw manure in his face.

"Not the friendliest bunch of people, are they?" I ask.

"People here don't like outsiders."

"They didn't even notice me until now."

She nods and looks away, as if this is her fault. Her hair, so thick and straight, shimmers all the way past her shoulders. I could stare at her all day long.

"Glad you're in some of my classes."

"I'm sure you are," she says.

We reach the room.

"Well, thanks."

"No problem."

She says it the way an upperclassmen might answer a freshman.

Or an older sister her bratty brother. I want to say something witty, but nothing comes to mind.

I'm sure I'm not the first guy she's left speechless.


Every class I'm introduced to seems more and more unimpressed.

"This is Christopher Buckley from Chicago, Illinois," the teachers say, in case anybody doesn't know where Chicago is.

In case anybody wonders who the new breathing slab of human is, stuck in the middle of the room.

A redheaded girl with a giant nose stares at me, then glances at my shirt as if I have food smeared all over it. She rolls her eyes and then looks away.

Glancing down at my shirt makes me think of a song by The Smiths, "Half a Person."

That's how I feel.

I've never been the most popular kid in school. I'm a soccer player in a football world. My parents never had an abundance of money. I'm not overly good looking or overly smart or overly anything, to be honest. Just decent looking and decent at sports and decent at school. But decent doesn't get you far. Most of the time you need to be the best at one thing and stick to it.

I think about this as I notice more unfamiliar faces. A kid who looks like he hasn't bathed for a week. An oily-faced girl who looks miserable. A guy with tattoos who isn't even pretending to listen.

I never really fit in back in Libertyville, so how in the world am I going to fit in here?

Two more years of high school.

I don't want to think about it.

As the teacher drones on about American history and I reflect on my own history, my eyes find her.

I see her glancing my way.

For a long moment, neither of us look away.

For that long moment, it's just the two of us in the room.

Her glance is strong and tough. It's almost as if she's telling me to remain the same, as if she's saying, *Don't let them get you down.*

Suddenly, I have this amazingly crazy thought: I'm glad I'm here.


I have to fight to get out of the room to catch up to Jocelyn.

I've had forty minutes to think of exactly what I want to say, but by the time I catch up to her, all that comes out is "hey."

She nods.

Those eyes cripple me. I'm not trying to sound cheesy—they do. They bind my tongue.

For an awkward sixty seconds, the longest minute of my sixteen years, I walk the hallway beside her. We reach the girls' room, and she opens the door and goes inside. I stand there for a second, wondering if I should wait for her, then feeling stupid and ridiculous, wondering why I'm turning into a head of lettuce around a stranger I just met.

But I know exactly why.

As I head down the hallway, toward some other room with some other teacher unveiling some other plan to educate us, I feel someone grab my arm.

"You don't want to mess with that."

I wonder if I heard him right. Did he say *that* or *her?*

I turn and see a short kid with messy brown hair and a pimply face. I gotta be honest—it's been a while since I'd seen a kid with this many pimples. Doctors have things you can do for that. The word *pus* comes to mind.

"Mess with what?"

"Jocelyn. If I were you, I wouldn't entertain such thoughts."

Who is this kid, and what's he talking about?

And what teenager says, "I wouldn't entertain such thoughts"?

"What thoughts would those be?"

"Don't be a wise guy."

Pimple Boy sounds like the wise guy, with a weaselly voice that seems like it's going to deliver a punch line any second.

"What are you talking about?"

"Look, I'm just warning you. I've seen it happen before. I'm nobody, okay, and nobodies can get away with some things. And you look like a decent guy, so I'm just telling you."

"Telling me what?"

"Not to take a fancy with the lady."

Did he just say that in an accent that sounded British, or is it my imagination?

"I was just walking with her down the hallway."

"Yeah. Okay. Then I'll see you later."

"Wait. Hold on," I say. "Is she taken or something?"

"Yeah. She's spoken for. And has been for some time."

Pimple Boy says this the way he might tell me that my mother is dying.

It's bizarre.

And a bit spooky.

I realize that Harrington County High in Solitary, North Carolina, is a long way away from Libertyville.

I think about what the odd kid just told me.

This is probably bad.

Because one thing in my life has been a constant. You can ask my mother or father, and they'd agree.

I don't like being told what to do.

## 2. Milk at Midnight

The scream is loud and low and scares me right out of bed.

I fumble in the darkness, trying to remember where I am, why it's so cold, and why the ceiling is slanted and hitting my head as I stand.

I can see the cold moonlight reflecting off trees that wave to me through the window.

Another scream comes, and this time I wonder if it's Mom. Yet it doesn't sound like her.

It doesn't sound human.

I race out the door and down the stairs and hear another scream, and this time I know it's Mom.

The light in her bedroom blinds me. I find her in the corner of the room, shaking, her hands waving at something in the air, her eyes glaring.

She sees me and screams again.

I've never heard a bloodcurdling scream before in my life, but now I know where they got the name.

I hold her in my arms.

"Mom. It's me. Mom. It's Chris. Mom."

I say this over and over again as I hold her. It feels strange, I think, that this person so much shorter and smaller than me is my mother.

Eventually she calms down. Then starts to cry.

"I'm sorry."

"It's okay."

We sit at the small breakfast-dinner table. She's drinking a glass of milk.

"I hope I didn't scare you," Mom says.

"It takes a lot to scare me."

She knows this is true.

"What were you dreaming about?" I ask.

"The thing is … I don't … I didn't feel like I was dreaming. I know I was. It's just … it felt so real."

"What?"

Mom looks at me, then shakes her head.

"I don't know. It's nothing."

But the look on her pale face says something else. Maybe she's not lying. Maybe she just doesn't want to say because she thinks it might scare me.

Or make me scared about her sanity.

~~~~~~

My mom's not crazy. In fact, she's the sanest person I've met in this insane world.

My dad's the crazy one. Crazy for not loving her, crazy for leaving her, crazy for letting the divorce happen.

I don't want to talk about him or them. I want to talk about her. Tara Buckley is a cool name if you ask me. I like Chris, but I love Tara. It sounds both classic Southern and also modern and hip. Buckley is my dad's last name, but Mom is going to keep it. She lost enough in the divorce. She decided she'd stick with the name she'd carried around for eighteen years.

Mom is thirty-nine but looks ten years younger. If I had a dollar for every time someone has expressed disbelief that she is my mom … well, I'd be a rich kid. Which at this point in life would be nice. I think she's beautiful.

She used to complain about her upcoming birthday—the big four-oh—until she had other, more pressing things to think about. Sitting across the table from her, I see dark lines under her eyes. They're new. So is the lack of spark in her green eyes. And how thin she looks. And how faded her blonde hair seems.

I notice all these things now under the cold light above our little table. The first thing that I'd like to replace about this tiny little cabin are the lights. They seem like they'd be more appropriate in a dank prison than in a cabin nestled in the mountains of North Carolina.

The cabin is small. It doesn't have the dining room over here and the family room over there and all that. Basically, when you enter the cabin, you have the living room and dining room and kitchen all to one side. It's small. Cozy, my mother said. It had been large enough for Uncle Robert, but it was never meant to be a place a family lived in.

But it was the first, and only, place she thought of going after the divorce was final.

Mom grew up around Solitary, though she says she doesn't really remember it much as a kid. I wonder why she would want to come back to a place this remote, especially if she doesn't remember much about it. But she said that it's the only place where she still has family.

If you can really call them that.

The only *real* family member is Robert, and he's been missing for over a year. Sometimes I think she came back to find her brother and take him away from Solitary. Then again, I think a lot of things.

My mom is strong. At least, so far she's been strong. I know that deep down, underneath it all, she's sad. But sadness gets you nowhere in life. I think she would say that if forced to.

Sitting across from my mom, the lady known as Tara Buckley who has come to live in a cabin her brother abandoned for some unknown reason, I wonder if there will be more nightmares.

And I wonder what sort of visions brought out the screams.


## 3. NEWT


Have you ever seen someone swatted? Not struck in anger or patted in amusement, but literally swatted like a fly?

I'm in the hallway and still don't believe what I just saw.

It's Friday afternoon, and the hallways of Harrington High feel a little more energetic than usual. I think it's because everybody knows they're about to be let out, to have a nice two-day break. The thought of being away from this school is promising, but what kind of weekend awaits me is a whole other issue.

I'm pondering this as I see a pack of four guys walk up behind a small kid. They're wearing smiles on their ugly faces. One of them takes the palm of his hand and bats it across the kid's head, sending him sprawling onto the floor.

They just keep walking by.

Meanwhile, I stop.

And then I resume walking, toward the four big guys, toward the kid now picking up the pieces to his glasses.

As I'm about to help the kid, the swatter turns and blocks my way.

"Got a problem?"

Man, is this kid ugly. A big meaty face with large pork chops for cheeks stares me down. His eyes look like something in a frying pan; his forehead is dotted with sweat; his AC/DC T-shirt is far too much of a cliché.

"That explains it," I say, moving past him and bending over to help the kid.

I feel a hand on my shoulder, a strong hand that pulls me back.

"Why don't you just leave now?"

Something in me just, I don't know … ignites. Or explodes.

"You know what I think?" I say.

"I don't care what you think."

"I think that if I was born with such a homely face, I'd probably go around hitting people too."

The guy blinks several times, as if he's trying to compute what I just said.

I probably should try to figure it out myself, but instead my mouth keeps rambling. "What's the point? There are four of you. And do you even know him?"

"That's Newt," says a tall, skinny kid in the background. The rest of them laugh.

I turn and really see Newt for the first time. Something on his face startles me—did that cut on his cheek just happen? Then I realize that it's not a cut. It's a long, deep, bright red scar.

"Hey. I'm Chris."

"You're the new kid," says the big sweaty guy, hovering in my face.

"Are you the school bully? I've been waiting for one to pop up."

"Man, you don't even want to begin to mess with me."

"No, to be honest, I don't. Because you're bigger than me and sure, you could probably beat me up. But I can run faster than you because it looks like you've been wolfing down a little too much fast food."

Turns out Newt isn't the only one red faced. This guy is beet red.

There's probably a fifty-fifty chance I get decked, but for some reason, the big red-faced guy plays it cool.

It's about the guys behind him, about saving face.

Plus, I'm new. For all he knows, I'm a cage-fighting champion. He doesn't know that I've been in two fights in my life, and both of those I lost. Bad.

I help Newt to his feet. He's going to need a new pair of glasses.

Newt looks about ten, he's nerdy, and I can't help but feel sorry for him.

I can't stand bullies. I can stand a lot of things in life, but not people that pick on the helpless. Sad to say, Newt really fits that category.

Red-faced Ugly Boy still glares at me. "I'm going to tell you this one time and one time only: You come across my path again and I'll kill you."

"Fine. Let's make an agreement. I see you, and I walk the other way. I'll avoid you like the plague. But only if you don't go around acting like some hideous high school stereotype."

There the blinking goes again. I can see his brain not computing.

"I'm serious."

"Yeah, good," I say. "I am too."

"You have no idea where you are or who I am, do you?"

"Well, let's see. This is the backside of nowhere. So yes, I have an idea of where I am. And you're what crawled out of that backside."

This does it. The big guy lunges at me.

At that moment Mr. Meiners, my history teacher, walks past and breaks up the one-sided fight. He ends up taking a fist alongside his face before settling the guy down.

"Gus, you get out of here. Now! Boys, break's over."

Mr. Meiners has fire in his eyes and his voice. It looks as though he and Gus have butted heads before.

Gus looks at me and grits his teeth and starts walking away.

Where is he going? Is he just walking away after hitting a teacher? And is his name really *Gus?* I mean, come on.

The other boys leave me with Mr. Meiners and a paralyzed Newt.

"Newt, you okay?" the teacher asks. "What happened?"

"Yes, sure, I'm fine." Newt has a high-pitched voice that doesn't fit his obstinate tone.

"They were picking on him," I say.

"I'm fine," Newt says again. "Really fine."

"Look, Chris. You don't want to get involved with Gus."

"I wasn't trying to."

"No, I mean you *don't* want to get involved with him, okay? I'm serious." Mr. Meiners sighs and rubs his bearded jaw. "He's got a pretty good right hook."

"Who is he? Where I come from, kids don't get away with slugging their teachers."

"Yeah, well, that's where you come from. Gus isn't the one I'm afraid of."

I wait for more, but more doesn't come.

"You seem like a good kid," Mr. Meiners says. "Guys like Gus aren't."

I nod.

"Be careful, okay? You too, Newt."

Mr. Meiners walks away.

I'm left with the short kid with the scar on his cheek.

"So is this a regular thing? Gus giving you a hard time?"

"He means it," Newt says, looking at me with strange, wandering eyes. "About Gus."

"What about Gus?"

"It's his father."

"And who is his father?" I ask.

"Ichor Staunch."

It sounds like *ick* and *cur* put together.

"Ichor what? Is that even a name?"

"He owns most of the town."

"Does that include the teachers?"

"You don't want to mess with him." Newt is playing with his glasses.

"His last name sounds like Stench. Kinda fitting, huh?"

"I guess I should thank you, but I don't want to thank you for being stupid."

I look at Newt. "What year are you?"

"I'm a sophomore. I know I look younger."

"Why was I being stupid?"

"Because if you're going to mess with someone, you should first know who you're messing with."

"I've seen a hundred guys like Stenchy-boy before."

"No, you haven't. Not like Gus."

"I'll avoid him, no problem."

"Good. Because as much as I'd like to return the favor, I don't believe there's anything I—or anybody—could do for you."

With that ominous little warning, Newt walks away.

I can't help but laugh, shaking my head.

And as I start to walk to my class, I see a figure in the doorway. Jocelyn.

For a moment I stop, seeing the look on her face.

"Hi," I say.

*Lame.*

She looks at me and smiles, as if she's about to say something. But then she walks away.

I'm left there in the hallway, stumped, confused, but feeling like something just happened here.

I just can't really explain what.

## 4. SOLITARY

The beast lies in the middle of the street as if he's guarding the town.

I slow my bike down to a halt. It's a German shepherd, mostly black, with cold, menacing eyes. They bear down on me, daring me to pass.

I glance around for an owner, but there's nobody around.

A car coming the other way slows down and swerves around the dog, as if he has the right-of-way. The driver glares at me like I'm doing something wrong.

I pedal my bike toward the sidewalk, and then I hear it: the deep gargle of a growl.

The German shepherd stands.

Another car passes and honks at the dog, but the big brute appears to be more annoyed than anything else.

I get off the bike and try to roll it onto the sidewalk next to a small hardware store.

This time the dog unleashes a bark that is more like a sergeant shouting out an order.

He really doesn't want me around here.

I'm starting to reconsider my trip into Solitary and seriously
thinking about turning the bike around.

Until I see the man.

A big guy—hulking, swaggering—with reddish hair and a gray-
ish red beard walks out of the woods and across the tracks on my left
toward the street. I wonder if the long trench coat he's wearing came
from a thrift store selling vintage items from the 1930s.

He calls out in a voice even scarier than the dog's, and instantly
the German shepherd rushes to the man's side.

Two pairs of grim eyes now look at me as if I did something
wrong. I wave at the guy, then feel stupid for doing so and continue
on through the main section of downtown Solitary.


I wonder again why my mom chose to come back to Solitary.

There's nothing here to come back to.

The first time we drove through downtown she seemed to
barely remember it. She left when she was ten years old, the year
her mother died. Her father took Mom and her older brother and
headed north.

North proved to be tough for the family. Very tough indeed.

Strange that Solitary didn't mean enough for her to come and
visit—not even once—yet it's the place she moves back to.

Sometimes I don't think she wanted to move so much as to hide.
And this is the place to do it.

So far I haven't seen anything I recognize. No McDonald's or
Subway or Starbucks or chain of any kind. Not just downtown, but
anywhere.

Surely North Carolina has chains somewhere. Give me a big, fat Wal-Mart and a Whopper, and I'll be a little less nervous.

The downtown area consists of one block. A diner, a sheriff's office that looks like the one off that show with the kid named Opie, a place to get your hair cut (back home we call those salons, but this is no salon), a bookstore, a bank, a pub. A few other shops. They're all in various brick buildings, some beige, all polished and pristine. They look old and vintage, classy and clean.

Yet the place also looks abandoned.

Other than the shady character I just saw retrieving his dog, I don't see anybody else.

It's the middle of a Saturday. Where is everyone?

Our house is on the outskirts of Solitary, about ten minutes south of town, farther up in the rolling hills. The closest stores—gas, grocery, you name it—are all right here. On the gravel road our house stands on there's nothing except dense woods and a gushing creek cut down the hill that drops off from the main road.

Just as I lock up my bike and stand back up, I see her.

Jocelyn opens the door and steps inside the bookstore.

And I begin to think that I might be the luckiest soul alive.


"You don't have to hide," the voice says. "I saw you when you walked in."

I'm standing in front of a wall of books labeled SELF HELP. I turn and see Jocelyn walking over to another aisle in the store.

I decide it's impossible to pretend I just somehow wandered into The Corner Nook, a bookstore and café on the edge of the intersection off Main Street. I'm not looking for a book, and I don't drink coffee.

I find Jocelyn browsing through a shelf of books. A dark waterfall of hair seems to rush over the back of her T-shirt. Then I notice something startling.

A round, colorful tattoo on her inner forearm.

"Much of a reader?" she asks without looking at me.

"Not really."

"That's a shame."

"Looking for a book?"

"Either that or I'm deep in thought staring at the shelf in front of me."

I feel pretty stupid. For the second time this girl makes me feel like an idiot.

"I come in here all the time trying to find new authors," she says. "Sometimes I'm lucky."

She's holding a book in her hand, but I can't see the cover.

"So what'd you find?"

"Nothing."

"C'mon. What is it?"

Jocelyn looks at me, annoyed and unwilling to continue to play a game. "There. Happy now?"

It's a paperback novel with two figures embracing in what looks like more than just a kiss. It's called *Passionate Moon*.

I can't help but laugh.

"Looks like deep literature."

"I like all types of books, but I'm willing to admit it. I like romance. Even the slightly smutty kind."

"Oh, just *slightly* smutty."

"Did you come in here to make fun of me?"

*Actually, I came in here to admire you.*

"No."

"It's Chris, right?"

I nod.

"English-and-history Chris."

I nod again. Her hazel eyes seem to glow as she stares at me.

"Have a good first week?"

"Yeah. Most of my classes are pretty good. Well, English and history are."

"Nice."

"What?"

She goes back to looking at books.

"What'd I say?"

"Nice line."

"It wasn't a line—I was just being honest."

"Honesty can get you in trouble," she says.

"Yeah, I guess. But you never know if you'll have another opportunity to say the things you think but might not want to share."

Okay, I don't know where that came from. Getting past the initial awkwardness of standing here in front of Jocelyn, I feel more myself. But even I don't understand where *that* line came from.

It's like meeting someone famous. You get all tense and worked up and want to say the right thing even though there really is no such thing as the right thing....

Something in her face changes.

Her expression softens.

Just for a split moment.

But I see it. And it's something she can't erase or take back.

She turns her back, looking at more books.

And suddenly I feel stupid.

My embarrassment ends quickly with a ragged "Joss" yelled across the bookstore.

I turn and see a scraggly guy with watery eyes and dark bags underneath them. He's got a terrible drawl, like he's faking it. That's how bad it sounds.

I see skin on a tattooed arm that almost looks like it's falling off the bone. A hand is waving at her like a dog.

The guy curses and calls out for her again. I look at her and see yet another face.

First there was confident, beautiful Jocelyn, the one who strides around the school hallways ignoring everybody else. Then, for that brief second, there was soft Jocelyn. Friendly. Nice.

And now there's scared Jocelyn.

I see the color drain from her beautiful face.

"Excuse me," she says as she hands me the romance novel and rushes past to the front of the store.

The skinny guy, at least in his thirties or maybe early forties, wearing jeans and dirty boots and an equally dirty T-shirt, starts walking toward me, ignoring Jocelyn. She speaks to him, but he keeps coming my way.

The messy remnants of a half-grown beard and red eyes are suddenly in my face.

And I smell him.

He smells like too much liquor.

I know what that smells like.

"What are you doing?" he barks at me.

Jocelyn grabs the man's arm, and he backhands her across the cheek.

I stop breathing.

I've seen people hit before—guys hitting other guys. Just saw it happen this past week, in fact. But never have I seen someone strike with such malice, and never, ever have I seen anyone hit a girl.

*He struck her on her face. That sweet, perfect face.*

"What's your name?" he demands.

Everything in me wants to run. I should stand up and fight him, fight for her, but I can't. I'm taller than this guy and probably weigh the same, but the way he just slapped Jocelyn and the fire in those eyes and the smell under his breath....

He reminds me of the craziness I've seen on some cop shows, the kind of cranked idiot who drives his car into someone else's living room, then continues to bolt through the neighborhood without a single injury or clue.

"I said, 'What's your name?'"

"Leave him alone," Jocelyn says.

"Are you okay?" I ask her, finally breathing, finally doing something.

"She's more than okay," the guy says with a low whisper. "But you'll never know."

He smiles at me, and I see a chipped tooth.

I'm not kidding.

This has gotta be a bad dream.

He turns and takes Jocelyn by the arm and yanks her ahead, toward the door.

She doesn't turn around.

I want to follow, but I can't.

I feel like sludge.

I want to follow, but I'm too scared.

And I don't know what I'd do if I reached her.

# 5. THE WOODS

I can't stop thinking about her.

Sometimes drowning out the world with music helps, but not in this case. Every song I scroll to on my iPod seems to fit Jocelyn.

I wonder what happened to her after that guy pulled her out of the bookstore.

I wonder what she'll say when I see her tomorrow at school.

I wonder who he was, if he's the reason she's supposedly "spoken for."

I wonder if she'd ever go out with a guy like me.

I wonder what I'd do if I hadn't been able to bring my iPod, one of the few remnants of the past we packed up and brought with us in my mother's car.

I wonder a lot of things.

It's close to evening, and I'm exploring the woods surrounding our cabin. We're off a winding road that cuts through an endless forest. So far I haven't seen any trace of neighbors despite a couple of small cabins I've spotted along the way to ours. The driveway toward our cabin veers upward along a steep hill. Below the road the hill continues downward until it reaches the mouth of the large creek we can hear from our deck.

I'm exploring because I have nothing better to do.

Mom started drinking early today and was asleep on the couch this afternoon when I left to go outside.

Maybe that should make me sad, but I'm used to it. I wish I could take away her sadness. I know the booze sure won't.

The sunlight drips through the tall trees. It's starting to get dark.

I'm listening to the Foo Fighters and wish I could've been sixteen back when Dave Grohl was in his first band. Foo Fighters are great, but Nirvana was epic.

For a few moments I'm walking on a path that I don't even realize *is* a path. I figure it out and notice the way it cuts through the trees and the woods. It's an old path that hasn't been walked on for years, perhaps.

I keep following as it brings me deeper into the woods and higher up the hill.

The sunlight is fading.

I keep walking.

There are times when the trail seems to disappear, but a few minutes of searching brings me back to it.

I'm curious to see where it goes.

I probably should get back home before the blanket of night arrives. Getting lost out here could be a pain. Not dangerous— no, I'd find the cabin again. It just might take me an extra hour or so.

I keep walking and reach what appears to be the top of the mountain.

And there, in the shadows of the dense woods, stands a tiny cabin with dingy windows and wild growth surrounding it. Our cabin is small, but this one-story shack is really nothing more than a room with a roof over it.

I look around but know there's no one near me.

The cabin is barely taller than me, with one window next to the door. The roof barely slopes. I walk up to it and see a dead log blocking the front door.

As I glance around, taking in my surroundings, I notice that it's gotten a lot darker. Not because of anything sinister or spooky. It's just because of the setting sun and the quickly moving clock.

Without thinking about it, I try the door. It won't budge. Three nudges don't work either, so I kick it open.

Wood slices as the rotted lock crumbles.

The door swings open, and I smell something musty.

All I see inside is darkness.

And I suddenly feel very, very cold.

I look at the bumps on my arms.

I squint and look inside. I'm a little hesitant, because I don't want some big bear coming to greet me.

I don't hear anything, so I move inside.

My eyes adjust to the cold, dim light barely making it through grimy windows. Each side of the cabin has a square window on it. It appears as though there's just one room.

I see something in the corner. A bed. It's got sheets and everything.

I walk straight into a wall of cobwebs. I brush them off my head and face and wonder where the spiders are.

There's a small stove against the opposite wall. Next to that is a cupboard. There's a table and chairs on one side of the cabin, the bed on the other.

I'm shivering—it's so cold in here—in spite of my sweatshirt and jeans.

The light is growing dimmer.

I need to come back here with a flashlight.

I walk on a creaky wood floor. Dust seems to be hovering in the air. I examine the old stove, a square black thing blanketed in rust.

As I walk toward the bed, I notice something attached to the wall next to the bed.

I get close and notice that it's some type of chain, bolted into the wall of the cabin and maybe two or three feet long. At the end of the chain is a round leather piece.

For a second I stare at it before realizing what it is.

A shackle.

And it's at the foot of the bed.

I don't want to touch it. It fills me with dread.

I stare at the wall next to the bed and see markings on the wall, almost as if they've been cut out by someone.

Or maybe clawed out by someone.

The cold dread I'm feeling is only getting worse with the lack of light.

I decide to leave, come back another day. Or maybe not ever.

Just as I walk across the center of the rickety floor, something gives way.

For a second I feel light, like I'm flying.

Or falling.

Then I feel a sharp pain and a crack, and the darkness all around me smothers me until I'm out.

## 6. SINISTER AND CREEPY

*The man stands in the driveway, big and tall but completely weak. His eyes say it all. They're white with defeat.*

*He moves toward me, and I tell him to stop.*

*I don't want some epic, meaningful farewell.*

*"Chris—" he starts to say.*

*But once again I tell him to stop.*

*"Don't do this," he says.*

*I want to say the same to him but I already have, a hundred times.* Don't do this to us.

*The weak, blind, stupid man in the driveway claims he's my father, but he's nothing more than a living, breathing waste of an opportunity.*

*I want to tell him this, but I can't.*

*In the car an hour later, listening to my mother weep as she drives us away from the life that once was, I vow to tell that man those very words.*

I choke on the grainy air and the memory vanishes.

My mouth tastes like dirt, and I open eyes that sting.

My back and side throb in pain. For a moment I wonder if something's broken—I know what it's like to break a bone or two—but soon discover that it's just the impact of the fall.

I'm on dirt.

Fresh dirt, it appears.

*The kind that might cover a grave.*

I cough and keep tasting dust and grime on my tongue. Above me is the hole I fell through, the jagged opening of the floor.

I move and feel my entire body throbbing in pain. I'm going to be sore for a long time.

Something cool blows against my face. There's a breeze coming from in front of me, not above me.

*How can that be?*

Even as my eyes adjust to the darkness, there's nothing to see. The darkness is rich and smooth like chocolate.

I get on my knees and then stand, feeling my side and making sure a bone isn't jutting out.

Sometimes it's hard to keep my imagination in line.

My hands feel it again … the cold breeze blowing in front of me.

"Hello," I call out, not to see if anybody is there, but to see if there's a wall where it should be.

Just as I thought, there's an opening in the space directly across from me. I feel around and touch soil and earth. There is a gap large enough for me to walk through if I bend my head.

I hold out my hand and start walking, expecting something to block my way. Yet I keep walking.

I walk hesitantly for several minutes.

When I glance behind, I can barely make out the entrance to the walkway I'm in.

My hair brushes against dirt and roots above me. I wouldn't be able to stretch both of my arms out, this passage is so narrow.

*Someone dug this out.*

The question is why. The cabin looked as though it hadn't been touched for a long time. Was this underground passageway part of it?

I keep moving, feeling the air grow colder, feeling my breaths become more ragged. Perhaps it's fear, but I can't seem to catch my breath or suck in enough air.

I realize this is bad. That if something happened and the ground gave way, my mother would never see her son again.

Yet something draws me in, wanting me to see where this leads, hoping that this will produce something magical and miraculous. Or sinister and creepy.

I move onward until I hear the cackle.

That's what it sounds like. An echo of a sharp, strange laugh that seems to be coming from miles away.

Yet echoing down in this narrow passageway.

I stop and listen.

"Christopher," a voice whispers.

I turn and look behind me.

"Christopher."

The voice is low, whispered, yet sounds like it's far away and screamed at the same time.

"Christopher, come to me."

I swallow, and my mouth tastes dry, and I can feel the beads of sweat on my forehead.

I want to run, but am not sure which direction to go.

Again I think of my mother and why I shouldn't be here.

*You need to stay alive to take care of her.*

"Christopher," the voice says, then laughs again.

I bolt back to the place where I fell, and I scrape my arms and my face, and I finally reach the opening, and I tear through it and then see the way out above me.

For a minute I'm sure I'm stuck down here and I won't be able to get out....

Then I see the strips of metal that seem bolted into the side of the dark earth.

*Those are the rungs of a ladder.*

I don't hesitate as I start climbing.

These won't break.

I don't hear the voice again. Thankfully. As I get back up to the cabin, I wonder if I heard it in the first place.

Like I say, my imagination can do wonders.

I used to even believe that it could bring my parents back together.

But it can't do miracles.

## 7. So Not Right

Nonchalant.

That's what I'm going for in English class. Calm, relaxed, cool.

But Jocelyn and I both know I'm doing a horrible job at it.

Every time I've stared back at her—two rows away, three seats back—I see those eyes on mine.

There's no elephant in the room. It's a fox, waiting silently and watching with steady eyes.

Even at the end of the class I find myself moving slower than usual.

My hope is rewarded. I feel a tug at my shirt and hear a warm voice call out my name.

I turn toward her and nearly get trampled by a football player.

"Hey," I say.

Nonchalantly.

*You're not fooling anybody.*

We keep heading out of the room and reach the hallway where I see soft, seductive, sad eyes look at me.

"I'm sorry about the other day."

"Oh, no. That's fine."

The smile Jocelyn gives me is far too mature for a sixteen-year-old. Even that smile seems to contain an air of sadness.

"That was Wade. My step-uncle. Well, that's what he calls himself, even though he hasn't technically married my aunt, whom I live with."

Every word she says makes me blush a little more. I keep wanting to interrupt her, to say it's fine, it's not my business, it's really okay, I can pack up our things and drive her to California this afternoon if she'd like.

My face feels warm.

I'm such a loser.

"As you could see, Wade is quite the winner," Jocelyn says.

"I'm just—no—it's fine."

Seriously. What is coming out of my mouth? Words, yes, but barely. A jumble of third-grade nonsense.

"I'm sorry he was so rude. Believe it or not, that was Wade on a good day."

"So you live with your aunt?"

Jocelyn smiles again, brushing that long dark hair to one side and knowing that I'm changing the subject on purpose.

"Long story. I don't know which is the bigger nightmare: my parents' sad story or my aunt and her love life."

"My parents are divorced."

"Mine passed away. A long time ago."

"Wow, I didn't mean—"

"I didn't say that for sympathy. Really, it's fine. Aunt Helen—you know, you'd think adults might think things through before subjecting kids to a life of utter misery, wouldn't you?"

"Yeah."

"I better get going, but look—find us at lunchtime, okay? Do you mind?"

"Well, I was planning on having lunch with Gus and his friends, but maybe I can change my mind."

She laughs. "That's funny, but don't go there."

"What do you mean?"

"Mr. Meiners was right, Chris. You don't want to mess with him."

I'm about to reply, just to keep the conversation going, when Poe, dressed in all black as if it's Halloween, comes out of nowhere and puts an arm around Jocelyn and scoops her away.

"See you later," Jocelyn calls out.

Poe doesn't even say hi, which I'm already used to, having known her for almost a week now. The only time she seemed reasonably excited to be around me was that first day. Since then, she's been indifferent. Perhaps she's decided that I'm not as cool or unique as she thought. Or maybe it's just Poe. Who knows.

I want to ask what the deal is with Gus and why everybody is so afraid of him.

It makes me curious. And a little more defiant.

Gus doesn't scare me.

The only thing around here that scares me are those hazel eyes.


"Over here, Chris!"

Rachel's voice carries over the din of the cafeteria, where the scent of corn dogs and pizza hovers. I see messy blonde hair and animated eyes and a hand flapping, motioning me to come over. It feels like everyone is watching as I take my lunch over to where the three girls are sitting.

Poe is talking to Jocelyn and doesn't even stop as I sit down.

"Glad you found us," Jocelyn says.

"Yeah, it was really hard."

"How's your second week going?" Rachel asks as she pulls her chair closer to mine.

I can't help notice all the jewelry adorning Rachel—bracelets and necklaces and earrings. Her hair is curly in a way that looks more bed head than intentional. She's got a round face and a rosy nose that makes me think she'd be good as Santa Claus's daughter.

"Fine so far. No drama."

"Just give it time," Poe says in a world-weary voice. "There'll be drama, just not any kind that's interesting."

"Just ignore her," Rachel says. "The witching hour is almost here."

"Shut up."

Rachel ignores her. "She's just angry because her date is taken for the Halloween dance."

"Halloween dance?" I ask.

"Oh, yeah. They really celebrate Halloween around here. It's like some big festival. I'm just waiting for the farmers to bring their pigs in to sacrifice." Rachel giggles and looks at Poe. "For this dance, the girls ask the guys. And Poe had her eyes set on this little freshman boy."

"No, I didn't."

"Yes, you did. You told us last week that you were thinking about asking him."

"Thinking is not asking," Poe says.

"She was going to until we learned that he was already asked."

As Rachel and Poe argue, I glance over at Jocelyn. She rolls her eyes and smiles and continues playing with some grapes in a plastic bag.

"So who are you going to ask then, huh?" Rachel eventually says.

"Maybe I'll be like Jocelyn and not go."

"What am I supposed to do, then?"

"Have fun with *Lee*."

"He's a nice guy," Rachel says.

Poe looks at me. "I mean, come on. Lee? Only in the South, huh? The war is over, and you lost. Get real."

"If you think she's pleasant now, wait until there's a full moon."
Rachel makes a baying sound.

I can't help but laugh.

I also can't help but notice all the eyes watching me.

A part of me wants to stand up and ask what everybody's problem is. But listening to the girls talk—especially Rachel, who doesn't seem to care about being loud—I can see why people are staring.

But I wonder if there's more to it.

I find myself more and more glad this trio decided to befriend me.

"Maybe someone will ask the new boy here," Poe says.

I smile and avoid looking at Jocelyn. It would be too obvious. Too clichéd. Too much to look in her eyes.

She already knows.

"I'd be careful," Jocelyn says, as if reading my mind.

"Why's that?"

"There are some really scary people around here. Not just the guys. Some of the girls—" She fakes a grimace.

Rachel laughs. "Give me a break."

"She's being honest," Poe says. "Everybody here is just a little different."

"Good to know I'm hanging out with the right people."

Poe's ghostly white face looks serious, almost startled. "Oh, we're so not the right people, Chris. If you're looking for those, you're definitely sitting in the wrong place."

"I like where I'm sitting."

Jocelyn takes a grape and starts chewing on it as if to mask the smile on her lips.

## 8. The Gate

When I get home I find Mom passed out on an old fold-up lawn chair on the deck. It's a bit jolting because of where's she sitting.

Since our driveway juts up at a forty-five-degree angle toward the cabin on the side of the hill, our deck overlooks the sloping mountainside. It's not just a story off the ground. It's more like four stories. A fall would be deadly.

Someone consuming a bottle or two of wine might find a fall particularly easy.

I breathe in and call out for her to wake up, but it's not happening.

I scoop her limp body up like a corpse and carry her inside. As I put her down on the couch I make sure her head is propped up on one of the arm cushions. Blonde hair that used to be cut every few weeks looks uneven and faded. Strands glide over her nose and mouth, and I brush them back, the way she used to brush my hair off my face when I was little.

I lock the door, worried she might suddenly wake up and shriek and tumble over the deck.

A window is open, letting the afternoon light creep in.

I hear birds and the rustle of gentle wind and even the faint sound of the creek.

It should be peaceful.

Another sound yanks me out of my melancholy mood and calls me back out on the deck.

Far below, down through the trees, I can make out the gravel road below us.

I see a car coming, the first I've seen since we've been here.

It's not exactly a car. It's one of those massive SUVs that are used in the military. It's not even the smaller suburban version, but a black, shiny, hulking Humvee.

It rumbles past, leaving a cloud of dust.

I half expect a squadron of other vehicles to follow.

I wait and watch and listen, but nothing comes.

*Where was that thing headed?*

I want to take my bike out and see where this road leads.

Glancing back inside, I decide that I might take a bike trip a little later.

Mom won't care.

She probably won't even know.


I don't know if there's really any spaghetti in SpaghettiOs. I wonder if the O comes from the feeling you get an hour or two after eating them. Those tiny little chunks of hot dog surely can't be anything that was once living and breathing, right? Regardless, I can't help but love this wonderful and easy little dinner. Since Mom isn't cooking, it's my choice for dining.

It's already 6:30 in the evening and the sun is slipping away. Halloween is this coming Sunday, with the school dance the night before. As I pedal down the road through the shadows of trees, I wonder what it would be like to go to the dance.

It's not really the dance I'm wondering about. It's what it would be like to go with her.

*You have to stop this.*

Perhaps I should stop the dreaming, but I can still think about Jocelyn. I can still suppose.

*Just because she's being friendly doesn't mean she's interested in you.*

I know this. I've never been one of those guys who thinks that just because a girl talks to him or smiles at him or is nice to him means anything more.

Maybe it's because I'm new and I'm needing someone—anyone—to lean on.

Sounds corny, but I could use a little help.

I know that running into Jocelyn last weekend was complete luck. That's all.

She came to talk to me because of her step-uncle.

That's it.

I ride for ten minutes thinking things through until I reach the barrier.

I stop my bike.

With the hill sloping upward to my left and then heading on down to my right, I stand in the middle of the mostly dirt road facing a large gate. There are two stone blocks on each side, with a black wrought-iron gate between. On top of it are spikes. The gate opens at the middle.

There's a sign to one side: NO TRESPASSING.

And in smaller type underneath: Private Property. Violators Will Be Prosecuted.

Even though the barrier makes it impossible for a car to pass, I know I can slip right around it and keep pedaling.

The road continues on until it curves around the trees and disappears.

Now I'm really curious.

*This is where that big, honking Humvee went.*

I walk up to one of the stone blocks and peer around.

Something catches my attention, something that doesn't look like it belongs in the Carolina woods.

It's a black, square device that's planted in the ground.

It's about two feet tall.

A camera.

If someone is watching it, they can see my face peering down at it.

They can probably see the hairs in my nose, too.

I pick up my bike and decide to come back at another time.

I have plenty of time to check out what's farther down the road.

Next time I'll do it with the cover of night.

I'm propped up on my bed doing a bad job on my homework when I hear the stairs creak.

"I didn't hear you come home today."

*Maybe because you were floating in a sea of Merlot, Mom.*

I just nod and stare up at her.

She comes in and sits at the desk that's too tiny for a sixth grader and looks around at the narrow sliver of a room.

"I'm sorry," she says.

I'm not in the mood for a heavy conversation and nod again, accepting her apology for being dead drunk when her son came home from school. But she continues.

"I wasn't expecting this."

"Expecting what?"

Mom sighs. "I thought Robert was still around. I didn't really believe he was gone. I guess I was being naive and thoughtless."

"It's fine."

"You could have stayed in Illinois, Chris."

"I wasn't staying with that guy."

"He's your father."

"Technically."

"I still love him," she says.

"Good for you. I don't."

"Don't say that."

"He's not here to hear it. He never was around anyway."

"You don't understand."

"What don't I understand? Tell me."

"Don't get that tone. I'm just saying … I feel bad for dragging you down here."

"It's done."

She tries to ask about school and teachers and anything else, but my short, curt answers drive home the point.

"Do you need anything?"

I think for a minute.

*Yeah, I'd like you to be happier.*

"No," I finally say.

"Okay. Come on downstairs when you're done with your homework."

I hear the steps fade away and the television turn on.

For some time I fight staying up here and brooding and being angry.

Then I head downstairs.

I know I'm not the only person in this cabin who feels lonely.

## 9. FOUR OF THEM

These are the things I miss.

I miss Brady swinging by my house and picking me up in the BMW convertible his parents gave him on his sixteenth birthday. Brady's a year older than me but acts four years younger. He was always playing a new batch of songs he'd downloaded the night before, blasting them through outrageous speakers. He never understood the "album" concept and most of the time didn't even remember the band's name. Music in Brady's car sounded the way it should: loud, fast, riotous.

I miss the Tremont brothers, Lenny and Luke. Fraternal twins and stand-up comics who would inevitably make me laugh within five seconds of seeing them. We'd hang out before class and during lunch.

I miss dear, sweet Mrs. Williams: always encouraging me with my writing and my reading even though I gave a good C-minus effort in her class. She was like the grandmother I never had. (Though I doubt she'd appreciate that, since she's not *that* old.) I miss her smile and her gentle prodding. Even when I knew I should have done more, she was gentle, and she was so utterly consistent.

I even miss Trish. I miss the idea of what we had, though I still don't know exactly what that was, if there really was a *we*. I think of her tears when I told her I was leaving. I think of how I laughed and asked her why she was crying, since she had broken up with me a couple of months earlier.

"I never thought we wouldn't get back together, Chris. This is what couples do. They break up and then get back together. They don't move out of state and leave the other forever."

I miss my high school and the normalcy of everything. How I knew where kids stood and who they were. I miss the trends I knew and the path I was heading down.

Walking into Harrington County High, I realize I don't have a clue. The kids passing me might be poor as mud or wealthier than Brady's family. They might be kind or snotty or dorky or silly. They might be ten thousand things, but the fact is that every moment I walk by them, I don't know. I don't know anything. Sixteen years wiped away.

The slate is clean.

Sometimes that can be a good thing, but in my case it just feels like a headache.

I'm heading to my first class when I see a familiar face.

It's not the one I'm looking for, but I'll take it.

"You're here early," Rachel says.

"I'm taking the bus now. Last week my mom drove me."

"What? You don't drive?"

"We left Illinois before I could get my license."

"Ouch. That sucks."

"You're telling me."

"I'd pick you up, but you're the complete opposite way that I take."

"That's okay," I say. "Thanks."

"You should get Joss to pick you up."

"Maybe."

"I can ask her for you."

"No, that's fine." I glance around to see if Jocelyn is anywhere near.

"Hey—one thing Joss was asking about, but she's far too proper to come right out and ask you. Well—*proper* isn't the word. But I don't want to say *prideful,* because she's not, even if most of the school thinks she's stuck up. They think Poe is too. Just because they don't talk to everybody, you know?"

"What was she asking about?" I ask, lost in Rachel's stream of consciousness.

"What's your email address?"

I chuckle. "Don't have one. We don't have Internet."

"Seriously?"

"Yeah. Still trying to get used to it. Mom says we'll get it eventually."

"So like—there's no way to email you? How about your phone?"

"I left it in Illinois."

"Really?"

"Well … long story. I had a cell and busted it and my mom's making a point by not getting me another. What do you need my email for?"

"Oh, I don't. It's just—well, look, I'll let her tell you."

"Jocelyn?"

"Yeah." Rachel scans the crowded hallway. "Let me go find her. She usually gets here late. Hey—see you at lunch?"

"Sure."


I wish I had stayed home.

I don't talk with Jocelyn before or after either of our classes. Both times she slips in and out like a ghost. At lunch she's quiet and distant. Rachel dominates the conversation as usual, and Poe seems irritable. As usual. I try some small talk, try to make some kind of connection, but it doesn't happen.

Gym is the last class I have, and it's spent playing tag football with a group of guys who act like they're auditioning for the NFL. Back home I played soccer and ran track. This school doesn't even have a soccer team. Football is the big deal here.

At the end of class, with the bell signaling the end of another wonderful school day, I choose to put my jeans and shirt back on since I didn't get all sweaty. The locker room smells dank and old; the lighting is ancient, like it belongs in old army barracks. Just as I'm getting my duffel bag zipped up, I hear footsteps behind me.

There he is: Gus, with three of his henchmen, standing between me and the door.

He's smiling.

*Aw, man. Not now. Not today.*

"I thought I told you I never wanted to see you again."

Gus's cheeks remind me of the jowls of a walrus. Chunky black sideburns sandwich colorless eyes.

"Look, not today."

"Got somewhere to go? Perhaps with one of your lady friends?"
I stand there, holding my duffel.

Gus is the biggest of the four. He's an unhealthy big, fleshy and sloth-like. Doesn't mean he couldn't hurt me.

The one that makes me even more nervous than Gus is Ali, or Ollie, however the guy spells it. He looks as if he might be from South America, though I've heard him speak, and he sounds distinctly Southern. He's the opposite of Gus: all muscle, not in a body-building sort of way, but in a hurting sort of way. He was playing tackle football when we were supposed to be playing tag. I got sidelined by his arm a couple of times, even though I didn't have the ball. Imagine getting struck by a flagpole while riding a motorcycle. I still can feel the pain in my chest, and know I'll have a couple of whopping bruises there this evening.

The other two guys are country bumpkins.

There's a hallway leading back outside to the field, but the bumpkins go over to block it. Ali stands between me and the door to the school hall.

"What do you want?"

Gus laughs, then spits on the floor. "What do *I* want? You ask me now what I want?"

"I'm not looking for a problem."

"Maybe you shoulda thought of that when you decided to help your little gay friend."

I scan the locker room, but nobody else is around. It's a long, narrow rectangle, and I'm in the middle of it. The showers and the stalls are behind me.

"What is this? Is this what new guys get?"

Gus steps closer. I can already see dots of sweat on his forehead. I don't think they're out of any kind of nervousness. I think the guy is a habitual sweater. The meat in his veins is squeezing to get out.

"What are you hoping to get out of Jocelyn?"

I was still thinking about Newt. Jocelyn's name coming out of his mouth shocks me.

"What?"

"You like her?"

"Who says that's your business?"

He's now within an arm's length of me. "This place is my business. Jocelyn is my business."

"I'm not your business."

Gus laughs, the tip of his tongue rubbing the bottom of his teeth. "You're at the top of my list, boy."

For a moment, I hover above this little clichéd high school scene.

I'm standing there, bag in my left hand, the big kid in front of me. Behind him to his right by the lockers stand the other guys I don't really know. A little farther down toward the doorway stands Ali/Ollie.

Something comes over me.

I think it's not wanting my face punched in or doused in a toilet or worse.

I dig my right hand into Gus's throat and ram him backward with all the force a one-hundred-seventy-five-pound guy can muster. Gus definitely has a good forty or fifty pounds on me. He just stumbles and shuffles backward.

The momentum crashes both of us into Ali, who reaches out to

try and grab his friend. Gus is too heavy and lands on his back, with
Ali pulled down underneath him.

I do something I'm halfway decent at: hurdling. I vault over the
two guys and reach the door.

It opens with ease, and I bolt down the hallway, past students
looking at me with glances that ask what I'm doing.

*I'm getting out of here with my face and my backside intact.*

I reach the center of the square school and recognize the lockers
nearby. I scan the area and find what I'm looking for.

I decide to take Rachel's advice and ask for a ride. I can't take a
chance of running into Gus and his goons again.

"Jocelyn," I call out.

For a minute I think she's ignoring me.

Then she stops and turns.

And waits for me.


## 10. FREAKING OUT


"You look like a little overheated."

"I just got out of gym."

The red Jeep Wrangler rattles over the winding mountain road.
It's pretty beaten up, both inside and out. The ragtop above me has
a fist-sized hole in it. Jocelyn's driving makes me more nervous than
the confrontation I narrowly escaped.

"People don't shower after gym where you come from?"

"Actually I just had a run-in with Gus and his friends."

For a moment she stares at me while we ride around a steep corner. I'm about ready to tell her to look at the road when she finally does and then drives far over into the oncoming lane. Maybe she doesn't know that there are two lanes on this road even though no line cuts into the black asphalt.

"What happened?"

"I think he wanted to make up for our last interaction."

"When you stuck up for Newt?"

I nod.

The Jeep slows down a bit. Jocelyn glances over at me. "Chris … you don't want to mess around with him."

"Everybody keeps telling me that."

"You don't."

"I was getting ready to leave. He and his posse came out of nowhere."

"And what'd you do?"

"I escaped. And ran fast."

"Was Ali there?"

"Yeah."

"He beat up a kid really bad at a party last summer. Don't mess around with him, either."

"Let me state again, I'm not messing around with any of them. It was just—when I saw Gus do that to the poor little guy, I couldn't help it."

Once again, I see that look.

That look—there's something that she gives away. Something deep inside. Something that's there that I can't exactly explain or pinpoint. But it's beneath the beauty and the guarded expression and the air and everything else that makes up Jocelyn.

I'd like to think that it's interest.

Not just a "hey you're kinda cute" interest.

More of a common-bond kind of interest.

More like a "I get it and I get you" sort of thing.

There's something deeper down there.

I know this.

"It was a cool thing to do," she says to me. "But it was stupid."

"What's the big deal about Gus anyway?"

"His father owns half of Solitary, if not more."

"So he's rich."

"Not just that. The Staunch family has its hands in everything around here. *Everything.*"

"Okay. So what?"

"You live here, Chris. You live in Solitary."

"Yeah?"

She shakes her head and starts to say something, then remains silent.

"What?"

I can tell she's searching her thoughts.

"You have to be careful, just know that."

"I will," I say as if I don't have a care in the world.

"They'll hurt you and get away with it. It's not like where you come from."

"How do you know?"

"I just know," she says. "I know very well."

"I'm not looking for trouble."

"But you're wearing it with a capital letter on your chest. The best thing you can do is disappear."

"I already sorta feel like I have, coming here. You should see the street I live on."

"I'm serious, Chris. There are things about this place that you just can't—that I couldn't even explain to you. You wouldn't believe me."

"Try me."

"No."

Her response is short and swift, like a slap in the face.

"Okay."

For a few minutes, we drive. I tell her the roads to take to reach my cabin.

"I'm sorry," she says eventually.

"It's fine."

"You're a good guy."

I chuckle. "How do you know that?"

"I can tell."

"You don't know."

"Yes, I do. I know. I just know."

"Hey, the second street up there—past the sign—is mine."

Her face turns pale and registers disbelief.

"What?" I ask. I don't get anything about this day. Everything is just *off*.

"Are you sure?"

"Am I sure where I live? Yeah. Steeple Drive."

"Your cabin is on this road?"

"Is it just me, or is everything I'm saying slightly freaking you out?"

Jocelyn seems annoyed and doesn't say anything else as we drive down the road.

As we approach my driveway, I alert her to stop. Instead, she keeps driving.

"Uh, we just passed my driveway."

Those eyes stay focused straight ahead as the car zips along the dirt road until we eventually come upon the gate.

"I was going to tell you—there's a gate at the end of this drive," I say.

"The road on the other side of that gate leads to a rather large mansion. Want to know who it belongs to?" Her voice is angry.

I don't say anything.

"It belongs to your neighbor and dear friend, Gus Staunch. How's *that* for being freaked out."

"Seriously?"

She puts the car in reverse and zips it around, whipping my head against the side.

"Whoa," I say, taking the wheel for a minute.

"Don't you *dare* touch me!"

The Jeep jets down the street.

"I was touching the wheel."

We reach my driveway and she jams on the breaks, skidding the car to a halt. If I weren't wearing my seat belt, my lips would be stuck to the window.

"Jocelyn, what's going on here?"

"Get out."

"I'm sorry—I didn't—I was just trying to help—"

"I don't need your help, and I don't need your comments."

"This is all new to me."

"Yeah, well, I'm not your guidance counselor. You need to stay away from people who will hurt you, you got that?"

"Okay, fine."

"That includes me."

Again I'm stopped in my tracks, my mouth surely about ready to say something.

"Get out."

I obey. I climb out of the Jeep and stand in my driveway and listen as it rumbles down the road and away from me.


## 11. ESCAPING


The longer I'm in this cabin that once belonged to Uncle Robert—that *still* belongs to him—the longer I think that something strange must have happened to him. Something sinister or even supernatural.

If he did leave voluntarily, he decided to leave everything behind. Maybe the only things he took were the clothes on his back and the wallet in his pocket and the keys to his car (or motorcycle, according to Mom).

I think this as I'm rifling through one of the milk crates in the walk-in closet of my room. I glanced in here the day we arrived, but until today I hadn't looked through his stuff. On the floor below the shirts and pants and jackets all crammed together on hangers are three milk crates stuffed with records. Full-length vinyl albums, some double albums with fantastic artwork, some looking worn and frayed, others in spectacular shape.

Now I understand the stereo system in the corner with the turntable. When I first got here, I was psyched to see the large, waist-high speakers in each corner of the room until I saw what they were attached to. No iPod connection going on here. But tonight as I'm supposed to be studying, I'm surveying the tunes my forty-one-year-old uncle collected.

Turns out he had something in common with someone else in my family.

Musical taste. Maybe my father's only admirable quality.

The records aren't arranged in any sort of way I can see. I find some old Beatles albums, some Elvis, the Who, Pink Floyd. I wonder if they're all classics; I don't see anything current.

Then I spot a Nirvana album.

A Pixies record.

The Coldplay album piques my interest since it's so recent.

I put on New Order's *Brotherhood* album from 1986 and start making piles of the records. Is it bad to put Elvis with the Beatles? I make a separate stack for some of my favorites that I picked up from my mother: The Smiths, Depeche Mode, The Cure. There's a pile for groups I've never heard of: Hüsker Dü, Meat Puppets, Front 242.

There are newer releases that make me think Uncle Robert lived here recently—albums I have on my iPod, some I downloaded in the past year.

I hear a knock on the door.

"What's all this?" Mom asks. She's wearing a robe and has her hair in a towel.

"Uncle Robert has quite the collection."

She bends over and picks up an LP from one of my stacks. "I remember this group."

"Never heard of them," I say.

"Cocteau Twins."

"That how you say it?"

"I might have even been with Robert when he bought this."

"What do they sound like?"

"You should put them on and try it out. Just not too loud."

"It's not like we have neighbors who are going to complain."

"Yes, but you still have a mother who doesn't like to feel like her house is a rock concert."

She stays and listens to music with me for a while, the sounds exotic and otherworldly and powerful. Maybe it's because they're from another era, or maybe it's because they're coming from my uncle's record player, which actually sounds pretty amazing.

"He always loved music," Mom says. "If he could have chosen to be anything in his life, it would have been a musician."

"Why didn't he?"

Mom shakes her head, listening to the music, seeming to be in a far-off place. "It's one thing to have dreams. Or even the ability to pursue them. But you also need encouragement. Your grandfather was a loving man, Chris, but my mother's death really sucked hope out of him. He tried, but he just didn't have enough to pass around. I think I got the rest of what was left inside. Robert was pretty much on his own."

"Why'd he come back here?"

"I don't know," Mom says. "I just don't know."

"Why did you?"

"I wanted to get as far from your father as I possibly could. And the only place that seemed far enough away was Solitary."

Mom continues to sort through records with me as we sample the albums. The music seems to bring her back to another life, to another time, the way all good music does.

I feel like there's another universe just inside the closet next to my bed.

I know where I'll go when I need to escape.


## 12. I DARE YOU


I find the envelope dangling from a slit at the bottom of my locker.

The hallway is cold, the lighting hard, the students around me devoid of life. It's not eight yet, and once again I have time to kill before first period.

Ten minutes can seem like a lifetime.

The envelope isn't sealed. I take out the piece of stationery folded in thirds.

The handwriting is flowery and leans to the right.

I see my name at the top.

*Dear Chris,*

Again I scan the hallway around me to see if anybody I know is around or if anyone is watching.

*It's a rare thing to find a guy around here who is normal and who has stepped outside of this little tiny world—not only who has stepped out but who has lived there. The three of us—Rachel, Poe, and me—we're delighted that you've come to our wonderful little school.*

*I know that Poe might not show it, but she likes you. A lot. And Rachel thinks the world of you.*

*And I know I might not show it either, but I'm glad you're here. I really am.*

*I hope this doesn't come as a surprise—or rather a shock—but I'd like for you to go to the Halloween dance with me. What do you think? We could go with Rachel and her date—it would be fun! No pressure—you don't have to dance (half the kids don't dance anyway) and we can leave whenever you like. I can even drive if you want me to.*

*This way you could get the full Harrington High experience.*

*Don't want things to be awkward, so next time you see me, let's do this: If you're interested in going, why don't you ask me to go to the dance? I know the girls are supposed to ask the guys, but I believe it's the chivalrous thing to do.*

*If you're not interested, no harm and no foul. You don't have to say anything.*

*See you soon!*

*Jocelyn*

Even though her name is at the bottom, I can't believe it.

This is from the same girl who told me without hesitation to get out of her car yesterday.

The same girl who said that I need to stay away from people who will hurt me. And said that includes her.

I read the note again, scanning it for anything like "April fools!" or "just kidding!"

Maybe she feels bad about the conversation and this is her way of making it up.

But certain things just don't add up.

I laugh and grab my books and then head down the hallway, surely surprising the students I'm passing by with the big smile plastered over my face.

In English class I stare at her several times to get her attention. When she finally notices me, I nod to her in greeting.

Cold, blank eyes stare back at me for a moment, then move back onto the teacher.

After class, she slips out before I can get to her.

*What's with this girl?*

Maybe she's feeling awkward now. Things are always easier to write down in private. Things are always harder to say in person.

I look down the hallway but don't find her.

I head toward her locker but she's not there.

So I know I have to wait until lunch.

As if she has any question whether I'm going to say yes or not.

My glance back at her was surely enough of an answer.

So why didn't she wait for me?


I watch her for a moment, sitting at that drab table in the middle of the lunchroom, listening to Rachel talk.

So composed, so calm, eyes that seem as endless as an ocean. I'm mesmerized by her beauty.

I head toward her and don't even hear the voice next to me until its owner steps in my way.

"Going somewhere?"

The chiseled jaw of Oli is the first thing I see. He's about my height, maybe a little shorter, but he looks carved out of ice and stone. The T-shirt he's wearing is a little too tight.

Leaning against the wall is Gus.

"Perhaps going to hang out with your little girlfriend?"

I stand my ground. Two teachers are in plain view.

"They're not going to be around all the time," Gus says, reading my mind. "You won't always have a babysitter."

"I'm not trying to have a problem here."

"*You* are the problem. And unless you suddenly decide to take a sick year off, it's going to be a very big problem."

I get out of Oli's breath and face Gus. "So how's this going to end?"

"Who says it has to end?"

"What's it going to take? Beating me up so that everyone can see who's tougher than the new kid?"

"That makes it all seem so childish."

"Then what do you want?"

Other students are looking our way now. I wonder if this includes Jocelyn.

"Do we have a little temper?" Gus asks.

"What do you want?"

"You keep asking me that."

"And you keep neglecting to answer."

"Do I have to *want* anything?"

Just as I start to say something, I feel a hand on my shoulder. It's Mr. Meiners again. I must be on his radar, just like I am with half the school.

"I'm good, fine," I say, shrugging away from his touch and heading toward the girls.

The cafeteria suddenly seems quieter, with several hundred glances seeming to point my way. I sit down and realize I never got lunch from my locker.

The look I get from Jocelyn isn't the one I was expecting.

"What was that?" she asks.

"What do you mean?"

"That? Over there?"

"It was Gus being Gus."

"You sure don't listen well, do you?"

"Hi, Chris," Rachel says.

I nod at her, then answer Jocelyn. "I can't help where he comes and goes."

"Maybe you should pay attention a little more."

"Really?"

"Yeah, really."

Poe raises her eyebrows and takes a sip of her soda, enjoying the argument in front of her.

"I happened to be paying attention to something else."

"Do you want to get some lunch?" Rachel asks.

"No, I'm good."

"Maybe that's a bad idea," Jocelyn says.

"Yeah, I'd think so, but then again, I'm kinda confused."

Rachel is next to me digging through her lunch bag. "Fruit?"

Jocelyn is glaring at me. "Confused about what?"

"Confused about a lot of things. First and foremost, you."

"Nothing to be confused about there. Nothing you even need to think about."

"Really?" I ask.

She nods, looks away.

*What a total snot.*

This is crazy.

"Look, I don't have to go to the dance. It's not that big of a deal, okay?"

She blinks.

Rachel tugs at my arm. "Hey … Chris … do you want to just … can I talk to you for a minute?"

"I'm fine."

"What are you talking about?" Jocelyn asks.

"Nothing, I guess. Nothing at all. In fact, I won't ever mention the stupid dance again."

"Fine with me."

"Am I missing something here?" Poe asks.

"Nothing at all," I tell her.

"That's right," Jocelyn agrees. "Nothing."

"I never wanted to ask you in the first place."

"Ask me what?"

"You don't think I will, do you?"

For a brief second I see it.

A tiny glimpse of humor.

She's enjoying my frustration.

"Whatever you're talking about … no … actually, I don't."

"You guys, can we have a truce?" Rachel says, waving her arms between us.

"Okay, fine, fine. Just wait a minute. Jocelyn, I'd like to be your date for the Halloween dance this weekend. There. How's that?"

Rachel and Poe both look surprised as the hint of amusement continues to rise on Jocelyn's face.

"So I dare you."

"You dare me to what?" Jocelyn asks.

"I dare you to take me."

"Yeah, right."

"I know you won't. You're afraid."

"I'm not afraid of anything."

"Then I dare you to take me to the dance."

"Why would I do that?"

"Oh, I don't know. Because I think there's a part of you that wants to but that's afraid to actually go there."

"You have no idea what you're talking about."

"Okay. Then what's your answer?"

Jocelyn stands up and curses at me, then walks away.

I look at Poe and Rachel.

Poe clears her throat. "I've seen some lame attempts of trying to get Joss, but, buddy—that's gotta be the worst one yet."

She stands and follows Jocelyn, leaving me with Rachel.

"Sorry," I say.

"No, I'm sorry."

"You didn't do anything."

"Actually, I sorta … well … I kinda did."

Rachel rubs her arms nervously, then smiles in defeat. "I wrote that letter."

She almost trips over her chair in her hurry to get away.

## 13. MAKING TROUBLE

"Come with me."

The hand on my shoulder digs in and drives me forward before I can head into my history class. By the sheer force and surprise, I think it's Gus behind me. Yet my brain catches me up and tells me it's an adult.

I turn my head enough to see that it's some guy I've never met wearing bad pants and an even worse tie. Whatever hair he has left is slicked over in a way that seems to wave defeat.

The man guides me to the principal's office, where the door opens to reveal a group of adults.

There is the principal, Miss Harking, who said hello to me in passing on my first day. Next to her stands my gym teacher, whose name escapes me for the moment. He looks like the athlete who couldn't stand to let his high school days slip him by, so he simply stayed around to teach. And to pump iron. Next to him stands a cop. If we were back home I might think this guy is security at a mall, one of those "faux cops," as Brady called them.

"Young man, you are in serious trouble."

A part of me wants to turn around to see if Miss Harking is talking to someone else. The guy in the tie stands right next to her as if this is an intervention.

"Is there anything in your locker you want us to know about?"

I think about the bag lunch I brought and wonder if they're here for that. I shake my head.

"Can you tell me anything about that?" Miss Harking says as she points to her desk.

On it is a revolver, a short stubby kind that looks ideal for hiding in your pocket.

I glance at it, then at the stern faces in front of me.

"We got word this morning that someone saw you take this out of your bag and put it in your locker," the cop-or-not says to me.

"Who said that?"

"Does it belong to you?"

"No," I say with a bewildered laugh.

"You're in serious trouble, Chris," Miss Harking says. "We've called your mother."

"I've never seen this gun before."

It's clear they don't believe me. I stare at the tie guy who led me down here. He looks like he's been itching to take out his own teenage aggressions on someone for about forty-five years, and boom, here I come.

The outsider from Chicago, only here a week, is packing heat.

*Come on.*

"What are you doing with this, Chris?"

"That's not my gun. I didn't put it in my locker. What else I can say?"

"We've heard you've been making some trouble with some of the boys here," Miss Harking says.

"If 'trouble' is trying to avoid getting my face bashed in, then yeah, I've been making lots of it."

"And who has been trying to do this to you?"

"Gus and his buddies," I say.

The cop and my gym teacher look at each other.

"Did you bring this in to hurt one of them?" the cop asks, his nostrils flaring.

I want to flare mine back at him, but can't. "No. That's not my gun."

"You were suspended from your last high school for drinking."

The principal has done her homework.

"That's a lot different from carrying a gun to school."

For a few more minutes, they continue to drill me.

And I continue to say the following: "That is not my gun."

Finally my mother comes in, her eyes red and swollen. Sad to say, I can't tell if it's from being upset or being hung over. She gives me a hug, then stares at the other adults in the room. "What is going on here?"

"Mrs. Buckley, we received three different reports this morning from students who said they saw your son bring in a gun and put it in his locker."

"That's a lie," Mom says to Miss Harking.

"Have you ever seen this gun?" the cop asks.

"Of course not. Are you seriously saying Chris brought this in?"

"I didn't," I say.

"I know that. What proof do you have? Who said this?"

"We have three different sources—"

"Three? Where are they? Get them in here right now. I can tell you one thing. That gun doesn't belong to my son."

"There's going to be an investigation so we can find out if it does."

My mother curses in a way that both shocks me and makes me want to high-five her. She grabs me by the arm. "You're not doing anything with my son. He's not going anywhere with any of you."

"Ms. Buckley, there are certain procedures we have to follow—" the cop begins.

I would bet big money my mother could take him. She's not big, but she's scrappy.

"Your son has had some run-ins with some of his classmates."

Mom stares at me, then looks back at tie guy. "Run-ins? Like how? He's a new kid who sticks out like a sore thumb. Or should I say he's like the normal thumb on a sick hand. When do new students come in and make trouble?"

"It's happened before," the principal says.

"Well, it's not happening here. I can guarantee you that that gun is not my son's."

"But we have to—"

"You listen to me," my mother says, aiming her finger at the cop. "Chris's grandfather was shot when I was eighteen years old and not even out of high school. Shot with a random gun in a random shooting. Chris didn't tell you that, did he? He didn't tell you that he's vowed never to touch a gun, ever. Ever."

"Please, Ms. Buckley."

"No," Mom says. She grabs me just like Tie Guy did earlier.

I want to cry out that I'm not some animal who needs to be pulled around on a leash.

"You do whatever you must, but Chris is coming with me. You have a problem with this, I'll call my lawyer. You touch my son and I'll sue every one of you, and you'll end up on an NBC primetime special on the abuse of power in a hick town."

My mother storms out, still holding onto my arm. I walk with her in silence, bewildered and stunned.

We get into the car and she turns to me, red faced and breathless. "You look at me right now and swear, Chris, you swear that—"

"Mom, stop."

"Just tell me."

"It wasn't my gun. I swear."

"Then whose was it?" She pulls the car into reverse and almost rams a car behind us as she veers out of the parking lot.

"I have no idea."

But on second thought, I do have an idea.

It's an ugly idea, with an ugly face attached to it.

"Are you in trouble?"

"No."

"I mean with some other kids."

"No. I'm fine. Just typical high school stuff. Bullies."

"Why didn't you tell me?"

"There's nothing to tell."

We drive for a few minutes, my mother seeming to realize finally that she's not a superhero. I can see her deflating.

"Thanks," I say.

She grabs my hand. "They're not going to touch you. Nobody's going to touch you."

"Because of your lawyer?"

Mom looks at me and can't help the smile forming on her lips. "Like that one?"

"Yeah. I had to keep from laughing."

"I'd call him. If you were in trouble, I'd call him."

"Really? And you think Dad would actually help me out?"

"He'd help out if I called him," Mom says. "But he's the absolute last resort. Besides, there's nothing to call him about. That wasn't your gun."

"Yeah, but it was someone's. And whoever put it in my locker did it to get me in trouble."

## 14. CHANCE

The email goes like this:

> HEY, JOCELYN. SORRY ABOUT THE WHOLE
> EXCHANGE AT LUNCH. DID RACHEL TELL YOU
> ABOUT THE NOTE?

Her reply is short and sweet:

> YES. LOOK—I'M THE ONE WHO IS SORRY. I FEEL
> LIKE AN IDIOT. CAN I MAKE IT UP TO YOU? PICK YOU
> UP IN THE MORNING ON THE WAY TO SCHOOL?

The imaginary email.

Her imaginary reply.

I think of what it'd be like to have email or an Internet connection.

Maybe I should be thinking of something else, like how it's going to be back at school now that I'm known as a gun-toting gangster. But instead I think back to Jocelyn, about the conversation and misunderstanding at lunch. I think back to what Rachel told me and how I was looking forward to seeing Jocelyn during history class.

I never had a chance.

Life's all about chances.

Maybe I'm a little too young to fully appreciate this, but that's what it's about.

Chances.

And the element therein.

Dad used to tell me—well, *tell* isn't actually right, it was more like preach to me—that there was no such thing in this life as chance. That God controlled everything.

I wanted to say, "Yeah, well, if that's the case, Pops, then why did God put you and Mom together?"

I think it's easier not believing in God, knowing that Dad does. It's easier to pick a side.

Chance.

That's what I believe in. That's the team I'm on.

The random fateful chance that some guy comes across a grandfather I'll never know and puts two slugs into him.

The random fateful chance that one day I'll be accused of having a gun in my locker.

I'm full of questions. Were there rounds in it? Where did their investigation lead? Why haven't they called?

Most importantly, what's going on with Jocelyn?

I'm listening to the second side of an album by Love and Rockets. Strange stuff. I want to use the word *psychedelic* for it. It's like rock for creepy people.

I kinda like it.

I don't have the volume high.

I wish tomorrow would come. I wish I could talk to Jocelyn right now.

I think of ten thousand things to say.

I know that by tomorrow morning, I probably won't say any of them.

## 15. AUNT ALICE

Mom is dressed with her makeup already done and coffee in hand.

Usually I'm the one making her coffee, sometimes leaving for school without even hearing her stir.

"You taking me to school?"

Mom shakes her head. "I talked with the principal last night."

"And?"

"You're staying home today."

"They still think—"

"No," she says, stopping at the kitchen counter and directing her gaze toward me. "At least the principal doesn't think it was your gun. But they still need to talk to some kids, look into it. She said it would be better if you stayed home."

I sigh.

If this gets out, even if they find out it wasn't my gun, I'll be labeled as a troublemaker. Some freak.

Even more than a new student already is.

"We're going to see your Aunt Alice today."

I hear a rumble of thunder. "Any particular reason why today?"

"We should have gone last weekend."

I almost say, "Yeah, that's what I thought too, but you couldn't get off the couch."

Instead, I just ask, "What if the school calls?"

"They can leave a message."

I look at the box of cereal. It's some generic version of

Cheerios, as if you could get any plainer than that. I pour some into a bowl and find the milk.

"Are you going to take a shower?"

"Think Aunt Alice is going to care?" I ask.

"I will."

With a mouth full of soggy cardboard bits, I nod and mumble that I'll be ready in just a few minutes.

The only place the directions seem to be getting my mother is lost.

The glaze of rain coming down sure doesn't help. It feels like we're driving in the gray of clouds, turning down a wandering rocky road without a name only to have to back up and go miles over the same ground. We've been driving for half an hour.

"So Aunt Alice is your mother's sister?"

"Yes."

"Do you remember her?"

"A little. She was younger than my mother. I remember her at the funeral. She was a wreck."

"And nothing over the years?"

Mom shakes her head, squinting to see the messy scribbles of her own handwriting on the sheet of paper. "A card every now and then. I've spoken with her on the phone a few times. The last being just a month ago."

"How'd she sound?"

"Well, she gave me these directions. Which make about as much sense as she did." Mom puts the piece of paper in her lap and keeps driving.

"She ever marry?"

"No."

The *no* sounds like "not in a million years." Like Aunt Alice couldn't marry, like she has one arm and horns sticking out of her head and she talks in tongues. Or maybe has several tongues to talk with.

"My mother's death really had an impact on our small family. There were just the two of them—the two girls. Aunt Alice just—she never recovered."

"And she's the only family member around here?"

"There are several from the Kinner side of the family, my father's family. He had a couple of brothers, and I think their families are still in the area, though they'd only be cousins. I lost touch with them."

Without the directions in hand, it seems that Mom does a better job navigating. We drive down a dirt road and come to a small side road with a crooked old tin mailbox at the end of it. The numbers say it belongs to Aunt Alice. The driveway, if you can call it that, wanders way back into the woods. Our car passes over ruts in the muddy road, ruts that are turning soft and gooey like warm fudge. We eventually come to a one-story house that looks as though it's on its way to becoming one with the forest surrounding it.

"Seriously?"

Mom looks at me with a glance that says so much.

*Be quiet,* for one thing.

*Get out,* for another.

*Mind your manners* is surely in there.

And last but not least, *This is freaking crazy.*

Her sigh gives it away.

After several knocks on the crusted-over door with its welcome mat of dried paint chips, we hear a voice inside. We'd maybe look in the window, but it's dirty, dark like the clouds around us, unwashed for a century.

"Hello?" my mother says in a friendly tone.

"Inside," someone hollers in a not-so-friendly tone.

Mom turns the door handle, glances at me, walks in.

I start to get claustrophobic even before stepping foot inside.

If I thought that cabin I found in the woods was gross, this is something else. The smell of something rotten fills my nostrils, burning them. I don't know what death smells like, but this reeks of it. Mom turns just as I'm about to say something.

"Hello?" she calls out again.

We hear something crash in a room in the back. We're in the muted light of a living room, though it doesn't look like any kind of living to me. The glow of two windows creates shadows in the otherwise dark room. There's no light bulb lit. I half wonder if there's any power to light one.

"Aunt Alice?"

A round goblin comes out of the darkness of the hallway. At least that's what I see in my mind first, a round-faced figure hunched over, leaning on something.

As my eyes adjust, I see the woman. She's both overweight and tiny, if that makes any sense. It makes about as much sense as anything around her. She's short but round, with chunky arms and a couple of necks. By the way she moves, Alice hides half of her body.

"Aunt Alice, it's me. It's Tara."

The eyes widen. She stops, leaning on what appears to be some kind of walking stick.

"Tara?"

"It's Tara. Tara Kinner."

My mother's maiden name obviously rings a bell. I'm expecting the good ole "let me make you some biscuits and gravy" routine.

But Aunt Alice just stands there, leaning over, a scowl coming over her face. "What are you doing here?"

"Alice, I came by to see you. I want you to meet someone."

"Why did you come back?"

"Alice, this is Chris, my son."

*Thanks, Mom. Great time to be introduced.*

I stand like a complete lump and long for the days of simply being neglected in a classroom.

"You shouldna come back here."

Her voice is grainy, Southern to the core, almost hard to understand.

Mom looks at me.

"Hi," I say weakly.

"What do you want?" Aunt Alice asks.

I see the black outline of a crow in the corner, either a stuffed one or a carving. I swear I see its eyes blink.

Then the bird moves.

My skin and my heart move with it.

It flutters for a few minutes, then settles, having announced its presence.

If my mom is surprised or scared, she doesn't show it. "Do you mind if we stay for a few minutes?"

"This place isn't for you," Aunt Alice says, shuffling on toward the kitchen, which is separated from the living room by a half wall.

Mom points at me to sit down. I half expect to find bird poop on the chair or maybe a snake coiled up. I smile and stay standing.

Aunt Alice lights a couple of candles that make the place even creepier than before.

There's nothing in here that's pleasant.

A big frame shows a man who is as pale as a ghost with a bald head and an expression that makes me think he wants to kill the photographer. Then I notice that it's a painting.

"That's my grandfather," Mom tells me.

"Nice."

"Shhh."

Mom goes toward the kitchen. I can't help keeping my eyes on the crow that's resting on the back of a chair. It seems to be watching me.

"Don't have much around here," Aunt Alice says. "Don't get many stoppin' by."

"That's okay. We're fine. I just wanted to come by and let you know we're here."

Aunt Alice opens what appears to be an ancient refrigerator. My eyes take in more of the room.

I see a small table with a few pictures on it, some strange beads covering them, a woodcarving of an owl.

*That better be a woodcarving, 'cause if that sucker suddenly hoots, I'm outta here.*

I move toward the kitchen and past an armchair; then I turn and almost pass out.

A figure is sitting in the chair.

It's a corpse.

A rotting, stinking corpse.

It's the reason this place smells so bad, and the reason that I'm so out of here.

I jerk back and hit the wall and knock down something to the ground.

"Chris."

"Mom—did you see—"

But it's not a dead body. It's a mannequin.

A dressed-up mannequin of a woman wearing pants and a jacket. Dead eyes stare back at me.

I can just picture having a cup of coffee while sitting next to that thing. Maybe if I stay long enough, it'll start talking.

Mom keeps chatting with Aunt Alice while I pick up the framed stitching I knocked off the wall.

It's a pentagram.

I'm not sure what side was up or down. I forget what a pentagram stands for. Upside down or not, I'm beginning to think wonderful little Aunt Alice is into some weird stuff.

She lights more candles and proceeds to sit in the chair that the crow is resting on.

I lean against the wall, telling my mom I'm fine right where I am. Away from the mannequin.

"Are you Chris?" Alice asks me.

I was beginning to believe—well, *hope* is the word—that she hadn't even noticed me.

"Yes, hi, hello."

"How old are you?"

"Sixteen."

Her eyes grow dim. Even in a chair, she slouches, as if her back is permanently bent. I see spotted, fleshy hands rub something—a clear stone that's on a chain. It looks like a triangle.

"When are you leavin'?" Aunt Alice asks Mom.

"We're here to stay."

"You can't stay around here."

"This is our home."

"No home to you, not anymore. You should know that. You should know that by now."

"How have you been?" Mom asks her, ignoring her threats and warnings.

For fifteen of the longest minutes of my life, I listen to Mom try and engage the lady in this strange, smelly house in Nowhereland. The sound of the rain hits the metallic roof. My legs are tired, but I'm still okay standing. In case I need to run out of the door for any reason. In case the mannequin sits up and starts singing "Hello, Dolly."

"This is no place for him. For a family. For young'uns."

"Have you seen my brother, Aunt Alice? Have you see Robert at all?"

"Don't know a Robert."

"Bobby?"

Aunt Alice thinks for a minute, still rubbing that rock of hers.

I see something white come out of nowhere and slip between her legs.

A cat. Some big white ball of fur.

"He was around not long ago."

"Do you know what happened to him?"

"The mouth of the beast swallowed him up," Aunt Alice says. "Just like Jonah. Just like Annie. Just like it will swallow you."

Mom seems unfazed. "Did you talk to Bobby?"

"Death surrounded him. Death hung in the air around him like a broken halo. Death chased after him."

"What happened to him, Aunt Alice? Where'd he go?"

Aunt Alice suddenly turns to me, then starts to laugh.

I see missing teeth—either that or black ones. She starts to howl with laughter.

"Hell," she says in that southern drawl. "Hell. He stopped by just before he reached hell. Just like the two of you. Just like you."

## 16. This Life

I don't know whether I should laugh or shiver.

My mother plows down the long driveway from Aunt Alice's house. It's twenty minutes after the quote of the day involving us somehow going to hell. That was the climax of the morning as far as I'm concerned. The only thing that could have topped that would've been the mannequin standing up and asking me to play a game of checkers.

I'm waiting for Mom to say something.

When she does, it's a keeper.

"Well, that brings the term *dysfunctional family* to a whole new level."

We laugh. I mean *really* laugh.

Sometimes when life is so amazingly awful, that's all you can do.

That's one option, at least. It's either laugh or cry. We've done our share of both.

"Was she always that friendly?" I joke.

"She saw Robert. At least I got that out of her."

"Maybe she buried him in the backyard."

"Stop."

"Did you smell it in there?"

"Yes."

"That wasn't a normal smell. That wasn't the sort of something's-gone-bad-in-the-garbage smell. That was the sort of Dahmer-next-door smell."

"Stop it."

"I'm serious," I say.

"It's probably just some dead animal."

"Oh, well, in that case, it's fine."

My mom laughs at my sarcasm. "I didn't realize—I didn't know she was like that."

"What do you mean?" I ask. "You didn't realize Aunt Alice was completely whacked?"

"Stop."

"This was fun. Can't wait to meet some more relatives."

"Chris—"

"I'm not even going to say it."

"Then don't."

But of course I do. "I don't get why we came back here."

"I thought you weren't going to say it."

"Did I say that? Sorry, my thought spoke out loud."

"We've had this conversation a hundred times."

"And a hundred times, I keep getting the wrong answers."

"There's no right answer I can give you," Mom tells me.

"Sure there is."

"No. Because all you want to hear is that we're leaving this place. And that's not going to happen. We're staying."

"Even if that means we're going to hell?"

"Your Aunt Alice has some issues."

"You think?"

"Chris, be respectful."

"This just keeps getting better."

"What?"

"Everything. This place. This life."

"Stop it."

"I can't wait to get home and find out that the authorities are coming to get me. Maybe I'll be placed under house arrest. Or better yet, confined to stay a month with Aunt Alice."

Even though my mother doesn't want to, she laughs.

That's all either of us can do.

## 17. GIRLS

I peel the orange at the small table by the kitchen as I wait for my mother to get off the phone. When she finally thanks Principal Harking, I hold my breath and wait.

"It's all sorted out. The principal said that they ruled out that the gun belonged to you."

"Whose was it?"

"They can trace it back to a seller in Tennessee. Obviously there are no ties to you. The principal said that one of the deputies was going to stop by."

"It's almost seven o'clock."

"Maybe they'll stop by yet tonight."

"Doubt it. So that means I have to go back tomorrow?"

"You make it sound like a penitentiary."

"You haven't walked the halls."

"One more day and you have the weekend."

"Fantastic."

I can't help but think of the dance that I'm *not* going to.

It's not that I want to go to a dance. I'd go milk cows with Jocelyn if I could. Or do whatever kids around here do for fun.

"Chris?"

I don't notice the mess I'm making with the orange until Mom gets my attention. "Yeah?"

"Do you really think those guys you had a run-in with might have put a gun in your locker?"

"Yeah. I mean—I don't know. I'm not sure. I don't think it happened accidentally."

"You need to be careful, okay?"

"I've got the whole school watching me now. I'm probably safer than I was a couple of days ago."

"You have a point there."

I eat a sliver of orange. "You forget how fast I am."

"Don't talk with your mouth full."

"Sorry."

"You can't outrun everybody. I know, Chris. I've tried."


The phone call around nine o'clock makes me jerk even though I'm upstairs and only hear it faintly.

I wait.

It's not like we get many calls.

And calls at night are never good things. At least not for the Buckley household.

"Chris!"

I go downstairs and see the glow of the television as my mother holds the phone.

I miss our cordless. And my cell phone.

*And my life.*

I don't ask who it is. I spot a reality show on television as I take the receiver and walk back toward the kitchen. "Hello?"

"Chris?"

For a moment, I want to let go with a sigh of relief.

For a moment, I want to tell Jocelyn that it's about time she called, that it's about time she showed that she actually cares, that it's about time.

"It's Rachel."

"Hey," I say, surprised.

Trying not to sound too disappointed.

"You're a hard man to get hold of."

"I don't try to be."

"You need to get the Internet so you have email. Or at least get a cell phone."

*Maybe you'd like to loan me the money to do both?*

"Yeah, I know," I say.

"You doing okay?"

"Yeah, I'm fine."

"It's all over school about the gun."

"Wonderful."

"It wasn't yours, was it?"

"Sure. It was part of my collection. Actually, I was just cleaning my shotgun upstairs."

She laughs. I wish I had that laugh on my iPod. I'd play it whenever I felt awful.

"What's going to happen?"

"They said they found out the gun wasn't mine. Like that's a big surprise. They're letting me come back to school."

"We've been really worried."

I like her use of the plural.

"I tried to get Jocelyn to call," Rachel continues. "But of course she won't. She felt pretty bad about how she acted the other day, once she found out the truth."

"It's fine."

"I told her—and Chris—I mean, I know you have other things going on. But I feel really, really awful."

"It's okay."

"No, I do. We all do. Even Poe feels bad, if you can believe it. She doesn't show it, but really she's got a huge heart."

"It's really not a big deal."

"Well—so you're coming to school tomorrow?"

"Looks like it."

"I guess we can talk then. But I just—well, there was something I wanted you to think about. Something I wanted to ask you."

"What's that?"

Rachel pauses for a moment, and I wonder whether the line got disconnected. "Hello?"

"No, I'm here. Sorry," she says. "It's just … well, let me see how to put this."

"Just say it."

"Do you still want go the dance?"

"What?" For a moment, I think she's asking me. Doesn't she already have a date? Wasn't that why she wanted some other couple to come along?

"Let me rephrase that. Are you still willing to go to the dance? I know you said that you would. That you wanted to."

"With you?"

"No, no, no," she says, laughing. "With Jocelyn."

"Uh, that might be a problem."

"No, but that's the thing. It's not. She's willing to go."

"But last time she was talking about it—you were there. You heard what happened."

"But she didn't know about the note, Chris."

"It's really fine. I don't need to go."

"Just think about it, okay? Just—look, there's a lot about this school and this place and Jocelyn that you don't know."

"I realize that."

"Yeah, I know, but you don't *really* realize it. There are things—it would take way too long and it wouldn't make sense. Stuff about Jocelyn. Stuff that's just—I don't even get. Stuff about her family. And about her. She's really changed in the last year, Chris."

"What do you mean?"

"Just trust me. She's changed. She's different. But she's also … I don't know. She carries sadness with her like it's her child. Like it's her duty to have it. I can't explain it. I try to help, but I just can't. She's been with some winners, I tell ya. I could tell stories. Every man in her life has treated her the same—horribly. And I just want—I want her to have fun. I want her to actually have a little fun."

I don't know what to say.

"Look—just think about it."

I don't have to think about anything.

I don't have to because I know *who* I'll be thinking about later.

The same person I've been thinking about ever since meeting her.

"I'll go," I say.

"Thank you, Chris. I know that she likes you. I can tell."

"Oh, yeah. She's madly in love."

"You're different. She knows that."

"How do you know I'm not like those other guys?"

"I just know, Chris. I'm a good judge of character. Poe and Joss—they're *good* girls. They're quality. You'll find that out. I mean, Jocelyn is drop-dead gorgeous. So is Poe, minus the whole darkness thing going on. But underneath you'll find some pretty amazing girls."

I want to say something else, but I can't.

"Just find me tomorrow—find us. Don't mind Joss either. She'll surely be a little reserved. A little guarded. That's just her, okay?"

"And she knows about this? You sure she knows about this?"

"Yes."

"You're not playing matchmaker?"

Rachel laughs. "Oh, I'm sorta playing it, but Joss knows. She said it would be fine to go to the dance. For me."

"Okay."

Not the reason I'm wishing for, but I'll take it.

When I get off the phone, Mom looks at me from the sofa.

"What was that about?" she asks.

"I don't know. Girls. Hard to figure out."

"They always will be."

"Yeah."

I head to the stairs.

"Chris?"

"Yeah?"

"If you want to talk … about anything … I'm here. At least I'm trying to be."

"I know."

"Girls included."

I laugh and say goodnight.

Even though sleep won't come for quite a long while. I already know that.

I'm too excited to sleep.

# 18. FRIDAY MORNING

I discover that my locker is empty.

Not like I had a thousand mementos and memories stored inside, but I do need the books and notebooks that I left in there.

I head to the main office and explain my problem to a young lady at the main desk. She guides me to the small waiting area outside the principal's office. When the door opens I go inside to see Miss Harking.

"Good morning."

I nod and say the same, even though it's not really a particularly good morning for me.

"We changed your locker. We gave you one on the south side, the new lockers just installed a year ago. That way you'll have one that nobody will be able to get into. With some of the older lockers, we've had issues of people knowing their combinations."

I nod again.

"Of course, you have to understand our concerns when something like this occurs."

"Yeah."

"Did Deputy Ross come by to interview you yesterday?"

"No."

"He didn't? Did anybody?"

"No."

She jots a note on her desk. "Tell me something, Chris. Do you know who did this to you?"

"Not a clue."

"But you have any ideas? Do you think it might have been Gus or one of his friends?"

"I don't know. I know he's been after me. So, yeah, if I had to guess one person, it would be Gus."

"We spoke to him. He said he had nothing to do with it."

I nod.

*Did they think he'd admit it?*

"We'll keep our eyes open. If anything happens today, I'm just down the hall. My door is always open."

I leave with a slip of paper telling me the locker number and combination.

Three lockers down from mine, I see him. The little guy named Newt.

"You're back," he says, his eyes looking massive behind glasses three sizes too big for him.

"Hey."

"That your locker?"

"They gave me a new one."

"I thought you were expelled."

"Not yet," I say.

Newt appears to be using his locker door as a shield. He looks as if he wants to sneak inside the locker and shut the door.

"You're Newt, right?"

"Yeah."

I make small talk, yet every word I say makes him seem to shrink more.

"You okay?" I finally ask.

He looks around. The hallways are crowded over in this section.

"Yeah, I'm fine."

"You don't look fine."

"You just better be careful." He says it in a whisper.

"Careful of what?"

He does a double take and then turns quickly to shut his locker. "See you later."

I nod, glancing and seeing Gus and company heading my way. I'm sure they were roaming the halls looking for me.

I take out a book and turn my back toward them.

"Changed lockers, huh?"

Turning around, I shut the locker door with my books in hand.

The English book with its one thousand pages is big enough to make a dent in Gus's ugly meatloaf of a head.

"Easy, killer," he says as if he's reading my mind. "Just coming by to say hello."

I don't say anything. I just stand there, ready for something. Ready to fight. Or tear down the hallway.

"Got any special surprises in your locker today?" Gus asks.

I'm not taking the bait. I start to walk away.

"Hey. You. Turn around."

I stop and look back at him. Gus is flanked as usual by his buddies.

"I hear we're neighbors. You know that? So I don't have to just look forward to seeing you here. Who knows? Maybe I'll show up at your front door sometime."

This sounds like a threat.

I wonder if he knows it's just my mom and me staying at the cabin.

I want to tell him that I'll have a baseball bat waiting to greet his ugly face and ratty teeth.

Instead I turn around and head to class.

# 19. A Little Lost

This is teenage madness.

Trapped in a room knowing there's more outside.

Trapped listening to a teacher talk about Hemingway as if each sentence and word the man ever wrote had mythical importance.

Trapped knowing she is in the room with me.

Adults surely don't have to endure this, do they?

Forced to be somewhere they don't want to be, forced to not say all the things they need to say, forced to do things they don't want to do.

*That's the idea, boy. It's called corporate life. It's called the American dream.*

I hear grownups saying they'd like to never grow up, but isn't that exactly what we all want to do?

I see a big kid with watermelons for arms, dressed in basketball shoes, staring at the wall.

I see a bleached blonde chewing gum and doodling in her notebook.

I see a guy rubbing the sides of his gelled hair as if something went terribly wrong this morning. (If he asked, I'd tell him yeah, something went terribly wrong.)

Every one of these kids wants to grow up and get out.

My eyes shift back to Jocelyn.

Her hair is blocking half her face, but she sneaks a peek at me.

I turn back around.

Afraid and nervous.

Oh so young.

Oh such a teenager.

Even though I hurry, I don't reach Jocelyn as we go out to the hall. I see her white shirt and bare arms disappear with the rest of the students being swallowed in the black hole of the hallway.

That means lunch is the next thing I have to look forward to.

I curse in my head and go back to my locker. I see Newt standing there, looking like an FBI informant just before coming in.

"Here," he says, giving me a sheet of paper folded in half.

"What's this?"

"Shhh."

"Nobody's around, man."

For the first time I notice a scar on his arm, a lot like the reddish streak on his face.

"They're everywhere. They're listening to everyone."

I start to open the paper, but he grabs my hand. "No, no. Not here. In class."

"Class is better?"

"Don't let anybody see you."

He starts walking backward and runs into a guy in a leather coat who doesn't even stop. Newt turns and practically dashes down the hall.

I start to open the paper again, then decide to get my books and head to the next class, where I sit next to the wall close to the back. With a spiral-bound notebook half open, shielding the paper from the rest of the class, I open the sheet.

It's a copy—a rather bad copy—of a newspaper article, dated last year.

> Authorities have called off the search for Stuart Algiers after a month looking for the 16-year-old from Solitary, N.C.
>
> Algiers disappeared after telling his parents he was going to Colorado with friends over Christmas break. He never returned, and his friends said he never made it.
>
> The family, which declined to be interviewed, was questioned and has cooperated with the police.
>
> Algiers has a younger sister. She attends Harrington County High School, as did he.

I read it again, trying to figure out why Newt gave it to me.

Does Gus have something to do with this?

*Algiers.*

Have I met anybody with that name in my classes?

I fold up the article and plan on getting some details when I see Newt again.

Poe is the only one at our usual table. She sees me coming, so I can't back out. I drop my bag lunch on the table and sit down across from her.

She looks at me with suspicious eyes.

*What have I ever done to you?* I'd love to say. Instead I ask how's it going and make small talk.

Truly small, because it goes nowhere.

I'm still wondering about the article. So instead of more painful small talk, I launch the question like a unpinned grenade. "Have you ever heard of Stuart Algiers?"

Poe stops. Her eyes stop blinking, her mouth stops chewing, her body goes rigid.

"What?" I say.

She swallows and scowls at me. "That supposed to be funny?"

"What?"

"Who told you?"

"What do you mean?"

"Did Rachel tell you? What'd she say?"

"She didn't say anything. I just—I heard about him."

"So you had to go there, huh?"

"Go where?"

"You really know how to make a good impression, huh, newbie?"

"What did I say?" My curiosity is becoming frustration.

"You don't have that many friends at this place, you know?"

"Yeah, I've gathered that."

"So why are you trying to make another enemy?"

"By what? *What* are you talking about?"

To add to my nightmare, I hear Rachel's laughter approaching. I know I'm on thin ice.

Rachel sits down next to me with a grin and a greeting. Just as Jocelyn does the same across from us, Poe stands up.

"Did you tell him?" she snaps at Rachel.

"Tell him what?"

"Tell him about Stu?"

"She didn't say anything," I say again.

Rachel looks as bewildered as I am.

"Then how did he know?" Poe demands.

"I don't *know* anything."

"What happened?" Rachel says.

"You know—I'm sick of this. I'm sick of this place and I'm sick of people like you butting into things you don't understand and never will." Poe storms away leaving me with Rachel and Jocelyn.

Both of them look like they're attending a funeral.

"What?"

"What'd you say?" Rachel asks. "What just happened?"

"All I asked was whether she's heard of Stuart Algiers."

"Why would you do that?" Jocelyn asks.

*Oh, thanks for talking to me now.*

"I just—I was just curious."

"But why? How do you know about Stuart?"

"Joss," Rachel says.

"Well, I want to know."

"Someone showed me a newspaper clipping about him. He went missing last Christmas, right?"

"But why'd you ask Poe?"

"Why are you guys so defensive?" I ask. "I just asked a question."

"There's no such thing as *just* a question," Jocelyn says.

"Yes, there is," Rachel says.

"Who showed you that clipping?"

I scratch the back of my neck.

Newt had made it clear this was a secret.

"Who gave it to you?" Jocelyn asks again.

"Why?" I ask. "What's the big deal?"

"We can tell him," Rachel says.

"No, we can't."

"What's he going to do?"

"Nobody knows."

"A few people know."

I'm watching Rachel and Jocelyn talk as if I'm not there.

"It's not his business."

I stand up, then lean in close so that nobody else can hear what I say. "Listen—if somebody doesn't tell me what's going on, I'm going to get up and leave and never sit at this table again."

"Chris—please, just sit down," Rachel says, tugging at my arm.

"It's fine with me," Jocelyn says.

*This girl wants me to go with her to the dance? This is the girl who, according to Rachel, likes me?*

"Chris, listen, just sit," Rachel says. "Please? Listen, Stuart. He was a junior last year—and only a few people know this. He was seeing Poe for a while."

"Since the summer," Jocelyn adds.

"And that's it?" I ask. "That's why she went ballistic?"

"Nobody knows."

"So? How was I supposed to know?"

"They think that he died," Rachel says.

Jocelyn laughs in disgust.

"What do you guys think?"

"I don't know," Rachel says.

"He's gone," Jocelyn says. "And there's no point in bringing his name up. Especially around Poe."

"She loved him."

"No, she didn't," Jocelyn says. "Give me a break."

"She did."

"Sixteen-year-olds can't love."

"Yes, they can."

"Please."

Again I feel like someone just watching from the sidelines.

I want to ask how he disappeared and what people thought, but I decide to ask someone else.

*Thanks, Newt. Thanks for pushing me into hot, bubbling water and leaving me to tread water.*

"Maybe I should go find her," Jocelyn says.

"No, let me," Rachel says, standing quickly. "You guys can talk about tomorrow night."

Rachel smiles and leaves before Jocelyn can do the same.

Suddenly I feel the weight of five hundred students looking at us.

*I'm not imagining this.*

I try to ignore them.

"Look, I'm sorry for bringing up his name."

"It's fine," she says. "You didn't know."

"Maybe next time I can get the benefit of a shred of doubt."

"And maybe next time you can just keep your mouth shut."

Obviously something on my face shows how I'm feeling. The defiant look Jocelyn is showing suddenly deflates.

"I'm sorry," she says.

"It's all right."

"No, I just—I'm sorry. Look, I can be—I sometimes need to watch my mouth."

"I didn't know about Poe."

"I know. It's just that it's been really hard for her, and for all of us. There's just … just so much that could be said, but shouldn't."

I want to ask her more, but I'm feeling a little shy.

"Look—I know that Rachel talked with you, and I understand."

"You understand what?" I ask.

"About the dance. And it's cool. It's fine."

"It's fine … to go?"

"Yeah. She explained things."

I'm still a little lost.

"Explained things," I repeat.

"It's okay. I just hope—it's Harrington. It's North Carolina. There's not a lot of excitement at these things."

"That's okay," I force myself to say.

*Just shut up, Chris.*

"We should probably talk about logistics."

"Yeah, sure."

"When can I pick you up?" Jocelyn asks.

"Do you mind?"

"Of course not. Why should I?"

"I don't know."

"I can pick you up and we can meet Rachel and her date at school."

"Is this a formal thing?"

For a minute, Jocelyn thinks I'm joking. "Yeah, make sure you rent your tux and have a corsage for me."

"No, I know it's not like prom or anything—"

"It's a dance at Harrington. It's fine. Wear whatever you want."

"What time does it start?"

"How about I swing by your house around seven? Nobody says we need to be right on time."

"Yeah, okay."

Those eyes hook me, make me melt, make me dizzy, make me consider agreeing to anything she might say next.

"Chris?"

"Yeah?"

*I'll jump off a mountain for you if you want me to.*

"Really—I'm sorry for—for chewing you out a few times."

"It's fine."

"No, it's really not. It's just—" She looks around and thinks for a minute.

It's as if there's something she really needs to tell me. "I haven't always been like this," she says.

"Like how?"

"This—"

I thought she said something more, but I couldn't hear it.

"I better go find the girls, okay? I'll see you a little later."

"Sure."

I gaze after her long figure in jeans and shirt as she leaves the cafeteria.

It doesn't get old, watching her.

Nor does it get old wondering exactly how in the world I ended up going to a dance with her.

## 20. THE STONE WALL

Even if I do technically have a date to a dance tomorrow, I still find myself alone on a Friday night. I never used to be by myself on Friday nights. Back home there was always something to do. Someone having a party or going to see a movie or just hanging out.

Here there's nobody around to hang out with.

Nobody except a few groundhogs.

The evening is still young, and I've just finished helping Mom with cleanup after dinner. She tried something new—fajitas. Strips of steak and chicken along with undercooked onions and peppers put in flour tortillas along with cheese and salsa. They were fine. They didn't taste as good as they do at a Mexican restaurant, especially the little one we used to go to back home, but that's fine. I know Mom's trying to re-create it.

She's working on another large margarita when I tell her I'm going to go outside for a while.

Good thing she doesn't see the flashlight I'm carrying.

Even though the sky is still light, I know I'm going to need it.

I haven't forgotten about the little cabin in the middle of nowhere.

And I definitely haven't forgotten about the tunnel underneath.

The only thing it seems I've forgotten is how to get there.

I wander through the woods, going straight uphill behind my house, knowing it was this far up the mountain. But after twenty minutes of not finding it, I start heading right.

With each step it seems to get darker.

A clearing in the forest brush makes me stop for a moment. I discover a small trail with the leaves either gone or pressed down from use. It snakes alongside the mountain and heads in the direction I'm going.

Though I know deep down that the little cabin is far back where I started, I keep heading down this trail. Maybe I'll uncover something else.

Another ten minutes and I do.

In the middle of the dense trees of the forest, a ten-foot stone wall stands blocking my direction.

It heads straight up and down the mountain as far as I can see.

I almost don't believe it's real, so I touch it. The stone is cool and hard. It's very real, very unmovable. Very Middle Ages.

*Who would build something like this?*

I walk up the hill, trying to find a way around it. There are no entryways, no small windows looking in, nothing that can let me pass. I reverse direction, heading down the slope of the hill along the stone barrier.

I know who this belongs to.

This is part of the gate surrounding Gus's house.

Suddenly I *really* want to get over this wall.

I want to see what the house behind it looks like.

Who doesn't want to know what his neighbor's house looks like?

The gate I came across on the road below was just to prevent vehicles from going any farther. This stone wall is to prevent anyone from getting onto the Staunch property. To prevent people like me from snooping.

I decide not to go down the mountain too far. The closer to the road, the more likely I might run into someone. Or something.

*Like a camera.*

I head back uphill where I just came from, my legs getting a workout. It doesn't take me long before I come across a tree growing right next to the wall. I didn't notice it when I first passed. It's small enough to climb up, yet big enough to support my weight. Several branches jut out slightly over the top of the wall, which appears to be square and flat.

*This is going to be easy.*

Five minutes later, I land on the soft padding of the ground below.

I never even had to set foot on the wall. I just edged out on a branch and dropped over it.

As I look at the same scene facing me—just endless trees and bushes, now shrouded in dimming light—I have a not-so-great thought. *How am I going to get back to the other side?*

## 21. SLIVERS OF WHITE

I suddenly notice how cold it's become. Cold and dark.

My arms are bare in my thin T-shirt. I shiver and move on down the hill, walking slowly, making sure I don't fall on a branch or crash into anything.

Just in case someone is around.

*What if they have armed guards on their property?*

*What if security cameras are watching me now?*

*What if there are booby traps wired up somewhere?*

The animals in the forest have apparently all gone to sleep.

A slight gust—invisible, almost unheard—brushes up against my skin. I try to hurry up to stop feeling so cold.

I feel like eyes are bearing down on me. Not just from one direction, but from all around me.

Whoever is turning the lights to dim is doing a fast job of it. I consider turning on my flashlight, then decide against it, knowing it would attract attention.

There's a slight dip in the ground, and my foot plunges in, sending me falling. My face lands an inch away from a jutting tree limb. I know even in the growing darkness that the sharp edge could have done something nasty to my face. Especially my eye.

I stand up and brush the leaves and dirt off my shirt. I find the flashlight I dropped.

*Better start trying to figure out a way over the wall before the night swallows me whole.*

I've been walking downhill close to the wall. So far, I haven't seen another tree growing against it like the one that got me in here.

I stare downhill.

Beyond the trees, I see a reddish glow seeping through.

*Maybe it's the Staunch house. The one they don't want people to either see or come inside.*

I feel a dread come over me. It's as if the ruby glimmer down below is starting to glide up toward me like a ghostly fog.

I check alongside the wall for anything—an opening, something to stand on, another tree.

Then I hear the sound.

A slight rustling along the forest ground.

I stop and listen.

Then I hear something else.

I hear the clink of a chain.

A dog chain.

I think of Gus's face and the sign that says No Trespassing.

*What kind of dog would Gus get?*

I think of a pit bull, like the one we used to have in our neighborhood that was always in the news because of his love of biting strangers. They eventually had to get rid of him, something that caused a unified celebration along our block.

I hear a slight jingle and shine my light toward a group of trees nearby.

Then I see them. Slivers of white.

At first I think it's the dog's eyes. Then I realize that it's his teeth.

His mouth is open, panting, the sharp teeth ready to attack.

I back up, still facing toward the dog, moving slowly until I hit the stone wall.

*I'm an idiot, and this is what happens to idiots.*

I'm still holding the flashlight, but I don't think it will be much help in fighting off this dog.

It moves slowly toward me.

It's black or mostly black. I still can't see exactly what type of dog it is. I see its eyes. For a minute it seems as if …

*They're not glowing those eyes are not glowing.*

I stumble over something and almost lose my footing.

The dog growls.

As if to warn me. As if to say, "You can try and run and I'll even give you a head start, but your hide is mine."

## 22. THE BEAST

Things like this don't happen back in Libertyville, Illinois.

You don't get lost in the woods behind your house.

You don't get trapped inside a fortress-like wall ten feet tall.

You don't stumble upon demon dogs with glowing eyes.

I'm walking downhill next to the wall, my hand rubbing its rough texture as I move in the darkness with my head turned back toward the dog.

I swear that its eyes are glowing.

And there's something else.

*That's crazy. You're imagining it, just like the burning eyes.*

I smell something putrid. Something that makes my eyes water.

*Nothing smells like sulfur, that's just your crazy mind playing games.*

But I believe it because the hairs in my nose are telling me.

So far the big beast hasn't moved.

I keep slipping down the slope.

Then I hear a loud, gasping growl, a sound like something being shredded apart, like the top of a can being pried and popped open.

It's followed by a clicking sound, as if something in the thing's mouth or throat is recoiling.

*You're crazy it's not a thing it's a dog and it's probably as friendly as a Pixar movie.*

My breathing is ragged. I can't tell if it's my mouth sucking in air or the thumping of my heart.

I hear the thudding of steps, which sounds like the hooves of a horse digging into the dirt.

I run. And the thing behind me quickens its pace and launches itself.

Something massive flails against the tree to my left. I hear the small tree bend and shift as whatever the thing is stumbles and rolls around in the leaves.

I'm not just running now. I'm sprinting downhill next to the wall, trying to avoid anything in my way.

If my old track coach, who told me I never applied myself, could only see me now.

Whatever's beside me—the dog, the thing—is massive.

It's a big, black, hulking mess.

I hear it inhale in a high-pitched screech, then cough and start scrambling behind me.

The leaves and dirt on the ground sound like they're being rooted out of the earth, spit out all over the back of the forest floor.

The thing is breathing in and out like a hundred-year-old smoker with something sick and deathly in the back of its throat.

The smell—the smell hovers just under my nose and my mouth. I can taste it.

*Your imagination you can taste and smell your imagination there's nothing behind you Chris nothing at all.*

And then I start to lose my balance.

I'm going too fast and the slope is too steep and the darkness too black and I'm leaning a little too far in front.

And I hit a black metal object.

Something made of steel takes out both of my legs, cutting down my shins like a dirty kick might in soccer.

Now I'm soaring through the air.

I land on one shoulder and half my head, doing a somersault and then twisting and turning and landing in a half-buried rotting log that nearly swallows me as I finally come to a stop.

The dog—or the thing—is behind me, a little ways up the hill.

The eyes are now burning embers, fully on fire, enraged.

It's massive, the size of a bull.

*What if that's what it is—some random bull that's completely ticked off?*

Then I see what I tripped over.

It's a ladder.

The steel arms go to the very top of the wall.

*That's my ticket.*

The creature starts to move again, this time not running but rather slipping through the darkness.

Every time it moves it seems to change shape, like liquid, as if its shape is bending and changing to its surrounding.

*That's crazy, Chris. It's the darkness playing tricks on your eyes. Get up and get going on that ladder.*

Just as I get to it, the shape smothers me, the smell burning my nostrils and eyes, the hair wrapping around my feet and legs, something digging into my shoe and my foot.

Teeth.

They feel like scissors, a dozen of them tearing down and into my skin and bone and cartilage. I howl and in a crazy, mad gasp of desperation take the ladder and try to pull myself up on it.

The beast isn't letting me.

So I pick up the ladder from its bottom and manage to move it a little.

I hoist it up—it's heavy—and then I bring it down on top of the beast from hell.

The thick metal of the ladder hits something.

It sounds like a cantaloupe being dropped onto the street and splattering.

I bring the ladder up and down, again and again, hearing the sound of something hard digging into something soft, a knife digging into jelly, a pole scooping up thick mud.

Whatever had my foot lets go.

And with it comes a howl like I've never heard in my life.

It sounds like a baby mixed with an old man, both singing in unison in a coughy, sweaty, sickly scream of pain.

I lift up the ladder and drop it, again, again, again.

The massive beast underneath me and surrounding me suddenly explodes like a balloon full of black paint.

Liquid jettisons everywhere.

The scent is like raw sewage, making me dry-heave and cough. I look down and see a remnant of a gray cloud hovering in the air.

With trembling arms, I slam the ladder back against the wall and desperately scramble over it.

I don't even see the top of the wall as I flail blindly over it onto the other side.

It seems lighter over here. Not only in actual visibility, but in terms of being able to breathe.

I don't look back. I run straight through the woods, knowing that sooner or later I'll run into something.

Hoping that I'll see the lights glowing from my cabin.

Hoping that the darkness that hovers behind me is all in my mind.

## 23. CLOSED

"Chris?"

"Yeah?"

"Where've you been?"

"Just outside."

"Everything okay?"

"Yeah, sure."

It could be any exchange between any mother and son on a late Friday night. Any exchange where the mother stands outside the door to the locked bathroom wondering what's going on. Any exchange where the teen is in trouble but desperate not to give it away.

But instead of being drunk as a skunk or high as a kite, I'm trying to clean up a bloodied shoe and sock and foot.

The wound isn't as bad as it looks.

Thank God for my Adidas. Bet the marketers would like to know that they can also help fend off devilish dogs.

There are five cuts in the middle of my toe, all looking like dog bites.

*Not some bullish, crazy demon dog, Chris. Just a dog.*

The blood is coming out fast and furious. I've already used up a roll of toilet paper, and I've already flushed four times.

Making Mom surely wonder what my deal is.

"Are you sick?" she asks.

That clichéd image of the teen hiding something from his parents suddenly irks me.

*What am I hiding?*

*And why am I hiding it from her?*

"I'm not sick," I say.

But in a sense I am sick. I'm sick of being on my own and keeping things to myself and living and breathing behind a wall. Or a closed door or a closed room or a closed life.

*If things are going to change, I have to let someone in.*

I get off the toilet seat and unlock the door. Mom is there in her robe, looking notably out of it but nevertheless concerned.

She gasps when she sees my foot.

"It's better than it looks," I say. "It's just a dog bite."

"What?"

"Yeah, I know."

"What happened?"

I give her a quick synopsis of what happened, including the bit about the wall. I leave out things such as the dog smelling like sulfur and being the size of a bull.

I also leave out how I left things with the dog.

*I don't even know how I left things.*

"We have to get you to a doctor."

"No."

"Yes, right now. You don't know the dog. We need to get you a rabies shot."

"Mom—we can't."

"What do you mean we can't?"

"We don't have money for that."

"We have as much money for you as we need, Chris."

I stare at her, not understanding what she means.

A part of me thinks, *If that's the case, let's go shopping, starting with the nearest Apple store.*

"Mom, it's fine, really. Where are we going to go at nine on a Friday night?"

"We'll find a doctor. It doesn't matter."

"I'm sorry," I say.

She's probably thinking, *I need to put some clothes on.* Then, as she's walking down the stairs, *And I need to put some coffee on.*

## 24. CORNY AND CUTE

"Hey, Jocelyn."

"Hi. Didn't know you had my telephone number."

"Yeah. Hope you don't mind me calling. It's just—something came up."

"What's that?"

"Well, it's actually kinda weird, but—I was bitten by a big rabid dog that, if you want to know the truth, was possessed, too. Anyway, I went to the doctor late last night—had to actually go to his house, if you can believe that—and, well, I was given only a few hours to live. Sorry."

"That's crazy. That doesn't make sense."

"About the possessed dog?"

"No—about how you got this number."

"Yeah, well, anyway, Jocelyn, I just wanted to say—I know that I'm about to go to a cheesy dance with the hottest girl in school. And I know that it's just so ironic, not being able to go cause I've got rabies and am going to die."

"Yeah, that's crazy."

"Getting rabies and dying?"

"No. How you got this number."

Then the crazy dream I'm having vanishes in the dark like the dog from last night.

I open my eyes and see the wood ceiling above me.

It's Saturday morning, and I'm still alive.

Still planning on going to the big dance tonight.

Still going with the hottest girl in the school.

Not ready to die anytime soon.

And still without Jocelyn's phone number in my possession.

I'm pretty much useless on Saturday. I keep thinking I'm going to get a phone call—a real one, that is—from Jocelyn telling me something's come up.

I ride my bike to downtown Solitary, thinking and hoping I'll run into Jocelyn again. No such luck. Instead I get a hundred looks that all seem to say, *Go away. Go back where you came from.* I don't stay in the town long.

I spend most of the afternoon in my room listening to music. The bandage on my foot is tight and secure. If it didn't impact my bike riding, I'm sure it won't affect my dancing.

Mom eventually comes in to check on me.

"Everything okay?"

I nod, turning down the music.

"I haven't heard these guys in years," she says, picking up the Tears for Fears album *The Hurting*. "Robert loved this when it came out. I have every song memorized, he played it so often."

"They're pretty good."

"A little depressing, but then again most of this stuff is."

"Makes it even better."

Mom laughs and sits on the edge of my bed. "How's the foot?"

"A couple of toes just fell off."

"Just make sure you throw them away," she says. "I wouldn't want them getting stuck in the vacuum cleaner."

"We have a vacuum cleaner?"

"Well, it's on the need-to-get list."

"Can you add cable and Internet to that?"

"We don't *need* cable and Internet."

"You're killing me."

"Taking a break from being online won't kill you. It'll probably be good for you."

"Yes. Spending time listening to depressing albums from the eighties is so much better."

She laughs. "Excited about tonight?"

"Should be fun."

"Do I get to meet this Jocelyn?"

"I don't know. Not sure if she'll come to the door or not."

"I certainly hope so."

"I'm sixteen and don't even have my license. That's lame, Mom."

"Add it to the need-to-get list."

"Can I put 'a life' on there too?" I ask.

"Right after I get one," she says.


Turns out Mom gets her wish.

"Wow," she says, looking out the window down to the driveway. "She's beautiful, Chris."

It's funny when she says this. I'm looking at Mom, all made up, wearing dress pants and a blouse as if she's the one going out. All for the possibility of a brief greeting with Jocelyn.

My mom is beautiful. She really is.

"Yeah, I know," I say. "Get away from the window. She'll see you."

Mom waves. "Already has."

"Wonderful."

Soon I hear steps coming from our driveway to our deck, then a knock on the door. Mom opens it a little too quickly and greets Jocelyn in a voice that's a little too excited.

"Hello, Jocelyn. Such a pleasure to meet you."

*And please marry my son while you're at it. Your children will be so beautiful. If they take after you, that is.*

"Hi," Jocelyn says.

*Move, Mom.*

*Move so I can see her.*

I can see those eyes looking at me.

I can see the amusement in them.

Mom moves, and I see the rest of her.

*What's she doing wearing a frilly pink prom dress?*

"Hi," I say, trying to squelch the silly thoughts going through my head.

Jocelyn is wearing jeans and an indigo button-up shirt. She looks taller than usual and, like my mother, a little more "made up" than usual. Her hair is slightly different, with some of it up and the rest falling to one side.

The air in my mouth seems to go backward. Out of breath is not the right phrase to use.

*Out of touch. Out of my league. Out of my mind.*

"This is such a cute place," Jocelyn says, walking toward the small fireplace we haven't used yet.

"It belonged—belongs—to my brother."

"Really? I didn't know that." Jocelyn looks at me with a playful glance.

"I can give you a tour if you'd like," Mom says.

"Not a lot to see," I say.

Mom ignores me and shows Jocelyn around. I stay downstairs when they go up to my room. When they come down, Jocelyn still wears a humored look on her face.

*This is all so corny. I'm corny and Mom's corny and our little life in this little cabin is all just so corny.*

"Exciting, huh?" I say.

"I'd use the word *charming,*" Jocelyn says.

I can't tell if she's being honest or mocking.

Mom makes small talk, which makes me want to go back into the woods and see that dark devil dog again.

"We should probably go," I say.

"It was very nice to meet you, Mrs. Buckley."

As we head out the door, Mom's reply makes my lonely status all too clear.

"You too, Jocelyn. Come over anytime."

"Okay, Mom."

"You both have a fun time. And take your time coming home."

*Thanks, Mom.*

She's all but pleading with Jocelyn to help me with my loser life.

I head down the steps and walk around the side of Jocelyn's Jeep and climb in.

So many things I want to say but can't.

She starts up the car and then peers over at me.

"She's a lovely lady," Jocelyn says.

"Yeah."

For a moment, Jocelyn studies me. Then she takes my hand and squeezes it. "Relax, okay? That was fine. Your mother's just like you … cute."

"Cute, huh?" I ask as she lets go of my hand and turns the car around to head back down the hill. "Makes me feel like a puppy."

"Yeah, well, I like puppies, so consider it a compliment. I don't give lots, Chris. Especially to guys."

"Thanks, then."

"Come on," she says in a tone that I haven't heard in her since meeting her. "Let's try to have some fun tonight and forget about the rest of the world. Sound good?"

## 25. I Have Nothing

The school gymnasium is packed. The normal smell of tennis shoes and sweat is mixed with an additional odor: bad cologne. It reminds me of a guy we used to call Gift Cologne who would always wear a new kind of spray after Christmas and his birthday. I'm following

Jocelyn and can already tell that just being on school grounds has made her attitude shift a little. She's a little more serious, a little more guarded.

I guess I would be too if guys whistled at me the way they do her.

"I'm sure Rachel's already here," she tells me in a loud voice over the blaring music. "Look on the dance floor."

The song playing is exactly what I think of when I hear the term "country music." The singer has a deep drawl, the guitars are twangy, and the lyrics mention something about a pickup truck and a dog. I'm not joking.

*Bring back Tears for Fears now. Please.*

"There she is," Jocelyn says, getting Rachel's attention.

For a minute I lose her in the mass of bodies. Back at my old high school, dances were thought of more as a joke. They'd have a few student bands play, and it became more like a concert for indie groups than a dance.

*Guess there's not much else to do around here.*

I start looking for Jocelyn and then think about Gus and his buddies. But I don't find either in the crowd.

I feel a tug on my arm, and Rachel gives me a hug like a long lost friend. "You made it."

"Yep," I say.

"Chris, this is Lee."

A good-looking guy with short hair and a face that makes him look like a fifth grader smiles at me and says hi.

"He's a sophomore," Rachel says in a voice that already sounds like it's disappearing.

A new song starts playing, this one AC/DC. The room erupts, and everyone seems to start dancing. That includes Rachel and Lee.

But not Jocelyn. She moves her head and speaks into my ear. "I hate this song. Come on. Let's go see if they have anything to drink."

I follow her like a little boy wading through the crowd with his mommy.

Even in the chaos of student bodies jumping around us, I see the familiar stares.

*Glares,* I think.

People who look at me with complete and utter disdain.

I don't get it.

I don't get it because I haven't done a single thing to any of them.

*Why did Rachel want Jocelyn to come to this thing?*

I can't help wondering this as we stand and watch Rachel and her date dance and glisten with sweat and wave repeatedly at us. We hold our plastic cups of soda in our hands. Occasionally we try to talk, but it's too loud to hear anything.

The DJ plays either loud, bad country or loud, classic rock and roll. Every fifth song is what I call bad peppy pop—something that sounds like an overproduced song sung by someone who lacks talented and is not of age.

Guess it's easy to be a critic when you're standing on the sidelines.

After about half an hour of this, I ask Jocelyn if Rachel is going to dance all night.

"Yep. But we'll be able to talk to her at the party later."

I nod as if I know what she's talking about.

*A party?*

Suddenly I'm a better mood.

Suddenly I don't worry about this night ending with the two us standing and staring at the crowd in the middle of the gym.

"Such fun, huh?" Jocelyn asks.

"You don't like to dance?"

"Not here," she says, staring off at the students who don't seem to be anything like her.

Or like me.


Our first dance is—well, I'm not sure how to describe it.

I'm heartbroken in several different ways. For the wrong and the right ways.

I blame Rachel.

She's the one who comes up after the song and brings that ten-year-old with her.

They're beaming like newlyweds frolicking around in their love. Rachel hugs me again for some reason. And then the music starts.

A slow dance.

"Come on, Joss. Go dance."

"No."

"Come on. Oh, I love this song. Come on."

"Okay, fine."

And then.

Yes, and then …

The moment is etched in my mind.

Jocelyn takes a hand.

But it's not mine.

"Let's go."

The expression on Lee's face surely can't be as surprised as the one on mine.

I probably could fit a football in the gap between my lips.

I see Jocelyn wander off on the dance floor with its beating blue and red lights to slow dance with Lee.

*Slow dance.*

*Arms wrapped around each other. Slow moving and close and …*

Mine.

That's my dance.

*That's why I'm here, right?*

Then I hear the voice singing. It's a female singer—someone I think I've heard before but can't actually name.

It sounds like an older song, maybe a decade or two old.

I see those eyes and that face staring at me. As if she wants to make sure I'm watching her.

*Is she trying to get me jealous?*

"She's lovely, isn't she?" Rachel yells out.

*Lovely* isn't the right word.

And as the song begins to crescendo, a song that I've surely heard but don't recognize, I watch the couple dance and laugh and I feel jilted.

The words seem to echo my thoughts.

*"I have nothing—nothing. Nothing. If I don't have you."*

And somehow, in some way, I'm moved.

Not to anger, but something else.

There's nothing suggestive to this dance. It seems innocent and fun. And it seems like this is Jocelyn. *This* picture. Just a girl wanting to have fun. Wanting to give a guy the pleasure of dancing with her.

And watching me to make sure that I get it.

*Do you get it, Chris?*

No.

Nothing about this I get.

I don't get this gym or this school or this ancient song that's strangely bringing tears to my eyes.

*What is happening to you, man?*

It must be the pain medication I'm on.

It must be the rabies I'm infected with.

It must be the glorious sight of this girl with her sweet smile who's watching me, who's smiling at me.

Without her, I wouldn't be at this dance.

Without her, this entire place would be completely miserable.

I know.

I know now.

Not dancing with her, not dancing in her arms, but standing there staring and watching her finally let go and have fun—

This is when I know that this deep bubbling ache inside is real.

It's not just because she looks like she does.

I can't help that.

I can't.

But it's because she's human and real and strangely intoxicating.

"Well, that's surely blown Lee's mind," Rachel says with a laugh.

*Yeah. Mine too.*

## 26. THE CURIOSITY FACTOR

It's almost easy to believe that I'm back home at any party.

Almost.

For a moment I feel like there is hope for this place, for these people, for myself.

Yeah, that sounds horribly shallow, but that's what I'm thinking when I walk inside the house—I guess I can rightfully call it a mansion—and hear "The National Anthem" playing.

Not the actual national anthem, but the awesome live version off Radiohead's *I Might Be Wrong* album.

It seems like a cleansing after the beating I just took of Lynyrd Skynyrd and Kid Rock.

We followed Rachel and her date to the house after the dance. Lee is good friends with the guy who is holding the party: Ray Spencer. He's a popular senior I've seen around but never met in person. I guess for four years straight he's had this party. When Jocelyn tells me about it in her uninterested tone, as if I already know we're coming here, I pictured going to a tiny house where people are huddling outside in the back smoking and drinking beer.

But there's nothing tiny about this house. It's on the outskirts of Solitary, a fifteen-minute drive from the school. Even if held at gunpoint, I wouldn't have a chance driving back to the school or back home. The roads we take wander through the woods until we head up into the hills and arrive at a driveway that dips and circles around in front of the large mansion comprised of stone and logs.

Lights flood the outside. There are cars parked all along the road and the driveway. We find a slight spot next to what looks like a three-car garage-house next to the mansion, and Jocelyn parks. She seems familiar with this place.

I'm still just managing to pick my mind and soul off the dance floor from watching Jocelyn dance with Lee.

The house inside swarms with teenagers, some I recognize and some I don't. Jocelyn reads my mind as we're heading toward the kitchen past an immense wall decorated with family photos depicting perfection.

"A lot of these kids don't go to Harrington," she says. "Ray knows a lot of people."

I spot some kids holding beer cans, others holding cups that look like beer. I'm trying to figure out if this party if chaperoned or not.

When I get to the large kitchen, I see a spread on an island that doesn't look prepared by teens. It reminds me of the work parties my parents used to have catered.

It sounds like they're playing the entire Radiohead album. Awesome.

"Are his parents here?"

"I'm sure," Jocelyn says, continuing to lead me somewhere.

I follow her out an open sliding glass door to a deck. Floodlights illuminate the falling ground below. Jocelyn walks through some guys, who all smile at her and say her name. We get to the railing and look over it.

"You should see this during the day. Probably one of the most beautiful views in the country."

I just see the world falling into a sea of darkness below. I hear a familiar voice and turn to see Rachel.

"Hey, guys. Isn't this awesome?"

"This is Ray for you," Jocelyn says.

"Have you seen him?" Rachel asks.

"Not yet."

"Lee's getting something to drink. You guys want anything?"

"I'm fine," Jocelyn says quickly.

"Yeah, me, too."

"Look—excuse me for a moment," Jocelyn says, leaving Rachel and me alone.

"Just to warn you, she might be a little grouchy for a while. I'm sure it'll get better."

"Why?"

Rachel glances around, then brushes back her wild blonde hair out of her eyes. "She dated Ray for a while. Just a short while. Long enough, if you ask Jocelyn."

"Oh."

"Yeah. No chance she would have come here unless I was here. And you, too."

"Were they serious?"

"Serious? Lots of things with Joss are serious. But did she like the guy? Not really."

I nod. "What about him?"

"Oh, he was madly in love with her. Still is."

Rachel smiles, then spots Lee. She calls out his name and disappears into the crowd.

I stand out on the deck where some other kids, guys mostly, are talking and laughing and drinking.

I feel like a tool.

I wait for what seems like ten minutes or longer, then decide to head back into the house.

Maybe Jocelyn and Rachel are in the kitchen. Or somewhere else.

I search the kitchen and the open area next to it. A small table has a group around it with an assortment of food and drinks—mostly soda—in the middle of it. The room opens up into a family room with an L-shaped couch and a large television on the wall showing what looks to be a local football game.

I head into the next room, also full of kids.

Something's different here, however.

I feel it as soon as I step through the entryway.

There are three sofas all around a glass table, and everybody is circling and facing the table, watching what's going on.

At first I assume they're playing a game of cards or something.

But the faces suddenly turn, almost in unison—twenty-something faces looking at me like they're nameless, faceless, expressionless androids wondering what I'm doing here.

My skin prickles as I feel the chill in the air.

In the awkward silence I clear my throat.

I can't help glancing down at the table.

Just a quick peek.

I discover I'm right in one sense. On the table are about a dozen cards, larger than the ones my old buddies used to play poker. Their faces have all different colors on them, with images I can't make out from where I stand. I just know there are no numbers or symbols on them. No UNO or Old Maid emblems either.

Two stacks of the cards stand on the edges, their backsides completely black.

No—there's some type of small writing on each, like tiny cursive writing.

Suddenly I spot an ashtray. Yet nobody I can see is smoking, and there's no smell of cigarettes.

Something is glowing in the ashtray. Like a lit ember.

Then I feel a hand clap on my shoulder from behind me.

"Chris."

I turn and see Jocelyn, her face serious and pale and distressed.

"Get out of here," she says.

"What?"

She pulls me back into the family room and kitchen.

"I was looking for you," I say as we stand at the edge of a counter.

"You should've stayed put."

"What were they doing back there? What was that?"

"Nothing."

"Do you know?" I ask.

"It was nothing. Listen, just—dial down the curiosity factor, okay?"

I can't stop a nervous laugh. "I'm sorry, but I forgot to bring my tarot cards to the party."

"Don't."

"Don't what?" I ask.

"Don't go there. Those weren't tarot cards, okay? Just—just be smart." Jocelyn edges up to me and speaks in a whisper. "There are things around here you can't begin to understand. Things not everybody knows about. Just stay with me and don't ask questions or appear nosy, got it?"

I want to ask why she's whispering, but I don't.

I'm convinced.

I simply nod and stay there, quiet.

She smiles a sweet, sad smile. "Why do you do that?"

"Do what?"

"Just—you're impossible."

"What?"

"You're so easygoing, you know? Will you do anything I say?"

"Is that a bad thing?" I ask.

"No. I'm just not used to it."

"Getting your way?"

"Being listened to," Jocelyn says. "Being trusted."

"It's easy to listen to you. And trust you."

Jocelyn shakes her head.

"What?" I ask.

"You know—for being from the big city of Chicago, you act awfully naive at times."

"Sorry."

"No. It's—it's just ..."

"What?"

"Nothing."

"What is it?"

She shakes her head and sighs. "Fine."

"What?"

"It's endearing. Got it? I admitted it."

I laugh, and Jocelyn glances at me with mesmerizing eyes.

"What now?" she says.

"A compliment shouldn't be that hard to give."

"Yeah, well, you don't understand why I might be hesitant."

"No. But I have time."

"Time for what?"

"Time to learn why."

"Some things aren't worth listening to, Chris. Trust me. Some things you're better *not* knowing."

# 27. RAY

Ray Spencer is a snapshot of everything I want to be. He's good looking with messy—but not too messy—short blonde hair, the looks of a soccer player, and the smile of an actor. He looks like a poster child for Abercrombie & Fitch in his distressed jeans and plaid shirt rolled at the elbows. His handshake is firm, firm like a politician's. Not like that of a senior going to a high school in Nowhere, North Carolina.

He makes me feel about ten years old.

"Glad you could make it tonight. Has Jocelyn shown you around the place?"

"Not exactly," she says, standing right next to me like a bodyguard.

"Give him a tour," Ray says, his teeth practically glinting under the kitchen's canned lights. "You certainly know your way around here."

"We're fine right here." I can tell Jocelyn is annoyed and wants to end this conversation.

"I heard you had an interesting week," Ray says to me.

"Yeah, you can say that."

"Look—not everybody around here is like Gus. There are some cool people at Harrington—obviously you know that, because you're hanging around with a few of them."

"Ray here is the master of flattery."

"What?" he says to Jocelyn. "I'm being honest."

"Uh-huh."

"Where are you from again?" he asks me.

"Libertyville. A suburb of Chicago."

"My family's been to Chi-town a few times. Great place."

"Yeah."

The guy has an air about him, no doubt, but he reminds me of some of the guys back home. Of Brady, if Brady actually had some common sense. Even his voice doesn't carry an accent.

"I grew up in Colorado, in case you're wondering. Family relocated right before high school."

"Big change."

"It's all right. Going back there for college."

College is one of those far-off thoughts. I haven't even earned my license. College seems like it should be four years away, not a year and a half.

"So is Joss treating you well?" Ray asks with a smile.

"Sure."

"Shut up, Ray."

"What'd I say?"

"You know what you said," Jocelyn tells him.

"Joss, here, she's a feisty one. But that just makes her all the better, you know what I mean?"

"You can be a real jerk, you know that?"

Ray acts innocent, as though he has no idea what he said.

"Come on," Jocelyn says, heading toward the deck outside.

I start to follow her when Ray gets in my way.

"Hey, buddy—just a suggestion. Take it or leave it, okay? But I wouldn't get that serious if I were you. Joss is a lot of fun. *A lot.* But don't get too attached. She's not the one to hang your hat on. Trust me."

Without a word, I move around him to go find her.

I don't like the fact that he knows her better than I do.

Or the fact that they have a past.

I don't like the idea of this guy having had his paws all over her. He might look pretty and smell pretty, but that doesn't mean he isn't trash just like Gus.

The night air is cool, and I find Jocelyn standing by the railing looking off into the darkness.

"Where's Rachel?" I ask her.

"I don't know. I just—do you want to go?"

"Of course."

"I came here for her, and she's not even around. She's so lovesick over that little boy."

"Lee?"

"Yeah. One of Ray's boys, as I call him."

"We can go anytime."

She looks up at me with angry eyes. Her expression is tight and tough. "Don't you ever become like them."

"Like who?" I ask.

"Like all of them. Guys who think they're better than the rest."

I wish I had the courage to tell her that I'm not one of them and never will be.

I wish I had the guts to hug her and whisper that in her ear.

But though I believe this, I don't have the strength to tell her. I don't have the guts to show that belief.

"Let's go," she says.

"Home?"

"No. Let's just go."

# 28. Wounded and Wrecked

She drives for ten minutes into the winding country backroads that seem to get darker by the minute. We don't say much—not about the dance, or the party, or anything. The rock music in her car is loud, strangely making me feel worse than any silence might. Jocelyn eventually slows and heads down a small drive that is grown over with weeds and bushes. She stops in front of a small, abandoned wooden cabin.

If I was with anybody else, I might be completely freaked out.

Instead, I'm insanely curious where this is going.

"I used to live there, believe it or not," she says, the car lights still on and shining into dark holes that used to be windows. "I lived there with my parents. I've been with my aunt ever since they passed away."

"I'm sorry," I tell her.

"It's okay. I know that you get it."

For a moment, I start to ask why but then assume she's talking about the move and my parents' divorce.

Jocelyn turns off the engine and the lights, then faces me.

There's a bright moon out tonight. It's partially shrouded behind the trees and some clouds, but it's letting off enough light that I can make out her face and her lips.

I can't help but wonder what we're doing here.

She puts a hand on my leg. "You're a good guy, Chris. And I just want you to know—I get it. I understand."

I nod, lost, not sure what it is she gets or understands.

*Not that I care really. At this moment, she's touching me, and she's looking at me, and I might just pass out any second.*

"It's easy to feel like you'll never recover, but you will."

I start to shake. She feels it.

"Come here," she says, so comfortable, so in control. "It's okay."

But this just causes me to shake more.

She moves over and kisses me on the lips.

I've kissed girls before. A couple. But this just feels—it's strange. It's one thing to imagine this—and I sure have imagined this—but I'm feeling off balance sitting in her car in the darkness.

I stop the kiss before she does.

I move back and watch her eyes slowly open.

"What?" she asks in a soft voice.

"Nothing. I'm just—I'm sorry. I'm a bit—surprised, I guess."

"Why?"

"I just am."

"Have you never been with a girl before?"

"No, I just—well, I mean—"

Not only is my body shaking, but my words are coming out all mangled and messy.

Her hand wanders in the darkness. I suddenly realize that she's trying to undo my belt buckle.

"Jocelyn, no, come on," I say.

But she doesn't stop.

With a trembling hand I hold hers and put it back in her lap. Her eyes and her expression grow cold and confused.

"What?"

"Look, just, hold on. I mean—what's happening here? What's going on?"

"You're kidding, right?" she says.

"What?"

"Don't tell me you don't want this."

"Don't want—what? You?"

"Yeah."

"Well, I—I mean, yeah, of course, but I don't even know you."

"What do you want, a biography or something?"

Her tone and her words seem cruel, callous.

"You've wanted this since the first time you laid eyes on me, and you know it."

I feel like hyperventilating.

*What is happening here? What did I do, and am I really doing this? Am I really telling her no?*

But nothing about this seems right.

"Jocelyn—it's no big secret that I like you. Just like the rest of the school."

"Like the rest of the school, huh? What do you know about the rest of the school?"

"I'm just saying—"

"I thought you were different from the rest of them."

"Yeah, so?"

"So you have to be *that* different? Do you have to be such a gentleman and rub it in my face?"

"I'm not rubbing anything in anybody's face."

"You're making me feel like some whore."

I let out a crazy and angry laugh. "What are you talking about?"

"Let's just go home."

I put my hand on her arm as it goes to start the car. She jerks it back, putting a finger back in my face. "Don't you dare touch me. Don't you dare put your hand on mine."

*She's suddenly turned into a crazy woman.*

I hold my hand out. "Jocelyn, talk to me."

"What?" she yells as she starts the car.

"Please, don't—don't drive just yet."

"This was a mistake."

"What's going on?"

"This was a mistake. Going to the dance and going to the party. The whole thing was a mistake. I should've never said yes."

I shake my head. "You asked me to go."

"No, I didn't. You asked. First it was the whole Rachel thing, but then I know what you said to Rachel. I know what you told her."

"What'd I tell her?"

"I know about your family, Chris. I know about your father. I know he died just a year ago."

My mind is trying to catch up, but it's doing a lousy job computing. "Who told you that?"

"Rachel. She told me. And I just felt awful. Because I can relate."

"My father isn't dead."

"What?"

For the first time since I pushed her away from me, Jocelyn is looking at me.

"My parents got a divorce. My father's very much alive, still living in Illinois."

"But she told me that you guys ended up moving...." Jocelyn thinks for a minute, then curses. "I don't believe her."

"She lied to get you to go out with me."

"I'm going to kill her," Jocelyn says. "I'm going to strangle her. I mean it."

"I'm sorry."

"*You're* sorry? No wonder you were a little confused. I just—she told me you were still feeling down and still grieving for your father. And I just—I felt sorry for you. I could relate. And I just wanted you—I wanted you to forget. That's why—I didn't know."

"I didn't mean to push you away."

"No, it's fine. This whole night—it's just been a misunderstanding."

I take Jocelyn's hand in both of mine. "Please, just listen to me. You're right. Since the moment I saw you in that murky school, you've been the one sole bright spot in it. And I haven't been able to stop thinking about you. And everything in me wants this—wants you. It's just—I just—I can't, Jocelyn. I don't know what to tell you."

"You're shaking."

"Yeah, I guess I am."

"You don't need to."

"I feel like an idiot here. I feel like—I feel like a kid."

"Chris, stop," she says. "This was—I was just—I'm just really messed up. Look, you don't want to be with someone like me."

"But I do."

"No, you don't, Chris. Don't ruin yourself. I'm used goods."

"Stop it."

"I am," she says, her voice choking a bit despite the lack of tears in her eyes. "There's a reason those guys look at me the way they do."

"It's because you're beautiful."

"No, I'm not. You strip this away and there's nothing down inside. Nothing."

"Don't say that."

"It's true. I was just—I just wanted you to forget. And I guess I wanted to forget too."

"Forget what?"

"This life. I just wanted to escape for a moment. To leave all this emptiness behind."

I sit across from her in the car feeling wounded and wrecked and wasted.

I don't know what to say.

This is so beyond my comprehension that I'm beginning to shut down.

I can tell she's already shut down.

She backs up the car, and we leave the little empty shell of a house to the darkness.

## 29. SOMEONE, SOMEWHERE IN SUMMERTIME

There are a hundred things I want to tell Jocelyn—right after watching her car leave my driveway.

These words stalk me on Sunday as I count down the minutes until I can see her again.

I question everything I said and did. Every response I gave. Everything.

Doubt is a terrible thing, but there's nothing you can do with it except let it go. But that's not happening. Not on this day.

I don't feel like going outside. It's a bit chilly and overcast. I assume it's going to rain. It always seems to rain on Halloween. Instead I lose myself in Uncle Robert's music in the snug room upstairs.

Mom asks about last night, and I try to play it off cool. She knows something's up but doesn't pry. She knows it won't go anywhere.

The beauty in being a teen is that adults remember this and put you in a box. A box in which the bad can't be all that bad. A box in which drama is simply teen drama and doesn't necessarily count.

But it hurts and it counts. Just because you're sixteen doesn't mean you can't hurt.

Speaking of boxes, I discover another one filled with albums in the walk-in closet—more old eighties records. I listen to whole albums with fascination. The Psychedelic Furs. Peter Gabriel. Level 42. Information Society. Howard Jones. The Human League. A-Ha. Some of the songs are so unabashedly corny that I almost blush listening to them. Others sound poppy and fun. Some of them are magical.

Why go outside when I can lose myself like this?

I find a group called Simple Minds and play the album titled *New Gold Dream (81-82-83-84)*. The first song sends me somewhere far off.

As the music plays, I map out strategies in my mind.

What I will say and what I will do.

Knowing I'll say and do none of those things.

I'll still be in this room tomorrow, the songs still playing in my mind.

# 30. MORE SURPRISES

I want to look at my clothes to see if they're on fire.

I want to smell them to see if I accidentally rolled around in cow manure this morning.

I want to check my back to see if there's a sign that says DEAD MAN WALKING on it.

I want to figure out exactly why every single student I pass is staring at me.

This is worse than normal. And normal is bad enough.

I make it to my locker without seeing Jocelyn. I open it up and find a note taped on the back of the door.

*Not again, Rachel. This time whatever you're saying, I'm not buying.*

I open it up and read it.

> Chris,
> This is just to warn you … be careful. Be very
> careful who you trust. They're watching you,
> Chris. They're watching and waiting.
>
> A friend

The note is half of a sheet of paper that someone printed from a computer.

I reread it. *A friend.*

*Don't friends tell you their names?*

I wonder if this is from Newt.

When I see him I'll ask.

Surely it isn't from Rachel or Jocelyn.

Maybe it's from someone who doesn't want me to hang around them.

Maybe they're talking about Jocelyn.

*They're watching.*

Yeah? Well, from the looks of it, everybody's watching. Everybody's waiting.

I slide the note into my pocket and then grab my books.

The last thing I want to do today is learn, but I guess that's what I'm supposed to do.


"Hey, Jocelyn."

I've been waiting for her outside our English classroom and manage to speak to her before she goes in.

"Hi."

She doesn't look at me.

"Can we talk today?"

"About what?"

"About Saturday night?"

"No, that's okay," she says.

"Look—I just want to say a few things."

"That's quite all right."

"I'd feel better if I could."

"And I'd feel better if we just forgot Saturday ever happened."

She walks into the classroom.

I'd like to just wait out here for the next forty-five minutes.

Instead, I walk into the same room feeling stupid for even trying.


I'm on the way to my next class feeling like a product on a conveyer machine when I hear someone call out my name.

*Gus. He's decided it's about time to pay me a visit.*

But the voice sounds nothing like him, and when I turn I see Ray approaching in his cool jeans and shirt.

"Hey, man, how'd you score after the party?"

I look at him and don't quite know how to answer the question.

He laughs and hits me gently in the chest. "That's okay, man. I can imagine. I've been there. No need to share. Hey—I got a question for you. Wanted to ask you at the party, but you disappeared."

"Okay." My voice sounds weak.

"You guys find a church?"

I would have been less surprised if Ray had asked me if I had found a crack dealer.

"What?"

"A church. You guys go to church?"

"Not really," I say. "I mean, we used to. My dad wanted us to go."

"Well, cool. I go to this great church. You should check it out. It's called New Beginnings. The pastor there is amazing."

"Okay, yeah, great."

"I'm serious, man," Ray says. "It's really good. It's not like one of those regular boring churches out there. Promise me you'll think about it."

"Sure."

"Great." He smiles, and I think again how white his teeth look. "I'll see you around."

The last person I'd have expected to invite me to church would be Ray Spencer.

But every single day at this school brings a surprise.

And this day is only half over.

## 31. LUNCH BUDDY

This is high school.

The smell of bad burgers and gym class drifting in the air.

Nameless, faceless ghouls strolling by listening to iPods with blank stares.

Colorless bathrooms with red and black graffiti covering the stalls and cracked mirrors waving back.

A guy named Gus walking in the hallway and blocking the way, taunting you, trying to get something started.

A girl named Poe dressed in a black dress with Converse shoes and some kind of strange monotone top blocking the way to lunch with a disappointed stare.

All I want at this particular moment is to find Jocelyn and try talking to her.

Seeing Poe, I suddenly wonder if that's going to happen.

"What's up?"

"Hello, Chris."

"Something wrong?"

"Yeah, unfortunately," she says.

"Jocelyn?"

She nods, a look of glee on her face.

"I just want to talk to her."

Poe shakes her head. "Uh-uh. Give her some space."

I don't feel like getting into this with Poe. I start to walk past.

"Look, she doesn't want to see you."

I stop and turn. "What's that mean?"

"Well, let's see. I *think* it means that she, Jocelyn, doesn't want to see you, Chris. Yeah, I'm pretty sure that's what it means."

"You don't get it."

"I didn't have to go to some lame dance to get it."

"No, you really don't get it."

"Look, moron. Listen to me. I've sat and watched the guys at this dump come and go for two and a half years, treating Joss like some toy, some *thing*. Something they hold and put on a pedestal and then toss away whenever they feel like it. And we thought you'd be different."

My mouth hangs open for a second in disbelief. "You have no idea what you're talking about."

"Guys are guys wherever they're from."

"And so are girls," I say, walking away from Poe and going to get some food.

I'll have to find somewhere else to sit today.

"You mind?"

Newt looks up through his oversized glasses, away from the paperback novel he's reading, and shakes his head.

"What're you reading?"

"Dennis Shore. *Marooned*. Read any of his stuff?"

"No. I've seen some movies."

"The books are better. The books are always better."

I nod. He has a really ripe banana, some pretzels, and a half-eaten sandwich that looks like someone sat on it. The thing on my tray is supposed to be a chicken sandwich and fries, but I bet scientists would say otherwise.

"Hungry?" I ask.

He looks at me, then down at my plate. "You don't want that?"

"Not really."

"Okay."

He takes some fries and eats like a prisoner of war. Watching him, I suddenly get over my hesitation to sit with him. Instead of feeling sorry for myself, I feel sorry for him.

Newt, on the other hand, seems used to his life as a high school doormat. He eats as if nobody else is watching him.

Which they weren't, until I sat down with him.

"Girl problems?" he asks, mouth full.

"Yeah, something like that."

"Probably for the best."

"Hey—you know that article you gave me—"

"Shhh!" Newt shakes his head, and bits of fries fly from his mouth. "Remember what I said."

"About what?"

"They're watching."

"Look—did you give me this note today?"

"What note?"

I grab the crinkled thing out of my pocket and hand it to him. He looks around, then opens and reads it. He looks at me. "I'd never sign a letter like that."

"What? As a 'friend'?"

"That's right," he says.

"Well, okay."

"I say that whoever gave you this note can't be trusted."

"Really," I say with an exaggerated tone and look. "Maybe *you* can't be trusted."

"Don't mock me."

"You seriously didn't give me this note?"

"I *seriously* did not give you that note."

"What do you think it's talking about?"

"It depends on who gave it to you," Newt says.

"Maybe it's talking about *you*."

Newt ignores my comment and starts to read again.

"You know, maybe you've been reading a few too many horror novels."

"These are supernatural thrillers," Newt says the way a librarian might. "And furthermore, one can't read too many books."

"You gotta *live* life sometime."

"I plan to do so the moment I leave this town."

"Yeah, well, I hear you there."

I stare at the mystery meat and then put the bun back on top. "Want my chicken sandwich too?"

"Only if you don't," he says. In a millisecond half of it is in his mouth.

I get that feeling that someone is looking at me, so I turn around.

Seven tables away, Jocelyn is looking at me.

We stare at each other for a moment until a group of girls blocks our view. When the girls move past, I look for Jocelyn, but she's no longer there.

## 32. Things Can Only
## Get Better

I come home to a house that's been trashed.

Cushions are off the sofa. It looks like someone was picking at the fireplace and got soot and ashes all over the floor and the carpet. The table in the family room is overturned—I see broken glass on the floor.

"Mom!"

I search her bedroom and the small bathroom attached to it, then sprint up the stairs and search the two rooms up there.

"Mom, are you here?"

I keep calling out her name while I go back downstairs.

The kitchen is a disaster, with pots and pans all on the floor and food everywhere.

*Wait a minute.*

I see opened cookbooks, along with several bottles of wine on the counter.

A couple of bottles are in the garbage can.

Noodles in some kind of white sauce (that's now crusty-looking) are in the middle of the floor.

An empty wine glass is on the kitchen table.

Another one is broken on the floor.

It looks like there was a party here and I wasn't invited.

"Mom!"

I open the door to the laundry room, then let out a sigh of relief.

It's sad when seeing your mother passed out on the floor of the laundry room brings a sigh of relief.

Her eyes are swollen, with caked makeup smeared around them and on her cheeks. I can tell she's been crying.

*She's been raging too.*

I bend down and gently touch her cheek. Maybe it's morbid, but I'm just checking. Then double-checking to make sure.

*She's not dead, you idiot. She's just out like the drunkard she is.*

Mom is wearing a black dress along with high heels and a necklace. Her hair is up. I prop her up against the back wall, hoping that will revive her.

She's out.

Really totally out.

She smells sweet and sickly, a smell I'm slowly getting used to and quickly learning to loathe.

All around us in this tiny room are dirty clothes. Ghostly light spills in from the tiny round window above us.

I sigh and wipe the sweat off my forehead.

I've got a lot of homework to do, and none of it has anything to do with school.

The sun is gone and so is my appetite. If I keep this up I'm going to look like a skeleton.

It's close to nine, and I hear my mom's toilet flush. After carrying her to her bed and laying her down to sleep a few hours ago, I cleaned the place up as best as I could.

A light goes on. I'm watching one of the three channels we get on our television. I miss DirecTV. That along with a lot of other things.

She doesn't come out for another ten minutes. When she does, she's wearing pajamas. She looks tired, her face a bit swollen, her eyes vacant.

"Thanks," she says.

"For what?"

Mom glances around the room, then looks at me. "For everything."

I nod. What am I supposed to say? To be honest, I'm embarrassed about the whole thing.

"Guess my date never showed up," Mom says, trying to make a joke.

I nod, continuing to look at the television. It takes me a couple minutes before I start laughing.

"Sorry you had to see that," she says. "I didn't even know I had any of my dresses with me."

"You never know when you might need one."

"There are a lot of things I might need, but an evening dress isn't one of them."

Mom goes into the kitchen and comes back holding a glass of water. "Chris—listen to me."

"Yeah?"

"Tomorrow—tomorrow I'll start trying."

"Start trying what?"

"I'll start trying to live again. I'm sorry. I'm sorry you had to come home to that."

I nod again. It's all I can do.

"I need to find a job. Find something to do. Tomorrow—I'll get started on that, okay?"

"Yeah."

"Chris?"

I look at her.

"I know that—I know how I've been. I just—I just want to say that I love you. That I love how strong you've been."

I'm not sure what to say back.

"You have your father's strength, you know that?"

"I take after you more than him," I say.

"Maybe. In some ways. But you're still a combination of both of us."

"I wish I wasn't."

"Don't say that. I need that strength, Chris. I need it. It's sad to say, but it's true."

"Okay."

"I love you, you know that?"

"Yeah."

"It's going to get better," she says. "I promise it's going to get better."

I nod, but I don't believe her.

It's November, and winter is still approaching.


## 33. Playlist for a Loser


The week crawls by.

Jocelyn remains a stranger despite several attempts to speak with her.

Every day repeats the same track listing.

There's side one, since this obviously must be a record I found in my uncle's cabin:

1. "Ship of Fools" by Doves (for the bus ride)
2. "Losing Touch" by The Killers (for everything before second period)
3. "Something" by The Beatles (for English class)
4: "Did You Ever & Do You Still" by Sean Torrent (for after English)
5. "Shut Your Eyes" by Snow Patrol (the next couple of hours)
6. "Shot in the Back of the Head" by Moby (for lunch with Newt because he sorta reminds me of Moby)

Then side two:

7. "Invisible Sun" by the Police (after lunch)
8. "Heartless" by Kanye West (American history)
9. "Last Goodbye" (Jeff Buckley) (trying to talk after history)
10. "Driveaway" by Great Northern (for the bus ride after school)
11. "Go It Alone" by Beck (getting home)
12. "Until the Night Is Over" by M83 (for everything after sunset)

She's built a wall, and there's no ladder around to climb up over it.

I had one chance, and I blew it.

The week is a blur.

A nightmarish blur.

The worst thing in the world is the silence. The stares, the secrets, the solitude.

I'd rather be chased by a rabid dog in the middle of the night than ignored and left alone.

At least Mom gets a job as a hostess at the local family restaurant in town.

At least I have Newt to eat my food at lunch and swap witty comments with at the locker.

I'm stranded and marooned like Robinson Crusoe. The rest of the school is made of savages. Newt is my Friday.

The guys back at the old school would laugh if they could hear me. But then again, so would anybody else. That's okay. My thoughts are sealed up. There's nobody to listen to them anyway.

As Friday begins to fade away, I am approached by Ray the Politician. That's what I'm starting to call him, at least to myself. My friends and I used to always have names for other kids. Perhaps this is payback.

*My name is Loser, and I'm wearing it proudly.*

"Hey, Chris, here's that program I told you about," he says, handing me a colored flyer from his church.

"Thanks."

What else can I say?

"There are two services on Sunday. You guys should check it out."

"Sure."

At this point I'm willing to try anything.


## 34. All the Puzzle Pieces


"Just stop, please, for a sec."

I'm blocking her way and making a fool of myself. If she goes around me, that's fine. I'm not going to tackle her.

"I just want to talk."

It's Friday, and she's headed out toward the parking lot. I know I'm dangerously close to missing my bus, but there are worse things that can happen.

*Like having her leave me in complete confusion all weekend long.*

"What do you want?"

"What'd I do?"

The porcelain doll face looks down.

"Jocelyn, please, look at me."

"What?"

"I'm sorry."

"What are you sorry for?"

"For—for everything."

She rolls her eyes.

Again, I'm not getting it. I'm not getting this.

"Please, just—just hear me out, okay?"

She remains there as students pass by, every one of them looking at us like we're a car wreck in the middle of the interstate.

"Look—this is my third week here, okay. And I don't know all the rules and the ins and outs and all that. I just know that I think you're really amazing. And really special. And I just—I'd like to show you that not all guys are complete morons, and I thought—I thought I was doing the right thing, but I didn't mean to hurt you or do anything that you didn't want—"

"Just shut up."

"What?"

"Just stop. Stop talking. Okay? Just stop."

"Then what—I just wanted you to know."

"I know, I get it, okay? I get it. I got it last weekend and I still get it, okay?"

My mind tries to put the puzzle pieces in order. I'm not connecting, not computing.

And then, for a brief second, just a tiny sliver of a moment …

*There it is, once again.*

*I see it.*

*It's there, and I know it's there.*

"Jocelyn," I start to say.

But her eyes start to give her away and she shakes her head, says no, then rushes away.

I sigh.

I stand in the hallway that's now empty.

The bell rings, signaling that the buses have left.

I'm on my own.

I stand there for a long time, wondering what I did wrong, wondering what I should and shouldn't have said.

I have all weekend to think about it.

# 35. CHURCH

I hold the church flyer in my hand, wondering if this is a good time to bring it up.

Ever since the incident the other night when I found my mother in the laundry room passed out in her evening dress—there's an Oprah show for you right there—Mom's been acting different. She's been trying harder, acting sweeter, acting more like a mother should act. That and the job she's gotten have made things temporarily better. Even having to call her to pick me up from school yesterday after I missed the bus turned out to be no big deal. We ended up driving outside of Solitary (driving for what seemed to be half an hour) to grab a bite at McDonald's.

I've been waiting today to ask her.

I know she's going to be leaving soon to go to her new job. It's close to eleven in the morning.

The brochure seems to burn in my hand.

Maybe that's because the whole church issue is ultimately what did it for Mom and Dad.

Some relationships go south because of an affair or because the love is not there or because of some other big issue. But the thing that did it for my mom and dad ultimately was this.

The church-faith-God thing.

I chose to side with my mother.

But now I'm beginning to think again.

I don't know what to think. All I know is that Mom's not doing great and I could use a friend or two.

So what if I have to hear some preaching about God and heaven and all that?

It won't bother me.

I certainly heard enough of it living with Dad.

*You say God is love and God loves us, but what about you, Pop? What about you?*

I shove the thought away and go downstairs.

I smell something that's unfamiliar in this house.

Perfume.

Mom is in the bedroom getting ready.

"Can I come in?"

"Yeah, sure. Just finishing up."

I go inside the small room that certainly doesn't resemble the "master bedroom" it's supposed to be. I sit on a stiff bed that buckles in the middle. It lets out a groan when I relax on it.

"You look pretty," I tell her.

She does. She's wearing some casual pants and a light white sweater. I'm sure she'll be the most glamorous hostess that restaurant's ever had greeting customers.

"Thanks."

"I got a question about tomorrow."

"Yeah?"

She's putting on an earring, so she's not looking at me.

*Get it out. Just get it out, Chris.*

"Well, a guy came up to me at school—a guy named Ray Spencer. Really cool guy. A senior. He was the one who had the party."

"Uh-huh."

"Anyway, he was asking me about going to his church tomorrow."

Mom stares at me as if the bed swallowed me up inside it.

"And?"

I can already hear her tone. It's defensive, the kind that can't help coming out.

"Well, it's just—I don't know. I thought it might be good to go."

"And why is that?"

"Mom, relax."

"No, Chris, you relax."

"I'm relaxed."

*But not really and you probably know it, don't you?*

"Why do you want to go to church?"

"Mom—this has nothing to do with Dad."

"Okay."

"It's just a guy—look—he just seems really cool, and he seems like he's being nice."

"What's he trying to do? 'Witness' or something? Save your soul?"

"Easy."

"Chris, please."

"I just thought we might—"

"No, no," Mom says. "We're not going to do anything. I'm not stepping foot in a church."

"I'm just thinking it might be good to meet some other guys."

"You're free to go if you want."

"What do you want me to do? Walk there?"

I can see it on her face. She's not going to go, and she's probably not going to even take me.

"It's fine," I say.

Mom looks at me. "Chris, come on."

"No, it's cool."

"Don't do this to me, not now."

"Okay."

"Look, if you really want to go, I'll drive you there. Deal?"

"Yeah, that's fine."

"Chris."

"It's fine. It's cool."

"Where's this coming from?"

*It's coming from the fact that I had to choose between the second coming of Moses or you, and I chose you. But that meant I suddenly have no friends and no life. So this is coming from me wanting to actually have a life.*

"Nowhere," I say.

"I gotta go."

"Okay, sure."

"We'll talk later."

"Yeah, that's fine."

There's always later.

## 36. CONFUSION

New Beginnings Church is difficult to find, even with the small map on the brochure. The tiny drawing doesn't include the miles of dense woods surrounding this area. Twice Mom and I drive by the road we're supposed to turn down. We eventually find Heartland Trail and head down the dirt road through hilly terrain until we reach a cleared area at the top of a flat hill that reveals a large white building with a dagger of a steeple.

It's a lot bigger than I thought it would be. Mom drives to the front of the building where there is a sidewalk circling the entrance. We see a family of four walking through the glass doors.

I feel the urge to ask Mom again, but I won't. It's enough that she drove me here.

"Want me to be here a little after noon?"

"Maybe I can find a ride home," I say, feeling guilty for asking her to make two trips out here for me.

"Well—if you can't, just call me. I don't mind picking you back up."

"A cell phone would be nice. Or you could just stay."

She lets out a *yeah, right* kind of laugh. I glance at her. She's strong and she's stubborn, and there's no way anybody is getting her through those doors.

"Okay, I'll touch base later."

I walk through the doors and see a welcome booth in front of me. A sign says in bold type COME AS YOU ARE. I wonder if that's supposed to be a quote from the Bible or from Kurt Cobain. Music shakes from inside the sanctuary. I look and see what appears to be more of a gymnasium than the inside of a church. On the stage are a group of singers along with some guys jamming out with guitars and a drum set.

I scan the foyer, but Ray is nowhere to be found. I see a small area with sofas, windows peering into a nursery, and a coffee and lounge area.

The place doesn't look too bad.

A firm handshake greets me at the door to the auditorium. I'm handed a bulletin that has *New Beginnings* plastered all over it, similar to the one Ray gave me.

There is a picture of a family on the cover. A father and mother holding hands with their son.

*Nice image. Maybe there are families here that actually have all their units still intact.*

I shuffle into the darkness of the crowd and find a seat near the back. This not only looks like a gymnasium, it is. I can see the basketball hoops propped up and the wood floor beneath my feet.

I'm thinking there might be five hundred people here, if not more.

I was expecting something smaller, something more old-fashioned.

Then I see Ray.

He's playing bass up on the stage. He's jamming away, singing the lyrics to the song, having a good old time.

I envy the guy, the look on his face.

It's so peaceful.

I wonder if I can get a little of that.

Just a few minutes after the guy who appears to be the main pastor walks up on the stage and starts talking, I begin to feel it.

Dizzy and dangling and out of breath.

I feel like I'm hanging onto a rope—not the kind you're strapped and locked into, but a thick strand of rope dangling out high above a gorge. I feel like the ground beneath me is moving, falling away. Yet even as I sense it I can see everybody else around me, the same dark bodies and faces, staring up at the light of the stage.

The pastor wears jeans and a dress shirt that's not tucked in. He's got spiky hair that looks highlighted and thin black glasses. He certainly looks like he's trying to be cool. Not sure if he does indeed look cool, and no idea whether he really is.

"Good morning, everybody. My name is Jeremiah Marsh. Thanks for coming out on this beautiful November morning. Welcome to New Beginnings Church."

He recounts a story about his young daughter getting up this morning that gets everybody to laugh. He talks in a manner that's like conversation around a dinner table with your family. Nothing about what he says seems anything less than sincere.

Yet I'm sitting here listening (or trying to listen), feeling like I've been drugged.

No, not drugged. Poisoned.

I can feel the sweat beads on my forehead and my cheeks. My neck, too. I have a dry taste in my mouth. The sickly dry taste that comes right before you throw up. I need air. I need water. I need something.

There's a lady sitting next to me, probably in her fifties, laughing away and acting like she's listening to the president. I glance at her, and she gives me a delirious smile that makes me a bit nervous. More nervous than I already am.

"So today let's talk about something that we hear over and over and over again. Your neighbor."

Pastor Jeremiah Marsh keeps talking. I notice he's wearing a headphone mic. There is a small podium near him, but he never uses it. He doesn't carry a Bible or notes or anything else. He waves his hands like a conductor as he speaks.

I can hear something else. Something that's faint, low, almost humming.

It sounds like a rumbling drone.

As if the church is sitting on some kind of ticking bomb, or a reactor of some kind, trembling at its force.

I wipe the sweat away. I don't want to get up and leave—that would be too obvious. But I'm fighting passing out.

Every now and then I focus on what the pastor is saying.

"And sometimes you don't even want to simply go outside and greet him."

This sounds like the "treat your neighbors as you would yourself" talk. I've heard that one before.

I shift in my seat and glance up a few rows at a pretty blonde. It's almost as if she knows I'm glancing at her, because she looks back at me.

"—and then sometimes you decide that the best thing to do is puncture the wound as quickly as you can."

I glance at the stage. I see the moving hands and the moving lips, but suddenly don't seem to quite hear what the pastor is saying.

*He didn't just say that. He didn't just say* puncture, *did he?*

"And the thing to ask yourself is this: Who watches over you? Who watches what's in your heart? You know, when I was fourteen years old living in Greer—"

I was hearing things. He's just talking like any pastor. The people around me are listening. I'm almost hyperventilating for some reason. I feel like a bad flu and cold and virus are all coming over me. I'm not sure what to do.

"So sometimes you take everything you think is yours because in the end, we leave with all we can get. So you need to take and ignore the rest."

Again, I focus on the stage and try to figure out if what I'm listening to is real.

The pastor keeps talking.

"We all come from different backgrounds. Different races. But we're all one. Like the U2 song says, we're all one."

*Now he's quoting a U2 song? This guy is seriously trying hard.*

I must be making things up in my head.

Someone behind me clears his throat. I want to turn—the urge to turn is incredible—but I force myself not to.

"It's okay to let down your guard if you need to. Because sometimes, sometimes my dear friends, death is the only option we have in this life of ours."

*What?*

I look around to see if anybody else is wondering what this guy is talking about.

"We near a time of thanksgiving, but shouldn't we always carry a heart that's thankful? That's giving? That's loving? That is the right way, my friends."

I clear my throat, and it sounds like I'm wheezing.

*I need water.*

The pastor keeps talking about being nice to neighbors and family and being real. It all sounds nice and fine and real.

I'm beginning to see double.

I finally stand up and start to walk out.

The voice behind me continues.

"But it's best that when we're faced with uncertainty, we act swiftly. We act promptly. And don't let yourself down. Don't act like you can't or won't. Because in the end, it's our job to give up a life in order to keep it."

*You're losing your mind, Chris. You're making up these words.*

"Don't fear darkness, friends," Pastor Marsh says. "Fear the light that tries to burn it out. The deeds inside can be covered and hidden, and that's what we all need. Because night is coming. Night is coming for us all."

As I leave the sanctuary, I hear applause.

I make it to the doors and stumble outside into the brilliance of midday, feeling like a prisoner gasping his few last breaths of life.

## 37. CHANGING LIKE THE MOON

I manage to mingle with the churchgoers when the music begins playing and they start filing out. I feel better after getting some air and sun and then having some coffee to try to revive my senses. I don't even like coffee, but I need something to jolt me back to sanity. I don't know where all that craziness came from, but don't have time to figure it out.

Soon, as I'm biding my time looking around in the crowd, I hear a voice call out my name.

"Hey, you made it," Ray says.

"Yeah."

"Wasn't that awesome. He's a great speaker, huh?"

"Yeah, he was good."

"See me up there? I've been playing with them for a while. It's fun. Sometimes we even do concerts. Nothing that big, but still something, you know?"

"Cool."

Ray introduces me to a few people and says hi to a bunch more as we stand in front of the coffee area.

"Hey—did you drive here?"

"No. I—I still need to get my license."

Ray laughs. "How'd you get here?"

"My mom."

"Want a ride home?"

"Yeah, sure. That'd be great."

"No problem. You want to have lunch at my house? It's always a big gathering, but nothing fancy."

"Okay, sure."

"Cool. Pastor Marsh usually comes. You gotta get to know him. He's really a great guy."

I nod. I decide to not tell Ray what I was hearing.

My mind sometimes plays tricks on me.

Maybe it has to do with my dad and the whole church thing and my hesitations toward God and all that.

*Or maybe this is God trying to tap me on the back and say that He really does exist.*

But I doubt God would do that by frightening me.

Ray tells me he's got a few people to see; he'll be back in a minute.

I'm not sure what to think about going to his place at lunchtime.

But it beats going back home.


Ray drives me to his house in a VW Jetta that still smells new. He jams tunes from the iPod he's got connected to the stereo, listing a dozen groups I've never heard of. I feel behind in everything. I don't know anybody, don't have my license, don't have money, don't know as much as I should, don't act the way I should.

But Ray seems oblivious to all of that. He seems eternally "up."

This is the second time I've been to this monstrous house, and the second time I've seen it full of people. This isn't Sunday lunch; it's a holiday celebration. It appears that half the people at the church must have come over for lunch.

After navigating through the adults, Ray shows me his room.

It's pretty much how I might have imagined a really sweet room to be. That and more.

A flat-screen television hangs on one wall. Of course, two different video game systems are on a shelf underneath it. Several framed posters hang on the wall. One is of the group Phoenix, with a minimalistic artistic shot that looks like an album cover. There's lots of sports stuff, including lots of indications that his favorite team is the Denver Broncos. I see three tennis rackets, a shelf of really awesome caps, a collection of trophies on his dresser.

Do they really hand out trophies anymore?

I wouldn't know. I've never really been a trophy sort of guy.

"Here—this is what I was telling you about," Ray says as he finds the CD and hands it to me.

"They're a local group?"

"Oh yeah. Awesome. They're going to be huge. I played you a couple of their songs."

We talk music for a while. I tell him about the music festivals I've gone to in Chicago, one of the few things that seems to be able to impress him. Soon we leave his room and head back to the kitchen.

I spend the next half hour meeting strangers and listening to adults talk with Ray. I'm never ignored—Ray always does a good job of introducing me. Everybody in the house seems to know and love him. Why not? I'd probably hate the guy out of jealousy if I didn't like him so much myself.

We eventually take plastic plates full of a day's worth of food outside on the deck. Now I'm able to see the incredible view below. It's breathtaking. I follow Ray to some empty chairs and sit next to him.

"So what's up with Joss and you?"

I almost choke on the piece of chicken I'm trying to swallow.

"Nothing."

"Things go bad after the party?"

"No, it's just—nothing's going on."

Ray nods and takes a bite of his potato salad. He eats like he's in a hurry.

"Look, the thing with Joss is this: It's easy to fall in love with her. I sure did. Everybody does. You have to be careful."

"Careful about what?"

"Careful about her. The girl has got—she's got secrets. She's got some really deep-rooted issues. I mean, we all do, right? But not like her."

"What sort of secrets?"

"They wouldn't be secret if you knew about them, you know?" Ray smiles. "Secrets. Stuff about her family. I don't know—she wouldn't tell me. I've just heard things."

"Like what?"

"Curious, huh? Just things. Things she's been involved with dark stuff. The sort of things we shouldn't talk about, not here."

Ray glances around, says hi to someone passing by, keeps eating like a famished man.

"What do you mean, dark stuff?"

"Maybe another time, all right? I'm just trying to warn you."

"People have been warning me about her ever since I first spoke to her."

"Doesn't surprise me. Our school's not that big. People talk. Rumors, secrets, all that. A lot of the kids who don't live in Solitary don't really know what they're talking about. But it's just—you're new, you don't have a clue."

"Thanks," I say.

"No offense. Not like you're clueless about life. Just about
Solitary. I can see any guy coming to this place and being gaga over
her. I sure was."

"What happened?"

"Issues, man. Like major crazy issues."

I think back to the last week, to the conversation in the car, to
my last few interactions with Jocelyn.

It's easy to believe Ray.

"Man, I'm still crazy about that girl. But she changes like the
moon. Some days it seems like she's full, you know, when she's just
alive and amazing. And other times, it's like she's empty. Nobody's
there. I don't know why. Guess that's why they have medication
and doctors and all that."

I suddenly don't feel so hungry.

It's strange, but I feel almost guilty talking about Jocelyn with
Ray. Even if she doesn't want to talk to me.

Ray finishes his plate and tells me he's going to get another. I
nibble on my food and listen to conversation in the background
and try to picture my mother here.

It's impossible. I can barely even picture myself here.

A minute or two later I see the pastor walking toward me.

A dread suddenly comes over me, and I have no idea why.

It's like I'm worried that he's going to ask me about God or my
faith or my family or something else that perhaps I need confession
for.

"Can I sit here?"

I nod and smile and suddenly have an urge to jump off the
deck and fall several stories below.

## 38. Help and Guidance

"I don't believe we've met," the pastor says in a calm, warm manner. "I'm Jeremiah."

I shake his hand. "Chris."

"Friend of Ray's?"

I nod, suddenly feeling light-headed. The guy has a baby face, the kind that probably could never grow a beard, with tiny lips and a narrow jaw that makes it appear like he's smirking all the time. His hip glasses glint in the sun.

"New to the area?"

I nod again.

The pastor looks around. When I follow his glance, I see there are only a couple of people left out here, and they're starting to walk away.

*Where'd everybody go?*

"Solitary is a good place, a quiet place," Jeremiah says between small bites of his salad. "I grew up here, then left for a while to find the world. Learned that the world is no different from here. It's just faster. And louder."

I try to swallow, and some potato salad seems to get stuck in my throat. I wonder if Pastor Marsh knows CPR, because I might need it.

"Is your last name Buckley?"

"Yes," I croak out, taking a drink of my soda to help loosen the potatoes.

"What's your mother's maiden name?"

"Kinner."

"Tara Kinner?"

"That's my mom."

"I knew it," he says with a smile.

*A creepy smile that gives me an icky feeling that I can't explain.*

"You look just like her," the pastor says.

"Yeah."

"How is she?"

"Good," I say.

*If good means downing bottles of wine every day.*

"You're not going to believe this, but your mother and I were in the same class at the grade school."

"Really?"

"Yes. Until she moved away. Ask if she remembers me. She probably won't. I was a little nerd back then. Even in grade school your mother was beautiful."

I nod and force a smile. I want to get up since we're the only ones on the deck now, but there's no way to delicately do that.

"Where are you living?"

"We're at my uncle's cabin."

Jeremiah nods, taking a bite and quickly chewing the way a mouse might. Every time I look at him, something seems off.

I have no idea why. He looks normal.

*Something's not right.*

"I haven't seen your uncle for some time. It's Robert, right?"

"Yeah. He sorta vanished."

Instead of finding this surprising, Jeremiah takes a sip from his glass of water in a casual matter. As if he already knew that.

*Probably does, since this is such a small place.*

"Did you know your Uncle Robert?"

"Not really."

"How old are you, Chris?"

"Sixteen."

"That would make you a junior then, correct?"

I nod.

*Where's Ray? Where's anybody?*

"Any other friends you've made at the school besides Ray?"

He waits for an answer, giving me a hard look that forces me to answer it.

"No, not really."

"No one? No one at all?"

"No," I say again.

"There is a lovely young girl I know named Jocelyn Evans. Have you met her?"

I stare at him, feeling like he has his knee on my chest and is pressing down. The oxygen inside of me is suddenly gone. My head feels dizzy, down, suddenly despairing.

"Sure, I've met her."

He nods. "Of course you have."

Adults can talk to kids this way. Even if you're sixteen, you're still always behind.

I don't know what to say.

"I'm sure you've probably been told by different people to be careful, right?"

"It's come up," I say.

"And?"

I shrug, looking into the closed screen door where I hear voices and laughter but don't see anybody.

"Have you taken their advice?"

"Do you know Jocelyn?"

"I know most of the people in this town, Chris."

I feel bumps on the back on my neck. And on my arms.

*Something in the way he said that …*

"She's just someone I've gotten to know."

"You know what a pastor's job is, Chris?"

*The way he says my name. It's almost the way my father used to say it.*

*It's too familiar, too close.*

"No," I say because I have no idea what else to say.

"It's twofold. It's to help. And to guide. Some people need encouragement to do the things they need to do. Others need their hand held. Which one are you?"

"I don't know."

"And sometimes, when people don't want their hands held, they end up falling on their behind. That's what I want to prevent, Chris. Can you understand that?"

"Is this about Jocelyn?" I blurt out, surprising myself.

"This is about you."

"What about me?"

"A new kid who needs help. And guidance."

"Yeah, sure."

He looks at me, dark brown eyes that almost look black, peering from behind his spectacles. "Do you need help? Or do you need your hand held?"

"I just—I don't—"

"Because I want to help you, Chris. You and your mother. I'm here to help."

"Okay."

"The last thing I would hate for you to do would be to lose your way."

"I'm not lost."

"We're all lost, Chris. Every one of us. The difference between me and most other pastors is that I'm honest. I tell the truth. And the truth is this. Do you want to hear it?"

I nod, feeling like I have a knife stuck up against my temple forcing me to stay here, forcing me to comply.

"The truth is that sooner or later, we all die. It's inevitable. But we do have choices when it comes to that. We can be afraid, or we can embrace that inevitable dark last breath."

I seem to have stopped breathing. I'm just looking at him, probably shrinking down in my chair.

It's only when I hear the sliding screen door and Ray's voice call out that I suddenly start to breathe again.

Pastor Marsh touches my arm and holds on to it.

"Think about what I've said, Chris. Tell Tara I say hi."

I force myself away from him and follow Ray back into the house.

I just want to get out of here, far away from Jeremiah Marsh and his foxlike glare.

## 39. QUESTIONS

I'm sixteen. Some people think that's young, but it's not *that* young.
I've had sixteen full years to get to know the person I live with each
and every day, and there's one thing I know about myself.

I don't like being told to do things.

I'm stubborn.

I take after my mother in that way.

My father forced the faith issue, and she drew the good old line
in the sand. She said *no way* because ultimately she doesn't like being
told what to do.

It's way past midnight, and I can't sleep in this dark room.

I'm listening to Cocteau Twins because it's dreamy and light, but
it doesn't put me to sleep.

It gets my mind spinning and spiraling just like the songs
themselves.

I'm thinking about everybody telling me to stay away from
Jocelyn. Everybody, including Jocelyn herself.

I would probably feel more inspired to stay away if everybody
and their brother didn't tell me to.

I think things through. Why Jocelyn? Why is everybody so
against me seeing her? What is the big deal?

*More like what's the big secret?*

My mind can wander and imagine. But the more it does, the
more it makes me curious. The more it makes me want to find her
and figure her out.

*And protect her.*

The voice that whispers this is another voice, one deep down, one that's foolish and that nobody except me hears. It's crazy. Protect her from what? And how would I do that? How can I have anything to do with her?

*Figure it out.*

I don't like this voice. It's one thing to be curious, another to be crazy.

It's November, and I've managed to finally start to fit in. I've got Ray on my side, a decent guy (not to mention popular and wealthy). I've got Gus off my back for the moment.

Jocelyn—what can I do about her?

*Don't shut the door.*

Yeah, that's fine, I tell this voice, but *she's* the one who shut the door. She made it clear that she doesn't want to have anything to do with me.

*Are you that stupid?*

I'm having a mental conversation with myself. Yeah, I'm that stupid.

*Don't give up on her, because she needs you.*

A part of me thinks this is stupid and dramatic. She doesn't need me. Nobody needs me. And if they did, heaven help them. What can I do?

Still, I hear Newt warning me. I hear her step-uncle threatening me. I hear the other voices, including the most recent belonging to Pastor Jeremiah Marsh.

Warning me against seeing her.

Why?

I want to know.

I want to find out *why* I need to stay away from her.

And knowing myself, I know that until I answer that question, I will do the exact opposite of what everybody tells me to do.

## 40. TWENTY-FIVE PERCENT CHANGE

If it worked for Rachel, it could work for me, too.

It blew up in her face (mine too), but still it worked.

So in the middle of the following week, nine days after the party (but who's counting?), I decide to write Jocelyn a letter.

I'd email her if I had an Internet connection. Maybe I'd get lucky and be able to chat with her online.

I'd text her if I hadn't broken my cell phone before leaving Chicago. Maybe she'd text me back, and that would break down the walls she's been building.

But instead of doing normal things that normal teens do, I have to get out a pen and paper and start writing.

JOCELYN:

PLEASE READ THIS.

I HAVEN'T BEEN ABLE TO GET TWO MINUTES OF CONVERSATION WITH YOU SINCE THE NIGHT OF THE PARTY.

I NEED TO EXPLAIN THINGS.

I'M USED TO HEARING ABOUT "THOSE GUYS." SOME OF MY

FRIENDS HAVE BEEN "THOSE GUYS." THE ONES THAT WANT ONLY
ONE THING FROM A GIRL AND THEY GET IT. I'VE SEEN GUYS TREAT
GIRLS PRETTY BAD, AND I HAVE ALWAYS PROMISED MYSELF I
WOULDN'T BE ONE OF THOSE.

I WANT YOU TO KNOW—I WAS SCARED. I WASN'T SURE
WHAT WAS HAPPENING, AND I INSTANTLY THOUGHT OF WHAT
I SHOULD AND SHOULDN'T DO. I'D LIKE TO SAY I WAS BEING A
GENTLEMAN, BUT TO BE COMPLETELY HONEST, I WAS SCARED.
THAT'S PUTTING IT MILDLY. I JUST NEVER EXPECTED THINGS TO
GO THERE.

I WANT YOU TO KNOW THAT I'VE NEVER MET A GIRL LIKE
YOU. EVER. SINCE THE MOMENT YOU WALKED UP TO ME WITH
RACHEL AND POE THAT FIRST DAY, I BEGAN TO THINK THIS.
BUT THERE'S SOMETHING MORE.

EVER SINCE SEEING YOU WITH YOUR STEP-UNCLE—I
JUST GOT THIS CRAZY URGE INSIDE OF ME. TO NOT BE ONE OF
"THOSE GUYS." INTERESTED IN ONLY ONE THING.

I THOUGHT I'D BE LETTING YOU DOWN IF I GAVE IN TO
THAT.

IT'S SOMETHING DIFFERENT.

WHEN I SAW YOU WITH YOUR STEP-UNCLE AND I SAW
THAT LOOK ON YOUR FACE—MAYBE I'M CRAZY, I DON'T
KNOW—BUT I HAD THIS URGE TO PROTECT YOU.

IS THAT INSANE?

I JUST WANT YOU TO KNOW THAT.

I JUST WANT A CHANCE TO GET TO KNOW WHAT'S BEHIND
THAT LOOK, AND WHAT'S BEHIND THAT HEART-STOPPING BEAUTY
THAT WALKS PAST ME ON A DAILY BASIS.

THESE AREN'T LINES—THEY'RE NOT ORIGINAL, BUT THEY'RE TRUE, AND THEY'RE EXACTLY WHAT I'M THINKING AND FEELING.

I JUST WANT A CHANCE TO KEEP GETTING TO KNOW YOU.

IT SEEMS LIKE EVERYBODY AROUND HERE— INCLUDING YOU—WANTS ME TO STAY AWAY FROM YOU.

BUT THE ONLY THING THAT HELPS ME MAKE IT THROUGH THE DAY AT THIS SCHOOL IS THE THOUGHT THAT MAYBE I'LL SEE YOU.

DON'T GIVE UP ON ME, JOCELYN. THAT'S ALL I ASK.

CHRIS

I put the letter back in my notebook and don't reread it.

I have a feeling that if I do, I'll tear it up.

I give myself a twenty-five percent chance of giving the letter to Jocelyn.

That percentage will probably go down by the time the sun rises tomorrow.

## 41. SKIRMISH

*Just when you thought it was safe to go back in the water ...*

I remember reading that the tagline for *Jaws 2* was one of the most popular ever. I can see why.

The phrase pops up in my head as I'm washing my hands and see the figures approaching in the mirror.

It's Gus and his boys.

I tried to talk with Jocelyn after second period, but she gave me the complete stranger treatment. She didn't know I had a letter for her, a letter I'm seriously contemplating throwing away.

The splotchy skin of Gus stands out under the cold, white light.

"You ever been hurt, Chris?" he asks me. "Like hurt really bad?"

Oli stands behind him, guarding the narrow passageway to the door. Oli is short for Oliver, I have learned. Newt told me.

Not that that's going to help anything at this moment.

I see Burt and Riley flanking Gus. They're average guys who get all excited when Gus pushes their buttons. Otherwise they're pretty harmless.

Gus, however, isn't.

I've been expecting this for a while.

"What are you going to do now, man? Where are you going to run now?"

My notebook and a couple of textbooks sit on the edge of the sink. I think about using the doorstop of a English book on Gus's face but know that I won't get far.

There's no window in this bathroom, not that I would have time to open and climb out of one.

The door opens, and Oli slams it shut.

"You're not looking so brave now, are you?" Gus says.

The bathroom isn't that big. There's a narrow entrance, which

Oli is blocking, then an open area with five sinks in it, then a half wall that leads back to the urinals and a set of four stalls.

Burt moves toward the back area.

I dash over to him, scaring him and slamming a shoulder against his puny side as I scram to the stalls. I don't have a plan. I'm just running.

I get in the last stall and lock it. The door is flimsy, and I know it will just take a good kick to open it. You can reach in underneath the door as well as get in above the walls.

This only gives me time to think.

*Come on. Do something.*

I hear them scampering behind me.

Gus curses at me, calling me names. The other guys are laughing.

I look at the white plastic seat. It takes two good jerks to pull it off.

"You really want to be hiding in a john, do you? You wanna know how gross those toilets are? Do you really want to know what that water tastes like?"

I'm holding the light toilet seat, and then I put it on the floor. Not sure what I'm going to do with it.

Gus taunts me some more, then says something under his breath to one of the guys.

I pick up the tank lid. It's heavy, white, ceramic.

Then I stand firm, a little ways back so the door can't strike me.

"Go ahead, Oli," Gus orders.

*This isn't going to be pretty.*

The door blasts open and slams against the side of the wall. As Oli regains his balance from kicking the door in, I rush toward him with the tank lid as a battering ram. It hits him square in the chest and sends him backward with a gasping cough.

The next few seconds are a blur.

I ran Oli into one of the other two—I think Riley. Burt doesn't know what to do and just stands there.

I wouldn't know what to do either if some crazy kid holding a tank lid from a school toilet came barreling out of the stall at me.

That leaves Gus, who looks at me still holding the lid and then backs off to find something to hit me with.

He launches a garbage can at me, but it simply rolls to my side. Then he grabs my stack of books and flings them at me.

I follow him because I want to get out of this bathroom with my teeth in place and my face intact.

Gus stays over by the sinks as I drop the lid on the ground in a loud crash and then rush out the door into the mostly empty hallway.

On my way to my next class, I realize my books are still in the bathroom.

So is my letter to Jocelyn.

## 42. BEFORE LEAVING

Later that afternoon, as I'm moving slowly through the masses trying to avoid Gus, I see two figures huddled near an open classroom.

I can see Mr. Meiners looking down, his arm around someone.

Then I see her.

Jocelyn.

She's got her hands in her face. One hand wipes her eyes.

Tears.

I wonder if someone she knows died.

I stop and nearly get trampled by the herd behind me.

"Watch out," some girl says.

I want to go to Jocelyn, see what's wrong.

*She doesn't want you knowing.*

I lurk around the lockers on the other side and watch them.

Jocelyn continues to cry. But then she does something else, something strange and baffling.

She laughs.

The tears she's crying—I can't tell if they're tears of sadness or of joy.

Or maybe both.

# 43. MAGIC

Time scrapes by, the same needle on the same side of the same album turning around and around.

Mom comes and goes, doing a little better, staying busy. But sometimes I hear her come back home really late and then I see her the next morning and know her habits haven't changed. I don't have to smell her breath to know. Drinking somewhere other than home is still drinking. To avoid a lecture, she promises that we're going to get cable and Internet.

I'm sixteen years old. I should be the one getting lectured.

Classes remain the same. Schoolwork remains the same. I'm uninterested and uninvolved. The same way 99 percent of the students are regarding me.

Jocelyn is a stranger. And all the words I summed up and scripted in a silly little letter remain missing, just like our brief friendship.

If that's what I can call it.

Rachel reaches out to me, just as Poe seems to try to cast an evil spell on me every time I see her. In my mind they balance each other out.

Every now and then I see Ray. He talks to me like I'm part of the crowd at a pep rally, shaking my hand or patting me on the back.

This is life.

This is how I spend my days.

I long to be twenty-seven and grown up. Why twenty-seven? It just sounds good. Not married—no way. But living in a house. No, scratch that. Living in a cool loft in a big city. New York, maybe Chicago. With a serious girlfriend. With a bunch of guys I like hanging around with. With a sweet car. And an awesome job that pays way too much.

Is this too much to ask for?

Maybe.

It feels like a mirage. Like the promise of water when I'm in the middle of a desert.

The days in that second week of November smear away, leaving empty slots on a calendar I ignore.

The weekend approaches, and with it comes the promise of getting away from here, of getting away from the reality that I don't have much to look forward to day after day.

Friday finds me alone at my locker, and I feel something touch my arm.

For the second time in a week, I see Jocelyn in tears.

"Chris ..."

Then she gives me a big hug.

When she moves away, I see something in her hand.

Then I realize.

My note found its way to her.

"How did you—"

But she puts a finger on my lips and stops me from saying anything else.

"Later."

"What?" I ask.

"Don't say anything. Okay? Not now. Just wait for later."

"Later?"

"Are you doing anything tonight?"

I chuckle. "Yeah, I have a double date I'm going on."

"Seriously."

"No."

"Then meet me at my locker at the end of the day."

"For what?"

She gives me a heartmelting smile that seems to say *I adore you* and *I'm sorry* and *I'm yours* all in some magical way.

Or maybe I imagined that.

Maybe I'm imagining this.

"Okay" is what I think I say.

Then she's gone.

## 44. THE GIFT

"Do you believe in God, Chris?"

These are not the words I'm expecting out of Jocelyn the moment the doors shut and she starts up her car.

"Why?"

"What do you mean *why?* Do you?"

As she backs out of the parking space, I wonder what to say.

"Don't think about it, just answer the question."

I commit. "No."

"You need to. You have to. You really have to."

She grabs my hand. She's beaming and seems to shake with excitement.

"What happened?"

"A miracle," she says, taking her hand back and brushing back her hair.

I stare at her lips for a moment and find myself getting lost in them.

"I tell you, it's a miracle."

"What is?"

"You, Chris. You're the miracle."

Either she's on some strange drugs or somebody has brainwashed her.

"I'm lost," I say.

"I know. It's fine. I just had to tell you that. And have to say that God works in mysterious ways."

"Why's that?"

"Because of you, Chris. Because of you."

We drive for almost an hour. Jocelyn says that she wants to get far away from Solitary, so she drives to Asheville. Mom and I drove through it on our trip here.

I try to press Jocelyn for more info, but none comes. She says she wants to talk to me face-to-face and tell me what's happened. As she drives, the sun starts to fade away and the shadows begin to smother the inside of the car.

"You hungry?"

"No," I say.

"Teenage guys are hungry all the time."

"I left my appetite at school."

*Along with reality.*

"Come on. Let's get something to eat. I've gone on a lot of dates here."

I think of all the "dates" I've gone on. I don't know how many actually count.

"A lot of older guys have asked me out. Some not knowing my real age. It happens, you know."

"Yeah."

But I don't know. I'm new to this.

We end up at a cool burger joint with modern furniture and snug booths and a rocking vibe. The burgers have unique pairings like pineapple and barbecue sauce or eggs and jalapeños, the latter of which I decide to try.

My questions are building.

Half her hamburger is gone before she takes a sip of her drink and then says, "Okay."

"Okay, what?" I ask.

"Okay, I'll tell you what's going on. I can see it all over your face."

"What?"

"Confusion."

"Yeah, well, for the last couple of weeks—"

"I know, I know," she says. "Just hear me out."

"Okay."

"How's your burger?"

"I want to hear you out," I say, adding, "It's good."

"You need to know, you do have friends at this school."

"What do you mean?"

"You said that everybody wants to keep you away from me. Not *everybody*."

"Maybe not Rachel."

"There are others too."

"Why do you say that?"

"Because someone gave me this."

She produces my letter, which looks like it's been trampled on and wrinkled and tossed about.

"Who?"

"I can't tell you who."

"When?"

"Today. This afternoon."

"Where'd they get it?"

"They didn't say. They didn't say anything except that I would want to read it."

"I wrote that a week ago."

Jocelyn touches my arm. "It's beautiful. I don't think anybody has ever said such kind things to me."

"I didn't even know if I was going to give it to you. Then Gus and his friends confronted me in the bathroom and tried to pound my face in, and I ended up running out on them. The letter was in my notebook and got left behind."

"It was unbelievable, what you said. I read it three times in a row. And that's when I knew."

"Knew what?"

"There's so much to tell you, I don't know where to begin."

She takes another bite and finishes it, never taking her eyes off mine.

"First off, first and foremost, I'm sorry about the last two weeks."

"Yeah, me, too."

"No. Don't you dare apologize, Chris. You didn't do a thing wrong. You treated me like a lady and you behaved like a gentleman, and my problem was that I didn't recognize it. That's my problem—one of many. But how you acted and how you've been—and now this note. It takes my breath away."

"You take my breath away," I blurt out.

"Thank you."

"That sounds corny."

"Not the way you said it. Not the way you looked when you said it."

"Probably like a ten-year-old."

"Maybe twelve."

"Maybe," I say with a laugh.

"This week has changed everything."

"How?"

"I can't explain. There's too much. I don't want to explain everything—not yet."

"Why didn't you talk to me these past two weeks?" I ask.

"Because I've been scared."

"Why? I'm not going to hurt you."

"No, I know that. I've known that all along."

"Then why? I don't get it."

"Because I've been falling for you and falling hard. And I finally realized it, and it absolutely terrified me."

Hearing her say that, watching her say that, terrifies me.

I can't believe this.

The last couple hours are all like some dream I'll wake up from.

*God, if you are up there, then please, please, please let me get what I want.*

"Then why did you ignore me?"

"Because I don't want to hurt you," Jocelyn says.

"You won't. How can you?"

"All I know is this. This is the truth: God sent you to me. He used you in the most amazing way ever. Do you believe in destiny?"

"I'm not sure. I'd say no."

"Yeah, well, I didn't either until it slapped me on the face, and I woke up and saw a beautiful, brilliant sunrise and realized that every day we have is a gift. And every smile that comes along is a gift too."

I'm totally lost.

Who is this person, and where did Jocelyn go?

"Not sure what to say."

Jocelyn finishes her meal, then puts the basket over my half-eaten meal. "Don't say anything. Just know this. You're the gift that came along. You and your words."

She stands then and urges me out of the booth.

"Where are we going?"

"You'll see."

# 45. TRUST

The night wind caresses us as Jocelyn winds through the neighborhood streets. She drives with purpose, knowing where she's going. I hold the door handle next to me and glance at her.

The picture is one that I believe I will remember until my dying breath, even if it's a hundred years from now.

Her hair swirls and blends in the darkness. Her eyes seem to radiate, their focus straight ahead, their windows shielding something deep and powerful behind them that I want to see. She looks like she's twenty-six, not sixteen. She looks like she's a woman who doesn't need to be with a boy.

She looks at me with a smile confirms that I shouldn't think such thoughts.

The old, expensive houses pass us by on old-school blocks with old trees towering above, all reeking of old money. It reminds me of some Chicago suburbs. Money is money anywhere. It's a beautiful thing to not be in that world, but to be here in the passenger seat, taking a drive and looking out and wondering where we are going.

Jocelyn turns on the radio.

The tune playing is perfect, and I know after two seconds that it will be our song.

She turns it up and keeps driving, not revealing anything, just driving and listening.

I never want to leave this moment.

"Here," she says. "This is what I wanted to show you."

"This is crazy."

"It's some view, huh?"

I look behind us at the towering stone structure that seems to hover with arms outstretched. The lights from the deck glimmer above us. In front of us, below the falling stairs and the lawns of the golf course, lies the snug and sleeping valley. The downtown of Asheville burns brightly to our left.

"This is called Grove Inn?" I ask.

"Grove Park Inn. Presidents have stayed here. It's legendary. Made of stone. They say it's impossible for it to burn down."

"Have you ever stayed here?"

Jocelyn doesn't answer. "This is one of my favorite views. When it's a clear night like this, you can see forever."

"It's amazing."

Slivers of stairs coil down from the hotel several stories above us. We stand in a small, fenced-in alcove that has two lawn chairs facing out. It's a private nook, one of many scattered around the falling hill.

"The restaurant above us is pretty spectacular," Jocelyn says.

"You've eaten there?"

"A few times," she says.

"Wow."

"Yeah. The sun sets while you're eating, and by the time you get dessert everything around is radiating."

"I can't imagine."

"I wouldn't be able to imagine either. It's a whole other world up there."

"What?"

"The people who stay here. Did you see all those cars in the parking lot?"

"No," I say.

"You didn't? Come on—you're a guy. Guys notice cars."

"My mind was on other things."

Jocelyn smiles. "From any other guy, I'd say *please*."

"Yeah, I know."

"But you're not any other guy."

"I don't think I am."

"I know you're not."

I don't know what to do, what I'm supposed to do. Should I hold her hand? Put my arm around her? It's a bit chilly here on the side of this mountain with the valley breeze blowing up.

"I wanted you to see something beautiful. Something amazing. There are lots of beautiful things around here. You just have to leave Solitary to find them."

*No, you don't.*

I want to tell her this, but it sounds like another line.

She continues. "I wanted to get away and have some breathing room, you know?"

"Breathing room?"

"Yeah, a chance to not worry about … about anything."

The way she says *anything* makes *me* worry.

"I know this is crazy, coming up to you at the end of school and kidnapping you."

"I volunteered," I say.

"I know. But after these last two weeks. I'm sorry, Chris."

"Okay. Thanks."

"But I don't want you to just know that. There's something else." She turns her whole body and faces me.

This is what it would have felt like to dance with her, to be so close, to smell her and feel her warm breath in the cool night.

"Can I trust you?"

"Yeah," I say quickly.

"No, I'm serious. I mean this—*can I trust you?*"

"Trust me with what?"

Her eyes move around, nervous. "Can I trust you with my heart?"

My mouth opens but only swallows a breath. I nod and don't move my eyes off hers.

"There are so many things about me you don't know. Things nobody knows."

"It's okay."

"No, it's not. Most of them are not okay. They'll never be okay. But when I hear you say that, I believe you. I believe that they'll be okay. And this faith—it just seems to be dropping onto me like a waterfall."

"You can trust me. I'm not going to hurt you."

"I'm not worried about me," Jocelyn says. "I'm worried about you."

Beyond the girl standing in front of me, the valley of Asheville hovers and seems to hold its breath, waiting to see what happens next.

"I don't want you to worry about anything."

She's just a few inches shorter than me. I move my head down a bit to kiss her cheek, touching her arm as I do.

It's sweet and innocent, and it's all I can think to do.

Jocelyn doesn't let me move away. She locks her arms around me and embraces me for a long time, her head leaning over my shoulder.

"I'm sorry," she whispers to me.

"It's okay," I say. "You apologized. It's done."

"No."

"It's fine."

She moves and faces me again, a look of fear on her face. "That's what you don't understand. It's not done. It hasn't even started yet."

"What are you talking about?" I ask.

"I can trust you, right?"

I nod.

"Then hold me. Hold me and don't say a word."

And that's what I do.

## 46. DOWNSTREAM

Something changes when the Jeep winds its way around the mountain roads into Solitary. It's not just something with Jocelyn. It's something inside of me.

Things feel different.

The temperature feels cooler. The darkness outside looks thicker. Even the street seems more desolated.

*Don't take me home, not tonight. I don't want to go there. I don't want to leave you.*

And yet that's exactly what I have to do.

Jocelyn puts the Jeep in park and faces me. "I can't promise you anything," she says. "How I'm going to be. What I'm going to be like over the next couple of months."

"Why do you say that?"

She hesitates.

"What?" I ask. I'm wondering if we're back to square one.

"You're a good guy, Chris. I just don't know what to say to you."

Then I surprise myself by saying, "You don't have to say anything, okay?"

She grabs my hand and leans over and kisses me on the cheek.

I tell her to call me if she can over the weekend. Something's going on with her—inside of her—and I can't know what.

At least not yet.

I step out of the car and watch her drive away.

As I head up the stairs to our deck and front door, I see the light to my mother's room go on.

Then I realize I never called to let her know I was going out with Jocelyn.

The next morning I find myself grounded.

Not that I didn't already feel grounded, stuck inside this cabin without Internet and without cable. A sixteen-year-old without a license or a cell phone, surrounded by trees and hills and the sounds of the creek flowing below us.

I'm grounded for the weekend.

Grounded from all the parties I'm not invited to, from the conversations I'm not going to have on the phone, from the Internet communication I lack.

Yeah, I'm grounded all right.

I was grounded the minute we moved here.

Mom didn't say much to me when I got home last night. She was tired and cranky. But one thing she did tell me, several times.

"I *need* to know where you're at, okay? You've got to let me know."

Yeah, this is the sort of thing a mother tells her child.

But the way she said it. It made me a little worried. Like there was something out there I needed to be worried about. Like there was something she was keeping from me, maybe for my protection or safety.

It's surprisingly warm today, maybe topping sixty or so—warm enough not to wear a jacket.

I wander around the house bored, listening to music and trying to find something on the three channels that come in on our television. Then I meander out on the deck and look out into the woods, listening to the stream below.

What I need is a dog.

That or a girlfriend. Or a life. One of the three would be cool.

After feeling the sun on my forehead and listening to the creek, I decide to get out and enjoy the surroundings.

I don't go behind the cabin, up in the hills with the small creepy cabin and the wall with the dog behind it.

This time I go downhill, down to check out the stream that I've heard ever since coming here.

It's only midday, so I don't have to worry about dusk.

Not yet.


The creek slicing through the bottom of the woods is about six feet wide, with towering trees that shadow its surface and jutting rocks and boulders scattered throughout. I skip from one moss-covered boulder to another, moving downstream, walking alongside it in the woods, then once again on its edge. It's serene down here, with slivers of sunlight piercing through the limbs above.

I walk for half an hour or more, occasionally getting my feet wet.

I forget where I'm going.

It's easy to do that, especially being out of view from the street above me, from any noticeable sign of life.

It's easy to just keep walking.

I reach a point where the water is louder. The creek bed narrows and juts to the right. As I hop from rock to rock, I see the hill dropping sharply where the creek turns.

It's a small waterfall.

I move to the side and have to climb uphill to see it.

The drop is about fifteen feet.

But when I reach the crest of the hill to see the waterfall to my right, I completely miss what's on my other side.

It's only when I turn that I see it.

The hill I'm on slopes downward to a bench. Behind that, leading up to the road above, are wooden steps planted into the dirt.

It suddenly dawns on me where I am.

*Is this part of Gus's property? Part of the gated-off section of land that is right down the road from my house?*

It has to be.

I make my way to the bench and can see that from there it's a scenic view of the small waterfall made by the creek. I walk up the side of the hill along the steps, slowly and carefully, making sure I don't hear anything coming my way.

Even before I reach the top of the steps, I can see it.

The immense lawn with grass as green as the kind the pros play golf on. The massive three-story house overlooking that lawn.

And the figure on the deck overlooking the grass.

I duck down and hide behind a tree. I'm not out of the woods yet, so they can't see me.

*You better hope they can't see you.*

I carefully move my head around the tree and look up to see who the figure is.

*It's Gus, and he's going to come down here and find you.*

I'm not worried about him. I can run faster than he can, that I know.

But it isn't Gus.

He's older, maybe Gus's father. He's balding with white hair at the sides, a serious face that stares up toward the skies. He's wearing what looks like a black robe, a cup of coffee in his hands.

I watch him for a moment as he stands there staring out beyond the trees toward the heavens.

Then he seems to close his eyes.

Like he's thinking.

*Or praying.*

Then he opens his eyes again, and this time it looks like they're staring directly at me.

I bury my face in the bushes in front of me and wait for a few minutes.

When I peer back around the tree, the figure is gone.

I can picture it being gone long enough to suddenly pop up in front of this tree.

I decide my little adventure into the woods has taken me far enough.

I head back up the creek toward my house.

Every few seconds, I turn around.

I can't help feeling that someone is watching me.

# 47. WHAT FATE BRINGS TO YOUR DOORSTEP

Mom worked all day Saturday and is working lunch on Sunday.

Ray talked to me Friday about going to church again, but I don't have a car, and it's not like I really want to go back. The only thing I do want to continue is my friendship with Ray. He's one of the only normal things around this very abnormal place.

At ten-thirty Sunday morning the phone rings.

Maybe it's Ray offering to pick me up for church. If that's the case, I'll change my shirt and make something normal out of my hair and go.

Even if it means getting the weird vibes and possibly talking to Pastor Freaky.

"Chris?"

The voice is definitely not Ray's.

She sounds weak, frightened, upset.

"Jocelyn? What's wrong?"

Her breathing is shaky and heavy.

"I'm scared."

"Scared of what?"

"I wake up scared. And go to sleep scared."

She's whispering, for some reason.

"Are you okay?"

"Yeah. I am now. He's gone."

"What? Who's gone?"

"I just called to talk."

"Okay," I say.

"Friday night was really nice."

"Yeah."

"I wish it could always be like that."

I'm about to say that it can be, but that would be a lie.

Friday night was a miracle, and those only come around at select times.

"What's wrong?" I ask.

"Everything."

"Like what?"

"Like the fact that I live with some crazy person who happens to be my aunt."

"What'd she do?"

"She was born. She decided to take care of me. She's a train wreck. A total and complete train wreck. Everything she touches seems to crash. Everything."

"Did something happen?"

"No, nothing specific. Not this time. Thank God."

"What usually happens?"

"You can't change who you are, what fate brings to your doorstep."

Her words sound more like a movie trailer than a girl talking over the phone to her friend.

"You must think I'm crazy."

"I think a lot of things, but I don't think you're crazy," I say.

"I'm sorry for calling."

"I was hoping you would."

"My aunt took the Jeep. Otherwise I'd come get you, and we could run away."

"Just let me know when."

"Really?"

"I'm grounded, by the way."

"For what?"

"For running away with you on Friday night. I forgot to call my mother, not that I have a cell phone to use and not that I could have gotten hold of her."

"I'm sorry."

"I'm not."

We talk for the next hour, the tone gradually lightening. I actually get her to laugh, something that is refreshing to hear.

I almost tell her about the house I saw yesterday, but I don't want to hear any more words of admonition.

I don't want anybody telling me what not to do, not even Jocelyn.

"I need to go," she eventually tells me.

"Okay."

"Thanks."

"For what?"

"For being there. And for not pressing. You can't believe how good it feels."

"How good what feels?"

"The fact that you don't need to take anything from me."

"Can I ask you a question?"

"Sure," Jocelyn says.

"What's tomorrow going to be like? At school?"

"Let's figure it out then. I can't tell you for sure. I can't promise anything."

"Okay."

"Okay," she repeats.

I can see the smile on her face as clearly as if she were standing right in front of me.

She's with me, even if we're separated by miles of wilderness.

# 48. THE DISCOVERY

The weird thing about this cabin—this room specifically—is that I get the feeling that Uncle Robert is going to be coming back any minute.

I keep discovering things that don't make sense.

Things that don't seem like a man going a trip would leave.

It's not just all his belongings. It's also where they are.

If he was living in this cabin by himself, why are most of his things up in this room?

There are clothes: T-shirts and jeans and shirts and jackets. Several pairs of shoes and boots. Boxers and socks. Everything.

And they're all up in my little room. Along with other things.

Some of the things I've found look brand new. It's not stuff that's old and outdated—it's stuff that hasyet to be used.

I don't get it.

*Was someone else living here with him?*

I'm thinking about this on Sunday night as I continue going through his stuff.

Call it boredom or fascination or both.

I keep feeling like the door is going to open and Uncle Robert will be standing there, breathless and delirious and angry.

I have no idea why I'm thinking this. Uncle Robert is someone I've seen over the years in bits and pieces. No idea why I get the feeling he would care if I was going through his stuff.

*And yeah, Chris, what's with the delirious and breathless thing?*

I get this feeling that he's in trouble. I know Mom thinks so too.

I've sorted the albums in a comprehensible fashion, putting the milk crates along the far wall that stands next to the walk-in closet. That gives me a little more room to try to go through the closet. There are lots of random things in here—an old photo album from Robert's high school days. Some shoe boxes with letters in them. A digital camera.

I still don't feel right looking through the letters or getting on the digital camera.

Why would Uncle Robert leave these things behind?

I stumble across a small black duffel bag and open it.

And then I know.

*Something happened to him.*

Inside is a toiletry bag full of the regular stuff—toothbrush, razor, cologne, deodorant. A couple changes of clothes. Some casual shoes.

Between a sweatshirt and a pair of pants, I find a gun.

It's heavy and black, a .45 of some kind, the kind that has a clip on it.

I can feel my hands shaking as I hold it. I look over my shoulder as if my mom is standing behind me. Then I put the gun back where I found it.

There are a few other notable things: a map of North Carolina, some binoculars, a knife.

*Was he planning on going hunting or something?*

Then in an outside zipper pouch, I find a couple of other things.

One is an iPod, the latest model, a lot thinner than mine. It needs charging. Then I find a pen-sized flash drive.

Mom calls me just then, and I stick the flash drive back where I found it and put the bag underneath a few other empty bags.

I close the closet door, wondering what happened to Uncle Robert.

Wondering if I should tell Mom.

For now, I decide to stay quiet.


## 49. SLIDING AND FALLING


There's another note inside my locker just like the last one, and it's taped on all four sides so it's impossible to slip off. I stare at the students passing me as I tear it off and save it for first period.

I make sure the letter is easy to access as Algebra 2 starts. I still don't understand how we're supposed to think about numbers and calculations this early in the morning. It's just not right.

The letter is just like before, typed and printed from a computer.

> Chris:
> The best thing you can do right now is mind your
> business and stay out of trouble.
> Don't be noticed.
> People are watching you.
> Go under the radar and go with the flow.
> And above everything else: Stay away from Pastor
> Jeremiah Marsh.
>
> > A friend

I look around to see if anybody is watching me. There's an occasional obnoxious glance, but nothing suspicious.

*Who's watching me? And why does this "friend" not reveal himself?*

I can't wait to talk to Jocelyn.

I wonder how she will act today.

I want to tell her what I found yesterday in the cabin.

One thing I know. I can trust her.

It's nice knowing that someone else is there.

This is a first.

I've always felt like I was on my own. Dad used to say that God watches over us and loves us, but I don't buy that. The more I think about it, I don't understand how He can love us, not in this sort of world. And I don't want Him watching over me.

But I want Jocelyn watching over me.

My dad wouldn't like those thoughts, but Mom would agree. Wholeheartedly.

I like the way Jocelyn watches me when I sneak looks back at her.

The way she waits for me leaving the classroom.

The way she slowly strolls on the way to our next period.

I like the way I feel when I am near her. The way I feel when I casually say "see you later."

I like the small smiles she gives during lunch as we listen to Poe and Rachel.

I like knowing that she knows. That she gets it, that she gets me.

I like everything about her and everything about this, and I know that I'm falling and I like that she knows this too.

I don't want school to end because I don't want to be away from her.

When she offers me a ride home, I like that even better.

This sort of thing goes on the next few days. Uneventful days. No more notes. No headbangers looking out for me.

I'm doing what the note said.

Staying under the radar.

Everyone's radar except hers.

The moments screech by when she's away, then evaporate when she's near.

I'm not in this place but somewhere else. I'm not sixteen but much older. I'm not Chris Buckley but someone better, better in a thousand ways.

I like all of this and feel like something has unwedged itself. I like all of this but don't want to mention that other word, the L word, because I don't get it. I don't think I know what that is. Maybe that's what I'm sliding into, but I don't think I'm there quite yet.

Am I?

"I shouldn't be doing this," Jocelyn says over and over.

"Doing what?"

But I know.

I'm not the only one sliding and falling.

She's slipping with me, holding my hand as we go.

## 50. THE EMAIL

Things are looking up.

Guess that means I finally found the rope leading up and out of this dark well I've been stuck in.

Guess that means I've finally seen the light.

It starts on Thursday afternoon, when I come home to a surprise. Not Mom sleeping in the fireplace or something bizarre like that.

No, this is a good surprise.

"I got something for you," she tells me.

Then she hands me a remote.

It doesn't look like the remote for our television.

I glance over and see the box on top of the TV.

"They put up a dish. So we now have ten thousand channels to choose from. We'll eventually upgrade the TV."

"That's awesome, Mom."

"And something else."

I wait, hoping.

Hoping to finally become a real teen again and have connection with the real world.

"We have the Internet."

I really want to hug her.

I really do.

"That's great," I say, resisting the urge to say *finally.*

I can tell that there's only one reason we got both services.

She's looking at the computer right now and beaming.

My laptop is a year old and connects easily. I spend the night online, looking at an old email account and looking at my completely blank Facebook page. I'm not one of those who suddenly went gangbusters with all the social networks out there. I tried them out, then quickly got bored knowing so much about people I didn't even know or *want* to know. I haven't missed them.

Some of the reminders are there. Some posts from friends, some photos with me tagged in them.

Reminders.

*It's easier letting go when you're not plugged in, not dialed in to the Matrix.*

But there are reasons why I've wanted the Internet.

The first thing I do is create a Gmail account under a made-up name with the password I always use for everything.

Torrent101

The last name of one of my favorite musicians along with the trusty 101.

Not totally secret, but then again who's going to bother breaking into something that has nothing to check out?

I find the address that I wrote down in my notebook when she gave it to me.

Then I send Jocelyn a quick note.

> HEY—GUESS WHO HAS EMAIL?
> CHRIS.

Short and subtle.

No reason to bombard her with some endless rant.

I wouldn't like that if I got one from someone.

Well, from Jocelyn I'd be okay with it.

I search Facebook and other sites for her, but nothing comes up.

This is how you can kill time. Searching for random people, seeing random pics, and scanning meaningless information.

It's eleven, and I haven't really gotten any homework done nor have I heard from Jocelyn.

*Guess I haven't really been missing that much.*

Mom knocks on my door, then opens it slightly.

"Everything okay?"

"Yeah," I say. "Just going online and seeing how the old gang is."

She comes into my room and sits on the edge of my bed across from where I sit at my desk.

"Do you miss the old gang?"

"Yeah. In some ways."

"I appreciate how you've handled things."

"Sure."

"I really do."

She's got that tone and that look. It makes me nervous. I'm afraid she's going to say something too deep, too meaningful, too vulnerable.

I never know how to respond.

So I say nothing.

"Find out anything new and exciting?"

"Brady went to the Bahamas with his parents."

"That's not new," Mom says.

"Or exciting."

She's about to say something, I know it. I can see it.

I can *feel* it.

I fiddle around with my laptop.

"Well, I'm glad we finally got you connected again."

"I appreciate it, Mom."

"Just don't stay up too late, okay?"

"Okay."

She leaves, and I feel a bit guilty for not talking longer.

I know she probably feels as lonely as I do.

Probably even more so.

I hear the pong of an incoming message, a sound I haven't heard in some time.

*She's emailing me back.*

I stare at the screen, then feel an invisible hand pound against my chest as I read the words.

> CHRIS:
> YOU'RE NOT WELCOME HERE.
> YOU NEED TO GO BACK WHERE YOU CAME FROM.
> YOU NEED TO STOP SNIFFING AROUND LIKE A
>     MANGY DOG.
> THIS IS NOT A PLACE YOU NEED TO BE CURIOUS
>     ABOUT.
> AND SHE IS NOT SOMEONE YOU NEED TO INTERESTED IN.
> YOU'VE BEEN WARNED.
> WE WON'T KEEP WARNING YOU.

I look at the message, but there's no sender information. Nothing.

There's no name, no info at the bottom of the email.

I try resending and replying and playing around with it, but there's nothing I can do to see who sent it.

I breathe in.

*It's gotta be a taunt from Gus. Maybe he's got some high-tech computer thing that knows I'm online and can see my info.*

I'm not a computer genius, but I know that's highly unlikely.

I reread the email, then turn off my computer.

I suddenly wish I wasn't connected.

The words haunt me when I eventually turn off the lights and try to go to sleep.

*Try* being the key word.

## 51. MIA

On Friday Jocelyn isn't around. I find Poe and Rachel and ask if they know what's up, and they say she's probably sick. That's all.

I don't sit with them at lunch. The vibe and mood are different when Jocelyn's not there. Instead I hang out with Newt. He continues to fill me in on the school and the students. He knows a lot.

I wish I had my cell. It's bad, I know. I just got Internet, and now I want a phone. No way that's going to happen anytime soon.

I wish I could call or text Jocelyn to see how she's doing.

I worry that something's wrong—something major. That she's somehow in danger.

I think of last Friday and how she stole away with me.

I've continued to think about that night every other moment of every other hour since.

*Now she's gone? I can't even explore the possibility of doing something with her tonight?*

I try to figure out a way to see her.

The first thing I do is borrow Newt's cell phone and tell my mom that I'll be hanging out with friends tonight.

I promise her I won't be too late.

Now I just have to figure out a way to get in contact with Jocelyn.

Either over the phone.

Or in person.

Before the last period, I run into Ray.

"Hey, man—haven't seen much of you this week—how's it going—missed you last Sunday."

He talks in short bursts, not sentences, like shotgun blasts of thoughts.

"Yeah, maybe it'll work out this Sunday."

"Let me know—I can pick you up if you need me to—should be a good one—what's happening this weekend?"

I suddenly get an idea.

"You know where Jocelyn lives?"

"Of course," he says.

The group he was walking with moves on down the hall. He's not so manic now.

"Does she live far away?"

"She's still in Solitary. Not far. Fifteen minutes, maybe less."

"Could you do me a big favor?"

"Most people I'd say no to, but I like you," Ray says. "What do you need?"

"Just a ride."

"To Jocelyn's place?"

"Yeah."

Ray laughs. "You sure you want to go there?"

"Why wouldn't I?"

He shakes his head, like I'm asking him to push me off a cliff. "No problem," he says. "Meet me in the parking lot at the end of the day. I'll try not to run late."

"Thanks, man."

"You're crazy, Buckley. That's all I gotta say."

I want to ask him why, but he's off before I can.

## 52. At Night

The driveway is nearly hidden beneath overgrown branches that create a mock doorway we drive through. It curves upward through woods until it stops just below a hill of grass and an unremarkable, faded-yellow one-story house. It looks like an orphan left in the woods, its three windows gazing dully at me. A set of stairs juts out beneath the front door.

"Here's the castle," Ray says in a way that I can't tell is mocking or simply honest.

I climb out. "Thanks, man."

"She know you're coming?"

I shake my head and shut the car door.

Ray is still talking through the open window. "You met her step-uncle?"

"Yeah."

"Just—be careful with that. He's a bit—well, you saw him."

"Okay. Thanks."

Before I have time to reconsider, he pulls away.

I feel like I'm being watched. Either from the windows or from the woods.

I feel a chill. My thin denim jacket isn't a lot of warmth. I rub my arms as I walk toward the house.

It doesn't look old and abandoned—it simply looks empty. There are no signs of life. I don't see the Jeep or any other vehicle. No garden tools or grill or garbage can. There's not even a welcome mat by the front door.

And no doorbell to ring.

I stand there for a moment, then knock.

I wait. Knock again, then wait. Try a third time.

Then I walk back down the wooden steps and wait.

As the sun fades away, a bit too quickly for my liking, I sit on those steps and shiver. I probably should get up and move around, but then I don't want to move.

I still feel watched.

I feel like someone's in the woods.

*Someone … or some thing.*

My mind is working overtime.

It's closing in on eight. I've been here for several hours, just waiting. Killing time.

Doing absolutely nothing.

Occasionally I've gotten up and walked around the house, finding nothing.

*What if Ray got it wrong?*

*What if she moved?*

*Or what if Ray is playing a practical joke?*

As the darkness and cold settle in, I know I need to get going.

Maybe Jocelyn's on a trip and just didn't tell me about it.

Maybe she doesn't live here.

Maybe there was a family emergency.

I know that if she did suddenly show up, with or without her aunt and step-uncle, I'd look pretty creepy sitting on the steps of the house she never invited me to.

*Nice surprise that'd be.*

I decide to walk back to town.

If I can find it, that is.

Halfway down the driveway, I see beams of light turning from the road below.

I dash off to one side of the driveway, heading toward some big trees that offer cover.

For a while I just lie with my back against the base of the tree, my body out of view. Then, when the lights move on up to the house, I sneak a peek.

I see the red glow of taillights from Jocelyn's Jeep.

The lights stay on as a figure emerges and cuts through them, heading to the front door.

The long dark hair gives her away.

Jocelyn walks slowly and carefully to the door and opens it.

Then the headlights go out.

Someone gets out of the driver's side. A tall figure.

*Is that her aunt or step-uncle?*

The way the person walks makes me think of the guy I saw on the street. I can still see him, can still remember his smell.

The figure walks into the house and closes the door.

I wait to see if anyone else emerges from the car.

If that's her step-uncle, then where's her aunt?

*Maybe she's inside.*

But I knocked several times; wouldn't she have let me in?

I stand behind the tree, staring at the shadowy structure in the trees. A panic fills me, and I don't know why. It's the same sort of feeling that I got when I was sitting in that church. A falling sensation, rising from my gut and bubbling throughout.

I want to run to the door and knock on it and let her know I'm there.

But it's nighttime. She'll wonder what I'm doing out here.

*If this doesn't fit a stalker profile, I don't know what does.*

I'm worried about her.

I'm worried about her being alone with her step-uncle.

I stay by that tree for what seems to be hours.

## 53. EMAILS

One plus about living around here: People driving down country roads pick up strangers.

I'm fortunate that I don't have to try and find my way back to Solitary. It's not the distance that concerns me. It's the risk of wandering the opposite way into South Carolina and having to backtrack two hours.

The other fortunate thing on that Friday night is finding Mom still at the restaurant. It's not a bad place. It's basically like one half restaurant and one half bar. When I enter the door, I see my mother laughing and talking with a woman behind the bar. It's good to see her joking around.

I make up some story about being dropped off, and Mom buys it.

I wait around for her for an hour. She gets the kitchen to make me a burger. Somehow she can tell I haven't eaten.

When we get back home, I check my emails.

Nothing.

I spend another hour debating and doubting and deciding.

Then I do it.

I type up another email and send it.

It's straight and to the point:

HEY JOCELYN.

EVERYTHING OKAY?

CHRIS

The bad thing with sending emails is that you expect replies.

Expecting can be a bad thing.

It certainly doesn't help sleep.

And it certainly doesn't get rid of the worry.

Thirteen hours later (but who's counting?) I get an email from her.

EVERYTHING'S FINE. PLEASE DON'T EMAIL ME AGAIN.

JOCELYN

I reread it to see if I'm missing something.

Seven words, that's all.

*But is there some hidden code in it?*

I act like the words are going to add up to something that says *I love you so please rescue me.* But I'm an idiot, because the words are what they are. They're simple and straightforward and to the point.

*Everything's fine, so don't worry anymore, Chris.*

*And oh, yeah, I never asked you to email me, so stop it.*

Back home if things like this happened, I'd ignore them and go on to the next important thing. Hanging out with friends. Going to see a movie. Going to a party. Going online to see the latest gossip and happenings and silliness. Going, going …

*Gone.*

But here the only thing I want to do is go to her. Go back to her tiny little house and see what's happening.

*What if that wasn't even from her? How do you know it wasn't her step-uncle? Or aunt?*

I breathe in.

I need air.

*How about going into the woods? How about a nice little stroll back there?*

I feel claustrophobic, like I'm stuck in a tiny elevator. I feel like there's nowhere to go if I'm outside, nothing to do, no one to see.

Ignoring the voices that tell me to stop everything and turn around and get out, I reply to the email.

WHAT'S GOING ON?

It's a bad one. Even after sending it, I know I shouldn't have. It's too direct, too in her face, too much.

Once again, the hours tick by until I hear from her again.

When I do, the following evening, it's even more simple and direct than mine.

NOTHING.

That's all.

A great way to think about starting the next week.

On a whim, just before bed that rainy Sunday night, as I hear the drops doing a tap dance above me, I check my email again.

There's another message from Jocelyn, but from a different address.

JUST WANT YOU TO KNOW THINGS ARE FINE. I HAD
SOME FAMILY DRAMA THIS WEEKEND AND WILL
EXPLAIN IT TO YOU WHEN I'M ABLE. CAN'T BE
SEEN ON THE COMPUTER—HE'LL FIND OUT. JUST
TRUST ME. I'M SORRY FOR NOT TALKING—WANT/
NEED TO TELL YOU THINGS. JUST KNOW—YOU'VE
BEEN WITH ME, CHRIS. THAT'S THE ONLY WAY I'M
GETTING THROUGH THIS. SEE U TOMORROW.

I wish I had a car. I'd find her house and knock on the door and take her away.

*No you wouldn't.*

Maybe I would. Maybe I'd at least consider it.

Maybe I would at least drive out in the rain and park in front of her house, contemplating taking her away.

Her words calm me even though they prove that something's wrong.

Something has been wrong from the day I met this girl.

Why her?

Why Jocelyn?

The day can't end or the new school week begin soon enough.

## 54. CRAZY IDEAS

I watch her coming up the steps to the school, and I make sure she sees me. Jocelyn doesn't walk the other way. She approaches me, and soon I understand.

"What happened?"

One long, sleek hand brushes over her eye, covering the bruise. Then she moves it and lets me see. There's a purple half-moon underneath the eye and rising up to her temple. It looks a few days old, with that slightly yellowish and faded look.

"Let's keep walking," she says.

We head down the hallway toward the lockers.

"Jocelyn—"

"Look, you can't email me. You can't do anything unless I okay it, you got that?"

"Who did that to you?"

"The guy you met that first weekend in town." She says this looking ahead, acting as if she's talking about the weather or the movie she saw this weekend.

"Your step-uncle."

"Yeah."

"Was that why you were out on Friday?"

She nods. "Looked a lot worse then."

"But what about—where's your aunt?"

"She's out of town. Nice little business trip."

"So then, how—what happened?"

She reaches her locker and opens it. I see a page from a magazine hanging up on the inside of the locker door showing a road heading into the woods. There's writing underneath that I can't make out.

"This isn't the first time, Chris."

"Yeah, well, maybe it needs to be the last."

"Listen, we can talk later—after school, okay? Not when others are around. Not with Poe and Rachel."

"Do they know?"

"Of course," Jocelyn says. "They're not idiots."

"Why would he do this?"

She laughs. "People do a lot of strange things when they're out-of-their-mind drunk."

"Listen, if you want—"

"I want you to just calm down for the moment. You can't do anything here and now, okay? Wade would kill you. He's stupid and crazy."

"But you have to let someone—"

"No. We'll talk after school. He's gone tonight."

"When does your aunt come back home?"

"Wednesday. The day before Thanksgiving."

I've forgotten that Thanksgiving is this week.

Guess I haven't been thinking of many things to give thanks for.

Seeing the discoloration on her sweet, beautiful face, I don't feel like starting now.

"Don't," Jocelyn says.

"Don't what?"

"Don't get any crazy ideas. I can see it on your face. You're an open book, you know that?"

"You sure aren't."

"No, I'm like that book you're looking for in the library but that's always gone."

"That's always checked out?"

Jocelyn shakes her head. "No. More like stolen. See you in English."

Even though I hear her words, I can't help them coming.

Those "crazy ideas."

I wade around in them, plunging deep and feeling the darkness.

I've seen and heard about things like this, sure, but never firsthand.

There were kids who had issues and problems at my last school, but when it wasn't in your face it was easy to forget about it.

The suicide attempt by the freshman.

I didn't know him.

The kid called out of class because something happened with his parents. Something like his mother shooting his father.

The kid was a bit crazy, so it all made sense.

I think of the lyric from the song I've gotten used to hearing by The Smiths. *I've seen this happen in other people's lives, and now it's happening in mine.*

This sweet, dark angel with her secrets and her scars.

I want to wipe them away.

I feel like I need to talk to somebody, but there's only two people I think of telling.

My mother. And, strangely enough, Newt.

But I can't. I don't think either will be able to do anything.

If Rachel and Poe have any concerns about Jocelyn, they sure don't show it. I have to listen to Poe bemoan her upcoming trip to New York to visit her relatives. Rachel complains about having to stick around here and endure a Thanksgiving with a houseful of crazy people. Jocelyn doesn't say what she will be doing.

"How about you?" Poe asks me.

Then suddenly something comes out of my mouth that I don't expect.

As if someone else is talking.

"I have a date."

"A what?"

"A date. Jocelyn didn't tell you? We're hanging out together."

Rachel and Poe look at Jocelyn. Jocelyn smiles, then nods and confirms.

## 55. The Prayer

"How far do you think a tank of gas will take us?"

Jocelyn glances over at me, an adult looking at a child. "Not far enough."

She's driving me home, though we don't seem to be headed anywhere close to my house. We haven't talked anymore since this morning. As I look at her profile, I can't see the bruise on the other side of her face.

"Are we running away?" I ask, trying to lighten the mood.

"You can't run away from things," Jocelyn says. "I've learned that the hard way."

"What's going on, Jocelyn? Is this all about your step-uncle?"

"Just …" She looks at the road, and then she takes my hand. "Just—please continue to be patient with me. Okay?"

"I just want to help."

"I know. And you are."

"How?"

"By being there."

"I'm not doing anything here."

"You're doing a lot, Chris. More than you can know."


She drives for ten minutes on Sable Road, the main stretch of road that flows into Solitary from the north and the south, then turns off onto a dirt road that doesn't look much traveled. We bounce around for several minutes until we reach a clearing with a wild, uncut field and a dilapidated old church that looks like a fire torched it. We park in front, and Jocelyn gets out.

I follow her along the side of the church. There are holes where there once were windows, rotting wood, weeds scattered around like stubble on an old man's face.

"Come on," she tells me.

The field is mostly full of overgrown bushes up to our knees. Jocelyn seems to know exactly where she's going. She heads straight into an open area surrounded by trees on all sides and stops about fifty yards from the church.

She kneels down.

As I approach, I see something sticking out amidst the tall grass and weeds.

A gravestone.

I reach Jocelyn. She's staring at a set of matching tombstones about three feet tall. I can't see the writing on them—they're too small and too dirty.

"I come here more than I should," she says, still looking at the stones. "You'd think that one of these times I'd actually clean up these stones. I never do. I always leave them dirty."

She touches them gently, as if she's touching someone's head. "I was only six years old when they died."

Deep down I already seem to have known this, but it still hits me hard. I look at the stones as if the bodies are right there in front of me, lying in open caskets with gazes planted toward the skies.

"Do you know I was actually baptized in this church? Can you believe it?" She sighs. "Amazing how things can change in ten years."

I look back at the church. The back wall is gone, with several blackened walls inside still clinging on for dear life.

"What happened here?"

"The church was small enough as is. When the fire happened, the few members that were left ended up meeting in secrecy. I guess that's what happened, anyway."

"Is this Solitary?"

She shakes her head. "No. We're actually not even in North Carolina anymore. My parents lived in Solitary but came here to church. This is where they got married."

I want to ask how they died, but I can't get myself to.

"Come here. Sit beside me."

So I kneel next to her.

"Do you want to know something, something crazy? I come here often and pray. Even with all the doubts I've had—I've still prayed. How crazy is that? Half the time I wonder if I'm just doing it for therapy or to make myself feel better. I don't know. Sometimes I think that maybe they can hear my prayers, that maybe Mom and Dad are somewhere around listening. It doesn't make sense, you know. If they can hear my prayers, why do I have to come here to pray? Same goes with God. I don't know. I just feel like—I feel like I *can't* pray back home, back in that darkness. But here, it seems different. Here it seems better."

I make out one name: *Joseph Charles Evans*.

"Crazy, huh?"

"I don't think it's crazy."

"I'm completely crazy, and so are you for liking me."

"Maybe," I say.

"Want to know something sad? I don't remember anything about my parents. Nothing. Six full years, yet I don't have any memories. And you want to know why? I think it's because of the ten dark years that have followed. Because there's just been—there's just been so much darkness...."

She begins to cry.

I don't know what to do, what to say, what to feel.

Yet I see my arm wrap around her shoulders and I feel her quietly cry against my chest.

I swallow, let her cry for a few minutes, and I don't say anything.

"Sometimes I think the darkness has swallowed up the light. That those ten years have sucked up everything good about those first six, you know?"

"I'm sorry," I say.

She moves away from me, her haunting eyes tearful, her bruise showing up more under the fading light of the sun.

"Then you came along," she says.

"What?"

"I got used to waking up and living and breathing in the dark, Chris. And then one day, your silly, smiling face came around." She wipes her eyes.

"Silly, huh?"

"Utterly silly. And utterly beautiful."

"Not sure about that."

"You're not infected, not like the others around here, not like me."

"Stop it."

"You're not. This place—not *this* place, but that place—that town. I'm telling you, Chris, it's evil. You can't know—I couldn't sum it up if I tried. That town killed my parents. I know that for a fact. And I have to live and breathe and walk around like it didn't."

"What happened?"

"Oh, they say it was a car crash. But something happened, something wrong. We're not in the big city around here. Things can get overlooked. Churches can burn down and life can move on like nothing happened."

"You think somebody did this to your parents?"

"I know they did. And I guess that's what I come back to, time and time again. I sit here and I pray, yet I know the truth."

"Which is?"

"God did this. Ultimately God let my parents down. God let them die. They believed in Him, that I know. I've heard bits and pieces from my aunt. They baptized me, hoping I'd follow in their shoes. Lot of good that did."

"Jocelyn—"

"The scary thing is that if—and I mean *if*—God is up there, then why? Why, God? Why would You let this happen? Happen to them? And now to me? Why?"

"What do you mean—" I say.

"And that's what I always thought, time and time again. I'd come here and I'd wrestle with belief, with wondering, with anger. And I prayed a prayer—I remember it specifically. I told God that if He was really up there, and if He really was all-loving and all-knowing, that I wanted Him to send me a sign. Not an omen—I've seen enough of those. But a sign. An angel. I wanted Him to send someone to show me—to remind me of the brightness. And you know what? The next day—the *very* next day—you showed up at school."

"Jocelyn—I'm far from what I would call an angel."

"But you were an answer to prayer. That I know."

I want to tell her that I'm not, that I can't be, but I see the belief in her eyes.

"I tried, Chris. Oh, I tried. I tried to ignore you and run away from you. I messed up, and I—you know, it doesn't matter. Not now. I just know that you really are an answer to that prayer."

"Maybe you should pray a few for me, then."

"I'm not saying I know all the answers," she says. "Because I'm not there yet. I'm not. But—but I just wanted you to know that."

We're alone, just the two of us. I no longer feel watched. I no longer feel awkward or young.

I look into hazel eyes and then see the glow of the sun beyond the crests of the trees behind her.

I move toward her face and kiss her lips.

She's still holding my hand, and as we kiss I feel her grip it tightly.

This is what I believe in, right here and now.

That I think I might love this girl.

And that I don't want her to leave my side for any reason.

Maybe, just maybe, I can help her in some way.

If that means I'm an answer to a prayer, so be it.

If I can, I'll be her guardian angel.

## 56. ECHOES

I stare out at the stars from the deck. It's chilly, but I still feel warm and light-headed from the afternoon.

I picture the field and picture her eyes and feel her lips against mine.

I replay the last conversation we had before she dropped me off at home, how I told her I was serious about seeing her on Thanksgiving. She told me she would see, that it would depend on certain things.

She said she would email me later tonight since she would be on her own.

I want to walk to her home and be with her.

I stare up at the sky and think about everything she said.

*An answer to a prayer?*

If only some of my buddies back home could hear that. They would laugh.

I almost want to laugh.

But another part of me wonders.

It makes me think back to my father, to all of his prayers and urgings and answers and leadings.

All his God-talk.

Why have I suddenly been surrounded by this notion of God in my life?

Not a go-to-church-on-Sunday sort of God.

No, He seems to be in my face every moment.

I don't want to think of these things every day. I shouldn't have to.

I know some of my resistance is because of Mom.

If God is up there, I blame Him solely for my parents' divorce.

It's easier not thinking about God. Anytime I do, it gets messy. I start feeling bad. I suddenly feel like I need to be better, that I need to believe, that I need to confess.

*I'm not a bad person.*

But I remember my father saying that we're all sinners. I

remember him talking about Jesus and about the cross and about death and resurrection.

I remember.

I just don't want to think about it.

It's just my luck. I fall for the hottest girl in school, and she ends up not only being the most tortured soul there, but she also ends up sounding like the ghost of my father.

*It doesn't matter if she ends up sounding like Mother Teresa or the pope.*

I know this.

It doesn't matter because I care for her, and I care deeply.

The things she said to me echo around in my head.


## 57. PLANS


"Do we have any plans for Thanksgiving?"

"Oh, I meant to talk to you about that."

I have a feeling I already know what Mom is going to tell me.

It's Tuesday afternoon, and she's off work tonight, and we're having some frozen dinners while watching television.

"I'm going to have to work half the day. But not too long. I figured we could do a Thanksgiving dinner that night."

"Sure," I say.

Maybe this is bad, but I'm glad she's working.

It helps with the idea I have.

I finish up the mystery Mexican dish on my plate and go upstairs to email Jocelyn.

She told me at school her step-uncle would be working tonight.

I clean up, and Mom asks what my rush is.

"Just want to go online for a while."

She nods, uninterested, picking at her meal and sipping at another glass of wine.

WHAT WOULD YOU THINK OF HAVING
THANKSGIVING DINNER AT MY HOUSE?

I wait for a while to see her response. It comes after a few minutes.

WHAT TIME?

LUNCH TIME?

LET ME SEE. I'LL HAVE TO COME UP WITH SOME
EXCUSE.

MAKE UP ONE. ANY ONE.

DINNER WITH YOU AND YOUR MOM?

NOPE, MY MOM'S WORKING.

There is another pause.

OKAY.

OKAY WHAT?

I'LL FIND AN EXCUSE.

I can't help but smile.

# 58. CREEPY

I wake up truly thankful on the very day you're supposed to give thanks. The plan is in place, and nobody knows except Jocelyn and me. It's not like we're running away to Vegas or anything (though if she asked I would probably say yes). My mom will head out around nine thirty or ten. Jocelyn will be coming by around eleven.

Worst thing that could happen is that Mom sticks around and has lunch with us.

It's not like she doesn't want Jocelyn around.

She would probably think it's a good thing, seeing her son with the gorgeous gal from school.

I go downstairs, but I'm not in the mood for breakfast. Instead I head outside to the deck to see what the weather's like. I'm on the deck for a minute when I see something odd.

Tracks.

Muddy tracks coming up our stairs and then stopping at our window. They proceed around the deck.

I'm wearing jeans and a sweatshirt since it's pretty cool out, but I'm in my bare feet. I tiptoe on the cold deck as I look to see where the tracks go.

This is probably stupid, because the person who made them could be waiting right around the corner where the deck wraps itself around.

Instead the tracks keep going and disappear where the deck ends and the forest ground begins.

I put my bare foot beside the track, a skinny white block on the dark wood. Whoever made the tracks was big. Gigantic.

The dirty tracks look like they were made by boots.

Not only was he big, but he also didn't seem to care much that he left a nice little trail behind him.

As I head back inside, I stop and notice how the tracks seem to make a resting place right by the window.

*Someone was watching us.*

And it had to be last night or this morning, because I know for a fact those tracks weren't there yesterday.

I go inside to tell Mom.


Before she leaves, I mention the muddy tracks to her again.

"I'm sure it's not anything," she says.

I wonder if she's saying this because she's running late or because she doesn't want me to worry or if she really, truly believes it.

I'm thinking A or B myself.

"So some creepy guy standing by our window looking in doesn't scare you?"

"How do you know it's a creepy guy? It might not even be a man."

"That would be even creepier, if a woman made those tracks."

"I have to go."

"Okay."

"We'll do dinner later tonight, okay? Make sure you take out that stuff and follow the instructions."

"Got it."

She glances at me, then gives me a nervous smile. "Keep the doors locked, just in case."

"Always do."

"I'll see you this afternoon."

I nod and instantly forget about the tracks.

I have a visitor coming over for lunch.

For what I guess I can say is truly an official date.


## 59. FIRST IMPRESSIONS


I hear the knock and stop for a second, breathing in.

Then I go to the door and open it.

Jocelyn stands at the door, a dark beauty in light blue. She wears a loose, long dress that falls down to her ankles and a jean jacket covering it. Her hair is bound together and falls to one side of her shoulder. I probably stare too long at her, because she laughs and makes a face, wondering if I'm going to let her in.

"Oh, yeah, come on in. Sorry."

Jocelyn enters and I'm a bit lost, wondering what to do, if I should take her coat or start eating or sit on the couches for a while and talk.

She gives me a hug. I awkwardly put one arm around her but feel nervous and unsure.

"Thanks for doing this," she says.

"You haven't seen what I've done."

"You invited me over. That's enough."

"Hope so, 'cause lunch isn't going to be anything special."

She laughs and walks over to the couch. "So your mother is working?"

"Yeah. Not that she would care if you came over. I just would rather—I'd rather keep it my own business."

"I told my aunt I was having lunch with Poe."

"In New York?"

"She doesn't know Poe's up north."

"What's your aunt doing?"

"She's probably hanging all over Wade. And he's probably half bombed by now."

"Sorry."

"That's fine. I'm not there, nothing to be sorry for."

I stand in front of the couch she's sitting on. "Your bruise keeps getting better. I can barely see it."

"Makeup can do wonders. And in the case of my aunt, so can denial."

I don't notice that much makeup—Jocelyn doesn't wear that much.

"Can I, uh—you want anything to drink?"

She laughs. "Such an adult thing to say. Yeah, I'd like a cocktail, please."

"Well, not sure—"

"Kidding. Anything you have is fine by me."

I get two cans of Diet Coke, and she takes one. I sit on the chair across from her.

"I don't have a disease, you know," Jocelyn says.

"Yeah, I know."

"Then come over here."

I sit next to her on the couch, and she moves her body to face me. She sips her soda and smiles.

"What?"

"Isn't this nice?" she asks.

"What?"

"Nobody around. Just you and I."

"Yeah."

"You wanna know what I thought the first time I ever saw you?"

"Sure."

"I thought, 'Uh oh. He might be dangerous.'"

"Yeah, really dangerous."

"I just hoped that you fit how you looked. And acted."

"And how was that?"

"I hoped you weren't another arrogant jock."

"Definitely not a jock," I say.

"You're a soccer player. Definitely a soccer player. But you're also definitely not arrogant."

"Guess that's a good thing."

"I'd prefer insecurity any day."

I look at my can of soda, then the surrounding room.

"You get so nervous around me, you know that?"

"Yeah," I say. It feels good to admit it.

"You don't have to be."

"You know what I thought the first time I saw you?"

"What?" she asks.

"I thought that you were the most beautiful girl I've ever seen."

"Stop."

"No. I mean it. And I still feel that way. Even more so. I thought that you—that there would be no way, you know. No way for you to be interested."

"I told you. I'm complicated."

"And I've told you, I don't care."

"I like that. Some things you're not so sure about. Like sitting next to me on the couch. But other things—like that. You're very certain."

I look at her and don't look away. "I'm very certain, Jocelyn. Very."

This would be a great time to kiss her, but I don't. I guess she would let me. In fact, I know she would. I can see it in her eyes. But I'm still—I'm hesitant.

For lots of reasons.

The moment passes, and she doesn't seemed fazed.

"You know, I don't smell a turkey."

"Yeah, well—I had to improvise. I have turkey, it's just the kind you get at the deli in slices."

"Awesome," Jocelyn says. "So we're going to reverse things and have the turkey sandwiches first."

"Yeah, sorry."

"I love it. That's the best part of Thanksgiving, when you're stuffed and you're not exactly hungry, but you have a fresh turkey sandwich at nighttime."

"Yeah, but you're probably not stuffed."

"I'm not hungry either," she says. "My mind is preoccupied with other things."

"Is that a good thing?"

"A very good thing. *He's* a very good thing. And he doesn't even realize it."

I feel warm and brush my hair back and have the urge to dive behind the couch.

"Plus when he turns red, his ears do as well."

"Okay, I think I'm going to keep getting things ready so I don't continue to look like a fourth-grade boy."

"You're cute when you blush."

"That doesn't help."

I stand and move toward the kitchen and hear her laughter.

It's a glorious sound.

# 60. ALONE

We sit on the floor in front of the crackling fire eating our sandwiches and potato salad and chips. It's a pathetic meal, but Jocelyn acts like it's the best meal of her life. She sits cross-legged with her dress spread out over the ground like a tablecloth and watches me as I talk about the school back home and stuff with my family. I suddenly find myself talking about my parents, a subject I never discuss with anybody.

It's a freeing thing, opening up like this and being listened to. Not judged or critiqued.

"What ultimately did it?" Jocelyn asks.

"Depends on who you ask. My mom blames God. Well, not even *the* God, because she doesn't believe in one. Just the idea of God. She blames God because my dad suddenly changed his life and his beliefs and didn't seem to have much time for what my mother and I wanted."

"I don't get it."

"Yeah, I don't either. It's just—he quit his job. Felt 'called' to do this and that, all while my mother ends up having to carry the load. It was too much. They argued all the time. My dad wanted my mother to find faith. But you can't force someone to believe."

"I know," Jocelyn says. "I know too well."

"The whole thing left a bad taste in my mouth."

"I can imagine."

"It's crazy—I'd never say this to Mom or Dad or—well, I guess to anybody. But it almost seems like—like it would have been better if my mom had found my dad cheating on her."

"What? Are you kidding?"

"No, listen. I know—that would've been bad. But this was like, like Dad lost his mind. He found God and then abandoned his family. I don't get it. Mom doesn't get it."

"You said she was the one who ended things."

"Yeah, because she couldn't deal with him following God. At least, if he was following some other lady, that would make more sense to me, because she's *there*. God—who knows?"

"There's this Christian radio station I listen to a lot. I like the music. They've got these commercials or segments that are different people reading psalms. It's kinda cool. They always make me want to—I don't know—find out more, figure things out myself. But I guess—well, that's a problem in itself. How can we 'figure out' anything? Faith is still about believing in something you can't see."

"Faith gives me a headache," I say.

"It shouldn't. It should set you free. At least that's what somebody keeps telling me."

"Who's that?"

"Just someone—someone who believes. A very strong Christian who's been reaching out—probably trying to save my poor, wretched soul."

"I don't think you have a poor, wretched soul."

"Oh, I do," Jocelyn says.

I study her face to see if she's joking, but she's not.

"I think we all do," she says.

"Hey, speak for yourself."

She slides over and finds my hand, taking it in both of hers. She studies it for a long time. Outside the sun has disappeared behind storm clouds. I see the light of the burning fire flickering over her face.

"What are you thinking?"

"Chris—I don't want you falling for me, okay?"

I start to ask what she's talking about, but she continues.

"Just—I want you—I want things to be like this, okay?"

"Okay. Me too."

"No, just like this. Like friends. Like really close friends you can tell anything. Or almost anything."

"That's cool."

"No, you don't understand. I don't—I've told you this. I don't want you getting hurt."

"You planning on leaving anytime soon?"

She smiles a beautiful, sad smile and grips my hands harder.

"You know the one thing about faith that makes it look—well, that makes it seem so appealing?" she asks.

"What?"

"It's this idea that we're not alone. That someone is up there who knows."

"Yeah, but does that mean He is looking out for us?"

She shakes her head. "I don't think it always works out that way."

"I don't either."

"But someone knowing everything—to me that's a pretty cool thought."

"Why?"

"Because then you know you're not totally alone."

"You're not alone, Jocelyn."

She looks at me, those hazel eyes so full.

"I think we're all alone. No matter who we are, we're alone."

## 61. BLACKOUT

Jocelyn's been gone for a couple of hours, and I can't stop thinking about her.

I can still see her hazel eyes looking up at me.

I can still smell her slight perfume.

I can still feel the kiss on the edge of my cheek before she left.

I can hear the sound of her engine starting, my face and hands and heart all feeling a warm kind of numbness.

I forget how quickly time passes as I check my email a hundred times. I forget that my mother's late. I forget to take out the stuff I should take out for dinner.

When the door opens and my mom comes in, I'm upstairs and suddenly realize what I've forgotten to do.

I tear down the stairs, but instead of seeing Mom I see the same cop who was drilling me about the gun in Principal Harking's office.

I try to stop halfway on the stairs, but my momentum causes me to stumble on the last few steps and fall on my butt.

An annoyed look stares down at me.

The door opens behind the cop, and my mother comes in, her face white and her eyes red and swollen.

"You okay, Mom?" I ask.

Another cop, this one probably twice the age of the first, with a thick, gray goatee, walks in behind her. I don't see any weapons in hand, nor do I see handcuffs or anything like that.

For a moment I have a strange thought.

*The gun upstairs. They're going to search the house and find the gun upstairs.*

Mom gives me a hug and tells me in a not-very-convincing voice that everything's fine. She walks over to the couch and sits down.

The first guy, the one I met at school, casually walks through the house and looks around.

"Hey, Kev, get the lady something to drink," the older guy says in a way that sounds like he's used to giving orders.

"Mom?"

"I'm Sheriff Wells," the goateed guy says as he shakes my hand. "You're Chris, right?"

I nod.

"Your mother had an incident downtown after work, but she's fine. We just thought it might be in her best interest to bring her home."

The other guy brings her a bottled water. He doesn't seem very interested in introducing himself.

"That's Kevin, a deputy with poor manners, but he sure does what he's told."

"I'm fine, really. It's okay." Mom sips her water.

"What happened?"

"Nothing."

"Mom?"

"Someone wanted to scare your mother—that's what we think happened," the sheriff says. "Someone was waiting for her when she got off work."

"Who? Where?"

I feel like I'm on my bike riding downhill without brakes.

"We don't know. Someone was waiting in her car and drugged her."

"*What?*"

"She's okay. Someone doused a rag or something with chloroform. It's harmless, just knocked her out for a few minutes."

"Did anything happen—"

"I'm fine."

"They didn't take anything that we know of," Sheriff Wells says. "We brought her to the doctor. She wasn't harmed. We don't really know why someone did this."

"Looks like you guys are having a bad start to your stay in Solitary," the cop named Kevin says in a Southern drawl. It sounds mocking.

"Shut up, Kev. Listen, Chris, do you know of anybody who would do something like this?"

I shake my head.

"Nobody at all? Any other run-ins you've had recently?"

"Just—what I mentioned when I went into the principal's office. Gus Staunch at school has been after me."

The sheriff cursed, then slowly shook his head. "Gus wouldn't do something like this. His father would tear his hide. No. Wasn't Gus. That I know for certain."

The way he said that makes me think the sheriff knows Gus, and knows him well.

"Anybody else?"

The only person that comes to mind is Jocelyn's step-uncle.

*But why would he do something like that?*

I shake my head.

Mom looks to be in a daze. I don't know what to say or do.

The sheriff asks me a few more questions, then stops when he sees Kevin walking up the stairs.

"Where're you going?"

"Just taking a look around."

He curses at the guy and tells him to get back down. Kevin follows like some trained, expressionless dog.

"Look, Chris, you keep a watch on your mother, okay? Here's my card—that's got my cell phone on it. Anything funny happens—anything—you call me, okay?"

I nod.

"Never heard of something like this happening around here, so can't understand if it's some locals havin' fun or if it's something else. So you keep me in the loop, you got it?"

Once they leave, I ask Mom to tell me what happened, but she tells me just as much as the sheriff did.

"One minute I was sitting in the car, and the next I was lying sprawled out on the passenger seat, my head throbbing. I must have been out only a few minutes, but I had no idea what happened."

"You didn't see anybody?"

"No. I just—I could feel something warm. Like—I don't know. I don't remember."

But I think she does remember and just doesn't want to tell me.

I go over to the door and make sure it's locked.

"Maybe we pass on dinner tonight?" Mom says.

"I can make you something. Anything."

"Maybe soup."

I nod.

"It's okay," she tries to convince me.

"Uh-huh."

"Come over here and sit by me."

When I sit down, Mom puts an arm around me. We watch television for a long time, not saying anything.

I can't tell which one of us is more scared.

## 62. A New Sensation

The email is waiting for me like a coiled snake ready to bite.

Even before opening it, I know.

As I awaken my computer it's almost like something else is awakened inside of me.

Something in the far reaches of my soul that I've never known or felt or even touched.

The email doesn't have a sender, just like the other.

It's simple, just like the other.

But this one is different.

Everything is different.

> CHRIS:
>
> THAT WAS JUST A WARNING TODAY. WORSE THINGS
>    WILL HAPPEN IF YOU DON'T LET THINGS GO.
> STAY AWAY FROM THE GIRL AND WE'LL STAY
>    AWAY FROM MOMMY.
> WE WON'T SAY THIS AGAIN.

I glance over it several times.

Words like *warning* and *worse* and *will* and *won't* stir something deep inside.

I tremble. Not out of fear but out of anger.

I want to see the sender, want to see his face. I want to look at the "we" behind this.

I was going to send Jocelyn an email, but I don't.

Not out of fear.

I'm too angry to do anything else right now.

And maybe, just maybe, that anger is covering this deep ocean of fear my little paddleboat is drifting over. Maybe. I don't know.

I know I have to calm down.

And then come up with a plan.

*Be smart, Chris.*

Because they're watching. Whoever *they* are.

They're watching, and they know.


# 63. Random and Profound

It's Friday, and there's no way that Jocelyn has any idea of how Thanksgiving turned out for me. I awaken that morning too early for anyone's good and can't stop thinking of Jocelyn and my mother and this place. I hope that the rest of Jocelyn's holiday was uneventful.

I vow to find out and find out soon.

I know that someone is watching me. One person, several people—I don't know.

I think of the email I got and consider again telling Mom or the cops. I think of Sheriff Wells's words: "Anything funny happens—anything—you call me, okay?"

Would I call the email funny? How about freaky? How about a quarter past frightening?

I don't know if I can trust the sheriff. I know that withholding information in the movies usually ends up getting a character in hot water, but I just don't know if I can afford to tell him. Something might happen to Mom, and I can't risk that. No way.

Then there's the issue of telling Mom.

I don't want her to worry.

Yeah, I know I'm the son and I'm sixteen and I can't do everything. I don't even have my license. But I don't want her worrying, and I'm still a bit nervous that whoever sent me this email will really do something bad.

I try to figure out how they might be watching, whoever they are.

Cameras in the house? Bugs that can hear everything we say? How about spies in the woods? It would be more than easy to hide out and remain concealed in the trees.

And what about those footprints on the deck?

If someone knows my email, then maybe they're monitoring that.

Same way with the phone.

I'm not a techie, and neither am I James Bond. No need to go crazy or obsessed or overboard.

But someone drugged Mom to make a point.

I change clothes quietly.

*Point taken, thank you very much.*

I spend an hour searching my room for anything that might be funny. Anything.

I find nothing.

I decide to write a note to Mom saying where I'll be when she wakes up later.

The sun isn't even up, so she certainly isn't.

I can get out of here and take a little bike ride.


The morning breathes cool air against my face as I ride in the fog.

It might be spooky or haunting, but it really looks beautiful.

I understand why they call these the Smoky Mountains. I'm literally riding through a thick mist.

I listen to random songs on my iPod. I love that out of 20,000 songs there can be one chosen for any particular moment. The reality is that usually the random songs are the ones that have the most meaning.

Even when things are random, they can still be profound.

The trees alongside of me stand like soldiers at arms. The road is visible for only a few feet in front of me, the sun somewhere rising but still unseen. I feel a mist covering my face as I pedal my bike.

I know where I'm going even if I can't see that far in front of me.

I like this feeling. If I can't see that far ahead of me, nobody else can see me either.

Well, maybe someone can see me now. But if He's really there He's been ignoring me for long enough, so a little longer isn't going to really matter.

When I reach the road turning to Jocelyn's, I decide to get off my bike and walk it the rest of the way.

I'm not going to go up to the door this time.

This time I'm simply going to be the lurker, checking to see who's at her house and hoping that I might get a chance to see her.

*Maybe she'll be taking an early morning stroll looking for berries and will suddenly see me.*

Right.

I walk down the driveway in the gloom and damp forest and see the house in a distance. I pull my bike up into the trees and then rest it against one, finding a place where I can hide out and spy.

Maybe this is what someone is doing to me. Who knows.

# 64. THE BURIAL GROUND

The sun settles in above me, above the dewy trees and fog-swept limbs. It seems like I wait for an hour or more, but I finally see what I'm hoping to see.

Not Jocelyn, but her wonderful step-uncle.

Wade Sims steps out of the door looking groggy and half dead. He walks to the small white car parked behind the Jeep. He starts it up and turns around, heading down the driveway and toward the road that probably leads him to work.

I know this is my chance.

Maybe Jocelyn's aunt is there—who knows. But I have to get to Jocelyn and tell her what happened yesterday.

She's the only one who might know.

Maybe she'll be able to explain who did this.

I sneak through the woods on the outskirts of the cleared area around her house. I exit along the side where only one window sits. I wish I knew which room belonged to Jocelyn. Then I'd do the good ol' pebble-against-the-window trick. I wouldn't even have to climb a tree to get to her.

I'm almost to her house when I hear the screeching of the front door. This sends me diving to the ground like some marine storming a beach. I land pitifully in plain view of the door, not close enough to the side of the house for it to shield me.

The figure on the top of the steps hovers as I bury my face into the long grass. As if that's going to help.

"Chris?"

I stare up and see a face looking both confused and amused.

"What are you doing?"

I'm sprawled out on her lawn early in the morning.

"Hi," I say.

"You're lucky, you know?"

"Why?"

"He just left," she says.

"I know. I'm dumb, but I'm not *that* dumb."

"Come on in. How'd you get here?"

"Bike."

"You're up early this morning."

"There's a good reason."

"Really?"

"Yeah." I reach the steps below her. "Well, maybe not good, but reason enough for me to come see you."

"Everything okay?"

"No."

"Come on in. My aunt's still asleep. Long night last night."

"You too, huh?"

Jocelyn rolls her eyes and keeps the door open for me.

As we enter the small house with the kitchen there to the right as you come in, I notice that Jocelyn is wearing her pajamas. They're plaid pants that match the blue and pink top.

Just seeing her like this ... it makes me stop.

She's adorable. She's like a Christmas present I've always wanted to find in the morning sitting under the tree.

*Don't you dare say that to her, Chris.*

"Can I get you anything?" she asks in a way that sounds like she's used to people showing up on her lawn first thing in the morning.

"No."

"You sure? You look kinda sweaty."

"Well—yeah, anything is fine."

"Helen usually makes coffee, and sometimes I have a little of it to wake up. I'm not much of a morning person."

"You look like one to me."

Her hair is wild, but only makes her look more attractive. She pours me a glass of orange juice and asks if that's okay. I take a sip and still feel nervous, wondering if we're being watched or overheard.

"What's going on?"

"Something happened last night. To my mom."

I tell Jocelyn what happened, explaining it in a voice slightly above a whisper.

"Who do you think did it?" she asks me.

"I was—I thought that maybe you might know."

"What? Why?"

"Because of last night. I got an email from someone telling me to stay away from you. That what happened to my mom was just a warning."

Jocelyn's expression changes. It almost like she's seeing someone die right in front of her.

"Do you think—maybe your step-uncle could be involved?"

"Wade?" Jocelyn shakes her head. "No. He's stupid and violent, but no—it wasn't him."

"Then who—why, Jocelyn?"

"You shouldn't have come over."

"I wanted to tell you. I needed to tell somebody."

"You didn't tell your mom?"

"No."

"Good."

"What's this about?"

Jocelyn stands up and moves to a window, looking outside. Then she holds up a finger to me, walks into the family room, and is gone for a while.

When she comes back, she's changed into some jeans and a sweatshirt.

"Come on," she says.

"Where are we going?"

"Outside."

"Out to where?"

"Just follow me," she says.

I follow her to the back of her lot and through the woods. The sun is warming things up a little, but it's still shadowy in the forest. After walking a few minutes up a small hill, I can see that we're following a trail. It soon turns into another, larger trail—almost like an old road that's been abandoned and forgotten about. It's level and heads through the woods.

We walk for a long time. Jocelyn is hauling, moving several feet ahead of me and not in the mood to talk. Every time I even try, she just tells me to be patient, to wait, to keep going.

I don't even know how long we walk. Maybe an hour, maybe more.

The road slowly but surely edges upward. We finally reach a place where the woods and the road open at the top of a clear mountain. She stops and holds an arm in front of my chest, stopping me from going any further.

I look out and see a small grassy crest in a shape of a dome.

"What's this?"

"We can't go any farther. I don't want to be seen. But if we were to keep walking up that hill, you'd find a series of large boulders with lots of little flat stones scattered all around them.

I look out, seeing the bright sky in the shadows of the trees. There's nothing ominous about what I'm looking at, yet the way Jocelyn talks builds terror inside of me.

"In the center of the large rocks is a fire pit."

I'm tempted to crack a joke because all of this is too much for me. But I keep my mouth shut and listen.

"Those stones—I believe, no, I *know* that they're basically gravestones. It's a cemetery up here."

"Really?"

"Yeah. The stones have inscriptions. Stuff I can't read or make out. But they're all kinda the same. And the fire—it's been used before. It was used shortly before Stuart Algiers went missing."

I look at Jocelyn.

I swear, if it were anybody else—and I mean anybody—I would laugh in their face.

"What are you saying?"

"I'm saying that—this is all going to sound crazy, but whatever … I'm telling you because I'm almost positive. I believe that Stuart Algiers was killed up here."

"Stuart—the one Poe was dating?"

"Yeah. Sometime around Christmas."

"How do you know?"

"Because of some of the things he told me. He didn't want anybody to know, especially Poe, but he told me. He told me about how the stone showed up in his bed one day and how the warnings continued and then he disappeared."

"What stone?" I ask.

"The stone that's out there. He showed it to me. I found it, Chris. I found that very stone. It's one that fits in your hand—a heavy, flat stone."

"And you think, what—someone left it for him as a warning?"

"I don't think it's a warning. I think it's like—a notice or something like that. A warning is to prevent something from happening. But there was never any intention of preventing what happened."

"How do you know he was killed?"

"He just disappeared. Just like that. And this town—this cursed, wretched little town—they didn't want anybody to know. I went to the police right afterward and told them everything. I told them stuff I haven't told anybody. I told them that Stuart was afraid because all these strange things were happening to him. They said it didn't make sense, and I know. But I told them to check this place out. They did and found nothing."

"But how do *you* know?"

"I spent one night digging, Chris. I found enough to know that there are bodies under there."

"Shut up."

"I'm serious."

"Then did you—you have to tell somebody."

"I did. I told the cops. Then suddenly everything changed. I was told to back off—guess in that case I was warned. And then sometime this summer, the same thing happened to me."

"What?"

"I went into my room and found one of those stones on my bed."

I stare at her and feel the air leaking out of me.

"And what's happened since?"

"What do you mean what's happened?" she says in an angry voice. "Nothing. Absolutely nothing. Except that a lot of people have started acting strange. As if they know. But of course I can't prove anything. I can't scream out about finding a rock in my bed, you know?"

"There's no way … you really think that Stuart was killed?"

"I didn't find his body.…" She stops and shivers and lets out a groan. "But I found part of a skeleton. And I know if someone came in and dug up all around this place, they'd find a lot more. I know that's where Stuart is."

"But why? What'd he do?"

"Nothing. Absolutely nothing."

"Then why?"

Jocelyn breathes in and looks at me. "What if it has nothing to do with Stuart except that he's a sacrifice?"

"A what?"

I'm not following this. My brain is on slow and is struggling to keep up.

"A sacrifice."

"Like for some cult or something like that?"

"Don't give me that look," Jocelyn says.

"What look?"

"A look that says I'm crazy."

"I didn't."

"You're giving it right now."

"This is just—all of this is crazy."

"Is it crazy that your mother was knocked out just to warn you?"

"Yeah, but—"

"But what? Somebody doesn't want you hanging out with me. Why would that be?"

I start putting the pieces together, but I don't like the picture that's forming.

"No."

"Chris—nobody knows about this. I didn't go back to the cops, because ever since I did, my life's been a living hell. I don't trust anybody. Aunt Helen—she's not involved in any of this, but I don't want her getting hurt. And you—I didn't want anybody else involved in this."

"Involved in what?"

"I don't know. That's the thing. I sound—I know I sound like a crazy person. I think half the time I am a crazy person."

"I just don't get—who—why?"

"Stuart Algiers told me that stuff in confidence, and he felt the same way. He saw things. He was experiencing stuff—"

"Like what?"

"Like—omens. Dark stuff."

"Have you?"

"Yeah."

I wait for her to tell me more.

"I just don't want you getting hurt," she says.

"Me? You don't want *me* getting hurt?"

"Or anybody else."

"What about you?"

"I don't know. I'm still trying to figure that out."

I grab her hand, then glance out at the grassy ridge beyond us. "This is crazy. Beyond crazy. Nothing's going to happen to you."

"Don't."

"Don't what?"

"I don't need you to be a hero."

I laugh. "A hero? You think that's what I'm trying to be?"

"Every guy has to save his woman. That's such a tired cliché."

"I'm not trying to be 'every guy,' and I'm not trying to live up to some stupid cliché. I don't want anything to happen to you for selfish reasons. You got that?"

"You can't do anything about it."

"I know I can't help it, but I'm serious, Jocelyn, and I mean this with everything I have—I love you. I can't do anything about that, but that doesn't mean someone's going to take that away from me."

She looks up at me and smiles and exhales.

"Chris."

She wraps herself in my arms and holds me tight.

"Nobody's going to do anything to you. And I mean it. And if we have to run away or dig a hole and hide inside, I don't care. We'll figure something out."

"You're not a part of this."

"I am now," I say. "I'm a part of you. Like it or not, that's the way things are."

## 65. ANGER AND GOOSE BUMPS

I eventually ride my bike home after we agree to meet up later.

There's something else she wants to show me.

As if she hasn't shown me enough.

I keep thinking of the gun I found in my bedroom closet, of the words my mother told the group at school. Telling them I would never use a handgun. Ever.

I thought that too. I believed I wouldn't.

But now I'm having a change of heart.

I'm relieved to find Mom home and awake. She doesn't ask where I've been. The small talk I make with her over breakfast is just that.

I spend the morning doing some rearranging in my room.

First off, I hide the handgun in a secure place. I put it under the bottom of my desk drawers in a place that can only be retrieved by lifting the heavy wooden desk up. Next I check out the room to see if I find anything else strange or interesting. I'm going through Uncle Robert's old clothes when I'm startled by Mom calling up to me that I have a phone call.

I run down to get it, thinking that it's Jocelyn.

"Hey, man, you busy right now?"

It's surprising to hear Ray Spencer's voice on the other end. It takes me a second to even place it.

"No."

"Awesome. Hey—just wanted to tell you about another party tonight."

"Okay."

He goes into detail about his friend having the party and gives me directions. I act like I'm paying attention and tell him I'll definitely stop by, but I already have plans of my own.

Of course I can't tell him that.

I can't tell anybody.

"Thanks for the call."

A part of me wonders if there's any coincidence.

I don't trust anybody.

"Make sure you come, man. It'll be good for you."

"Okay," I tell him.

When I hang up, I walk to my deck and look outside.

Why do I keep getting this feeling that we're being watched?

I don't know who or from where, but I know I'm not entirely crazy.

Something's going on here.

I need to figure out exactly what so I can help Jocelyn.


It's five and I'm heading out when I see Mom on the couch, still in sweatpants and a T-shirt, looking just like she did when she got out of bed. She holds a glass of wine; the bottle sits on the table.

"You going out?"

She looks and sounds a little too friendly, a little too relaxed.

"Yeah. Probably going to a party tonight."

"How are you getting there?"

"I'm riding my bike into town."

"Okay."

I stand there, watching whatever's on television for a few minutes. "You going to be fine?"

"Of course," she says.

"You sure?"

"I'm sure."

On my bike ride into town I wonder if things will ever be the same for her. The divorce was one thing, but my mom had a whole life back in Illinois. Other moms and friends she hung out with. A whole social life. Splintered and sunk so easily.

I feel a bit guilty leaving her behind, but I want to see Jocelyn. If there's an opportunity, I'll take it.

We just have to see each other in private.

I wish I could see my dad again to tell him what a mess he made, tell him that he should be there for Mom and that she shouldn't have to be working and living someone else's life. There's nothing here for her. At least I've found something. But Mom—she hasn't found anything, and it doesn't look like she will anytime soon.

The anger builds inside as I enter the main road of Solitary.

Anger toward Dad, toward what he did to us. Anger toward who he chose instead.

This all goes away when I see the figure coming out of the convenience store. Pastor Jeremiah Marsh.

He smiles in a strange, creepy kind of way. For some reason it makes my skin crawl.

"Hello, Chris."

I greet him and stop the bike at the edge of the sidewalk.

"Need to have you come back to church sometime."

"Sure," I say just to say it.

"You need to bring your mother, too."

"Okay."

"That a for-sure thing?"

"Well, I don't know—I'll have to check it out with my mom. She works a lot."

"Chris?" The voice sounds like someone on the radio.

"Yeah."

"Don't lie."

"Yeah, okay."

The narrow eyes study me from behind the glasses, his mouth revealing a mousy smile.

"There's enough love for everybody," the pastor says. "You just have to know where to find it."

I nod, not having a clue what else to say.

*There's enough crazy, too, so sell that somewhere else.*

"You have a good day, young man. Take good care of yourself."

Why is it that every single person I talk to seems to threaten me?

Is it just me?

Am I the crazy one?

I say goodbye and pedal faster down the main road.

I can't shake the goose bumps that cover me.

And the feeling that the guy I'm pedaling away from is worthy of them.


## 66. PIECES OF THE PUZZLE


Sable Road makes a straight line through the heart of Solitary, with the store buildings on one side and the train tracks on the other. As the tracks head on toward the opening in the woods, the street curves right and upward past a few more buildings (a garage housing a fire truck, a veterinarian's clinic, some offices) until it gets to a fork. I take my bike to the right, farther up the hill where the road stretches out and passes a long, one-story white building that looks new. I haven't been here before, but I know it's the library.

Jocelyn told me to meet her inside.

It takes me a good ten minutes to find her. If she's trying to stay hidden, she's doing a good job of it. I find her at the end of an aisle of books, pretending to read something. I greet her, but she shakes her head, then nods toward a window behind her. She starts walking, and I follow.

Before getting to the main area of the library, Jocelyn stops me and tells me to wait a few minutes, then to meet me behind the library. I do as she orders, my bike safely locked at the front.

A few minutes later, I crawl inside the Jeep, acting like I'm some wanted man making a run for it.

"Stay down for a little while," Jocelyn tells me as she whips the car back out onto the main street.

I stay crouched as much as possible as the car winds around the streets. Finally she says okay, and I sit back up.

We're driving on a rocky road I don't recognize. "Where are we heading?"

"You'll see," she tells me. "How was the rest of your day?"

"Boring."

"Boring is good, right?"

"Yeah, I guess so," I say. "It's better than something bad happening."

"I left right as Wade was getting home. He doesn't work tomorrow, so it's going to be a long night for him."

I want to ask her things about her step-uncle, but I can't. I feel like despite how much Jocelyn has told me, certain things are off limits. I wouldn't know what to say even if I got answers to my questions.

Sometimes it's best to keep questions to yourself.

"I shouldn't be showing you this, but I just have to."

"What?"

"You'll see."

"Any hints?"

"No."

The road goes through low-hanging trees that scrape the top of the Jeep. Jocelyn slows down as we turn left and go over a bridge leading farther up into the hills. After a few more minutes, the woods once again turning dark from the sunset, she pulls her car to the side of the road and shuts it off.

"We're taking a side way to watch. Nobody will know we're here since we're parking here. Nobody uses this road. People aren't supposed to drive over that bridge."

"Really?"

"Yeah. It's weak in spots. Doesn't stop me."

"Does anything?"

She smiles and climbs out of the Jeep.

I hear the sound of water. It's louder than the creek that's below my house. Jocelyn goes to the edge of the road and peers into the woods.

"This should be good. Come on."

It's hard to get used to driving for a few minutes and then being stuck in the middle of nowhere, in complete wilderness. The hill is steep just like the one around my house, and I watch my step as I go down the slope sideways. Jocelyn walks down the slope, stepping in a way that makes it seem like she's done this before. We walk for a few minutes, the sound of the gushing water getting louder and louder.

Soon I see where it's coming from.

The forest levels out for a while. Jocelyn stops, looks around, then finds what she's looking for.

"Right over here. Come on."

We reach a set of clustered trees and stop. She points in front of them, where the woods open up.

Even though the light is fading, I still can see the waterfalls.

They're mesmerizing, both in sight and sound.

In the middle of the woods against the side of the sloping mountain, some massive rocks create a series of waterfalls. I see three places where the rocks jut outward to form this, like a set of stone tiers. The water looks light and endless, its water falling down to the stream below.

I wonder if this stream is connected in any way to the one in front of my house.

"Those are Marsh Falls," Jocelyn says in a voice a little above a whisper. "This turns into the Basset River that gets really big farther down the mountain."

The water is very loud, and it's hard to hear her since she's talking in a faint voice.

If it was another evening I might think Jocelyn had brought me here as a romantic gesture, but the way we're peering behind these trees and the way she's talking make me think that something's about to happen.

"We have to wait for a few minutes."

"Wait for what?" I shout out.

"Just be patient. You're so impatient."

I laugh and shake my head. Just as I'm about to say something along the lines of, "You've brought me into the middle of the woods by a set of falls just after showing me what you think is a cemetery of murdered people, so yeah, pardon me if I'm a little curious," Jocelyn puts a finger on her lips.

"Just watch. But don't let them see you."

"Let who see me?"

My question is soon answered. Through streaks of sunlight that soften into a hazy, warm glow, I see a figure emerging from the woods to the right of the falls about halfway up. This allows me to see how big the rocks are, especially the top, which tower over the man.

I just see the figure—a man, dark-haired, tall, older.

Then he puts a hood over his head and steps on the edge of the second tier of rocks where the water from above is landing.

He ducks down and disappears beneath the white, cascading water.

"Who was that?" I ask.

"Just watch."

This same thing happens four times in the next few minutes. That means five men have come out of the woods in the middle of nowhere to go *underneath* these falls.

"What's behind there?"

She smiles, shakes her head, then looks back out to the falls. "Come on. Let's go back to the car."

"Jocelyn, wait."

"I'll tell you. It's too loud to talk here. I don't want them seeing us. I shouldn't have brought you here."

"Then why did you?"

"Because this place—those people—they might be able to help you."

We climb into the solitude where the sound of the falls can barely be heard. It seems a lot darker in her car now.

"That group meets there every Saturday night," Jocelyn tells me.

"So what are they, some kind of cult?"

"No."

"Then what?"

"It's a group of people—mostly men, a few women—who meet once a week. That's their church."

"Behind the falls?"

Jocelyn nods.

"Okay."

"Don't you get it?"

"The longer time goes by, the more I *don't* get."

"They're a normal church, nothing weird about it."

"How do *you* know?"

"I've been. A few times."

"What?"

"Yeah," Jocelyn says.

"Do they know all the stuff about—"

"No."

"Then why did you go?"

"I was invited by one of them. You don't just go. You get invited. They have to be very, very careful."

"Why?"

"Because worshipping God isn't liked very much around here."

"What about the big church—the one Ray Spencer goes to?"

"You've been to that, haven't you?"

"Yeah."

"Notice anything different?"

I don't want to tell her the things I thought I heard, the things I thought I felt.

*Why are you scared to tell her that? You can tell her anything.*

"Maybe a few things."

"There's no way of knowing that it isn't a church, a regular church."

"What is it?"

"They don't worship God there. You won't find the name Jesus Christ anywhere in that building, trust me."

"What?"

"Yeah. A few months ago I didn't really know, didn't really care. But it's just—that group—the ones we just saw—they're a small group that meets in private. If they were caught, they'd be in trouble."

"Like arrested?"

"No. Worse."

"Like—like what?"

She sits in the silence, and for a moment I study the outline of her face. This is surreal, all of it. The space and the soft sounds outside and the coolness of the evening and the disappearing sun.

"Jocelyn?"

"I knew it would be like this."

"Like what?"

"I sound ridiculous, I know."

"No, you don't."

"Of course I do. But, Chris—this is real. This place is real, and it's been real for a long time. And I just—I don't know. I'm searching myself. I'm trying to understand the answers."

"The answers to what?"

"What God is trying to show me."

Anybody else would get a complete wave of shutdown from the passenger side of the car at this moment, but it's Jocelyn. I still don't say anything.

"You know that six months ago, I truly didn't think there was a God. But this group—these people—they say that the Spirit—the Holy Spirit—is the thing that stirs one's heart. And for a while it's been stirring. Then I pray, and my answer comes true when you come along."

"I already told you. I'm not a guardian angel."

"Maybe. I don't know. I just know this: That group I showed you, I think they really have the answers."

"The answers to what?"

"To life and death and the big question that all of us have to consider. What happens when we die?"

"I don't want to consider it."

"Even if you don't, at some point you're going to die."

"Really?" I ask in a mocking tone.

"Death has hung over my head ever since I can remember. It shows up at my door time and time again. But those people—what they talk about isn't death. It's life. Eternal life."

"People like that usually like to talk about that really hot place that people—good people even—go to if they don't believe."

"I don't believe, Chris. Not yet."

"Sure sounds like it to me."

"It's not—not like what they have. What they have is different. It's like—it's real."

I think of my mother. I think of what she thinks, what she believes. And I know it's real too.

"Lots of people can have genuine beliefs. How do you know which one is right and which one isn't?"

"I don't," Jocelyn tells me. "But I want to know. I need to know."

"I know everything I need to know."

"Maybe that's easy for you. But I'm looking for answers."

I wish and want to help her but I don't have any answers. Especially for what she's looking for.

"That group of people—they used to be part of the church my parents went to until it burned down. This is where they ended up."

For a moment I think of what this means.

Suddenly I understand a little more of where she's coming from. The same way I feel about my mother is how she's feeling. Jocelyn wants to believe what her parents believed. She's searching for answers the way they were.

I get it now. Not fully, but a little more.

"I understand."

"Do you? Really?"

"Yeah."

"Listen to me," she says, tugging at my shirt for full and undivided attention. "This isn't the daughter trying to make sure that she believes in the same heaven her parents did in order to meet up with them later. They were a part of that group, Chris. Both of them. And they both passed away because of an accident."

Now I really get it.

"You think that's a coincidence? The same way that the thing with your mom and the warning about me are?"

My heart feels like it's been tossed off a cliff. My head spins like I'm bungee jumping.

"No."

"I want to put the pieces together. All of them. But every day it seems like the puzzle just gets bigger. And every day some of the pieces seem to go missing."

"What do you want me to do?"

"Help me."

"I'll do anything you want," I tell her. "Anything."

"Okay. For now, just—just be open, okay?"

"I will."

"For anything."

"I already am."

She starts the car and turns on the lights, then drives us through the darkness back toward civilization.


## 67. Messages and Plans


We sit on the edge of a cliff, staring out over the heads of trees capped by the light of the moon above and listening to the stream of the falls below. Jocelyn holds my hand and watches me intently.

"What is it?" I ask.

"You have to know when to let me go."

I'm a little confused, since she's the one who wanted to come here. "What do you mean?"

"I mean that it's okay to let me go. To let the memory of me go."

"The memory of you?" I ask with a laugh. "I'm trying to *create* memories. That's the point, right?"

"You have a good heart, and I just want to make sure that you share it with others."

"I want to share it with you."

"Don't be selfish," Jocelyn tells me, kissing me on the cheek. "And don't get too stuck. Too stuck or too scared to move on."

"Okay," I say, and that's when I wake up from the vivid dream.

I don't see Jocelyn anymore that weekend. Nothing eventful happens except for the two calls I get from Ray inviting me to church. Talk about being a disciple. Both messages are taken by my mom. I don't return the calls, and Sunday morning comes and goes.

By the time I arrive at school Monday morning after the four-day weekend I have an idea of how to possibly help Jocelyn out.

I need to get some answers.

I need to find someone who not only knows them, but will actually give them to me.

Someone who's not only below the radar, but who's effectively *off* it.

I find him standing at his locker like he always does, rearranging things. Probably to kill time.

"Hey, Newt."

He greets me in his usual nervous fashion.

"You got any plans after school?"

Newt shakes his head, then looks around to see if anyone's watching.

I'm beginning to understand a little more why this kid is paranoid. If he knows things, and he does, then he *should* be paranoid.

"Can we talk?"

"About what?"

"Stuff."

"Stuff pertaining to what?"

"Things," I say.

I think he finally gets it by the look on my face. The scar on his cheek seems to redden as if it knows too.

"Things," he says.

"Yeah."

"We can't do that around here."

"You tell me where then."

"My house is secure," Newt says in the tone of a secret agent.

I want to laugh, but then again, I don't.

Too many crazy things have happened.

I no longer think this kid is crazy.

Or maybe we both are.

"Is it far from downtown?"

"Not far enough," he says.

"Write down your address when you can. I'll swing by after school."

I open the letter that Jocelyn slipped to me before second period.

*Let's act like you've taken their suggestion. Just to be on the safe side. K?*

*Means no lunch or hanging out.*

*Communicate the old-fashioned way. Writing letters.*

*Just make sure you shred after reading.*

Without even glancing at Jocelyn, I begin to start tearing the note into tiny pieces on my desk.

Message received, loud and clear.

Thankfully, there are no run-ins with Gus, nor any guilt trips from Ray. The day is run-in free.

I move with the masses, standing in line and stepping in place. Doing what I should.

Whoever is watching is going to get bored because there's nothing to notice.

Meanwhile, I'm noticing.

I'm trying to notice anything and everything.

When I get home, I know that Mom will be at work. I grab my bike and the handwritten directions and head out.

# 68. NEWT KNOWS

I ring the doorbell, and Newt cracks opens the front door to the nice-sized two-story house.

"Go around the back," he tells me through the sliver in the doorway.

This looks like a relatively new housing development, one with maybe twenty or so houses in it. Everything looks like it's maintained carefully. I walk over lush grass and find a deck in the back. Newt stands by an open screen door and waves me in.

"Come on," he says as he guides me through a kitchen and toward the stairs going down. "Shut the door behind you."

We get to the basement. It's one of those that's been finished and transformed into an entertainment room. It's complete with the big screen television, a foosball table, a pool table, even a fish tank.

A part of me wonders with both humor and irony how many others come down to play games with the kid.

"Mom's out shopping and Dad's at work. But just in case, I wanted to come down here."

"You think someone's watching us?" I try not to look at the scar on the side of his cheek, though it really stands out under all the canned lights in the ceiling.

"They're watching *you*," he says.

"Who *are* they? And why are they watching me?"

Newt surveys the room, appears to be thinking. He's an odd little guy. Even simply thinking appears to be a strenuous, awkward act.

"People around here don't like outsiders."

"My mom lived here when she was younger."

"Doesn't matter if you have ties. You're outsiders. New kids don't last long."

"What do you mean?"

"I've seen them come in, and then the family moves away. It's happened every time someone new has come around here."

"But why?" I ask.

"Certain things just *are* around Solitary. Certain things are just accepted. That's the way this place is."

"Like what?"

"Like Gus, for one. He gets away with so much simply because of his father."

"So his father is some rich guy who everybody wants to brown-nose?"

Newt shakes his head. "No. It's more than that."

"What then?"

"There are adults that act like—I don't know. They act like they *owe* Mr. Staunch something."

"What?"

"I don't know. Even my parents. We don't talk about him, but when his name comes up, they act almost ..."

"Almost what?" I ask.

"Almost scared."

I think of the figure I saw on the deck, the feeling of dread that came over me. Of course I was temporarily trespassing on his land, so I had a right to feel a bit scared.

"I overheard my parents talking—people don't ever think I'm

listening because I'm little, you know, but I do—and someone mentioned Mr. Staunch in an angry way. Probably because they were drinking. And my father told the other man to be quiet. To stop talking like that. As if they couldn't say anything bad about him. It was really weird."

"Tell me something. What does this have to do with Jocelyn?"

Newt sits on the edge of the couch and looks down.

"Newt?"

"It's another unspoken thing. For the most part."

"Unspoken? Then how do you know enough to tell someone like me to stay away from her?"

"My parents told me the same thing. And someone told them."

"Why?"

Newt shrugs. "I don't know."

"You have to know."

"I don't. But the same thing happened with Stuart—the kid who disappeared—the one I showed you the article about. It was almost as if the very mention of his name was almost—well, like it was blasphemous. Before and after he disappeared."

"What? Why?"

"It's secrets. This town is full of them. Everywhere you go, every person you see, every corner—they're all full of secrets."

"What kind?"

"I don't know."

"You have to have some ideas."

"I have a lot of ideas, Chris. But the biggest idea is to keep quiet and to keep to myself. Just like my parents. Just like everybody else."

"But surely there has to be someone—some people who can do something."

"Who?"

"Your parents?"

Newt laughs. "No, no. My dad serves on several boards. He's Mr. Respected. And Mom is busy and—no. They're not going to say anything."

"But this kid—he just disappeared."

*Jocelyn says he was murdered.*

"People who have asked questions have disappeared too."

"Like who?"

"Rumors. That's all I know."

"Newt, listen to me. Jocelyn can't disappear."

"How are you going to stop it from happening?"

"How? I don't know. You gotta help me."

Newt looks around the room and fidgets. "I'm helping the best I can. The only way I can."

"But does this Ichor Staunch have something to do with these secrets—and that guy's disappearance?"

"Nobody will say that."

"I'm asking you."

"Yeah. Totally. But there's no way to know. No way to prove it."

"That guy lives right down the street from me."

"Then you need to be extra careful."

I laugh and let out a curse of disbelief. "What is going on here? I mean—where in the world is this place? Isn't this America? Things like this don't happen. Can't someone put out a rumor on the Web? Tweet about it?"

"This is a tiny town in the mountains of North Carolina. There aren't a lot of people around here. They're friendly, but they don't like outsiders. They all know each other, and they all keep their secrets to themselves. A lot of things can happen in a place where people live out lies."

"But why would someone—what does someone want with Jocelyn?"

Newt stares back at me.

"Tell me," I say.

But he doesn't. He can't. Or he won't.

He looks back at me, and I wonder if the scar on his face was there at birth.

I want to ask him, but I can't.

He's already helped me enough, and I don't want to pressure him anymore. To pressure him or to remind him of something that surely he doesn't want to be reminded of.

I sit on the floor and put my arms behind me and let out a sigh.

"One other thing you need to know," he says.

"What? What else can there be?"

"It's about Jocelyn."

I wait for him to tell me.

"That guy who's around her—the creepy guy who looks like he belongs in prison—Wade, is it?"

I nod. Newt continues speaking in his matter-of-fact way, no emotion clouding his face.

"Guys at school say that he does more than just hurts Jocelyn. That he does *a lot* more."

"That's a lie."

"I'm just telling you what I hear."

I curse, calling it vicious gossip.

"Maybe it is," Newt says. "Doesn't mean it doesn't happen."

"He's not going to touch her."

"You can't watch her all day long."

I leave his house feeling bewildered and confused and angry, but I should probably feel frightened.

# 69. INVESTIGATING

There is a small area in the library at Harrington High that has a computer area attached to it. It's laughable compared to the computer lab back at my old high school. I'm on a computer a little older than my laptop searching for something on the Internet.

I'm doing it here because I don't trust my computer. Someone already seems to know my every move, including any type of communication done on my laptop. If I start doing searches on it, that someone might find out.

I start my list with the following words: *missing people Solitary, North Carolina.* I narrow the search and use other words, like *students* and *children* and *disappeared.* After spending most of the study hall searching random news blurbs and articles, I've come up with a list.

Suddenly I feel nervous. I glance behind me.

*Big Brother watches and always will, Chris.*

If they did watch, they certainly wouldn't be able to read my scribbles on the piece of paper. That I'm sure of.

I look at the list.

STUART ALGIERS (17)—MISSING DURING CHRISTMAS BREAK

LUCY PENNER (13)—WENT MISSING DECEMBER 29 YEAR EARLIER

HARRY MARSHALL (16)—DISAPPEARED ON CHRISTMAS DAY TWO YEARS AGO

There are others, too, but none directly related to Solitary. At least not in bold letters. A guy who dies in a hunting accident. A man found frozen in his car after it broke down during a winter storm. An elderly woman shot by a burglar.

Three missing students in three years.

All between the ages of thirteen and seventeen.

All disappearing around the Christmas holidays.

The list looks way too long to me. Way too long to be coincidental.

If I knew someone to go to, I would.

*How about Mom?*

I fold the sheet of paper up and put it in my jacket pocket. Maybe I'll tell her about it, but she'll probably just tell me to stay out of it and be careful and all that. Or she might go to the police and spill the beans and get us into even more hot water.

I'm trying to avoid the hot water.

I slip a note to Jocelyn on the way to lunch, though I don't sit with her:

WHAT DO YOU KNOW ABOUT LUCY PENNER AND HARRY
MARSHALL?

At the end of lunch, she hands me her response:

*People said Lucy ran away from home. Never
believed it. Don't know anything much about Harry
Marshall. People said he was messed up. Maybe they
fall into the Stuart category. Do you think?*

As our class together begins, I shoot Jocelyn a look and nod at
her. I can see the paleness of her skin, the blankness in her eyes.

*That's fear, Chris. And it's something you probably smack of too.*

All throughout that class and the rest of the day, I try to figure
out what to do.

Who to tell.

Where to go.

Something's wrong with all of this. And Jocelyn might be next.

It sounds absurd, but so do many things that happen every single
day. They're absurd until they show up on your doorstep knocking.

*What about telling Dad?*

The voice comes out of nowhere, and I squelch it quickly. If I
could punch whoever said it, I would. There's no way I'd ask my dad
for anything. Mom could be going to a Turkish prison and I still
wouldn't reach out for his help.

Well, maybe if it was Turkish I would, but only then.

After last-period PE, I'm changing my clothes in the locker room, absorbed in thoughts. I don't even hear the guys behind me until it's too late. One second I'm by my locker staring into it, and then the next I feel arms grab me at both sides and something go over my head, and for a second I think it's a plastic bag that someone's going to suffocate me with. The room goes dark.

My arms are pulled and my hands are tied behind my back. I wrangle and wrestle and thrash, but whoever is holding me down is too strong. My scream is stifled by someone's big hand.

*It's Gus. It's gotta be Gus.*

Then I hear something tear and realize it's tape. They're tying my legs together now.

I manage to break my mouth away from the hold and howl out, "Stop it! Somebody help me! Somebody!"

But then I cough and choke as the hand cups something else around my nose and mouth. I inhale something strong, bitter, gagging. I cough more and then suddenly feel light and groggy.

In seconds, I'm out.

## 70. THE THREAT

"Wake up. Come on, boy. Wake up."

I open my eyes but feel like I'm still dreaming. My body feels like it's moving, my head swaying on the top of the surface of the ocean. Is it nighttime? Everything is still pitch black.

Then something hits the side of my face, and I open my eyes and know I still have something—a cloth of some kind—over my head.

"You there? You awake?"

I don't recognize this voice, but I know it doesn't belong to Gus.

"Yeah." My voice sounds scratchy and stuffy.

"Good. Very good."

I try to move my arms, but they're still behind me. My legs won't move either.

And I'm cold. I'm very cold.

"You're some kind of stupid, aren't you, boy? Don't you get it? Don't you even remotely care about things, boy?"

"What?"

"Now you shut your mouth, but make sure your ears are open and listenin', got it?"

I don't say anything, then feel a hand grab my head and shake it.

It's the equivalent of riding the roller coaster backward with the lights off after taking cough syrup.

"You got it, boy?"

"Yeah, yeah, got it."

The voice sounds older—Southern. No-nonsense. I'd want to say that it's an elderly voice, but the hand that just grabbed me felt like someone strong and big.

"You know what I hate, boy? It's headaches. I hate when they come on. I used to get them all the time. These brain-poppin' migraines. The kind that would make the lights go out. The kind that made you see ten thousand stars in yer head. You ever feel something like that?"

I shake my head, then utter "no" out of fear.

"And you know, that's what you're becomin'. A headache. A really annoying headache. But I'm not gonna let it get worse. It's not gonna be a migraine, I'll promise you that. You got that, boy?"

"Yeah."

He laughs and then mumbles a curse.

I hear shuffling. We're not the only people here, wherever *here* is.

The man's voice echoes the way it might in a small room. But it's cold. It's too cold to be inside.

"Eyes are on you a bit too much, and I gotta account for that. But sooner or later they won't be. And believe me, if you don't stop all this nonsense, you'll disappear like the rest of them. You got it?"

"Yes."

A blinding block of pain bashes against the side of my head, sending me to the floor. I feel hands grab my arm and pull me back up. I'm still wincing, still woozy, still trying to understand what's going on, when I hear the voice again.

"It's hard to know which you value more, Chris Buckley." The way the last name comes out sounds like someone picking food from his teeth. "Your mother's life or your own. We'll take both; it's fine with me."

I close and open my eyes, but it doesn't do any good. I still can't see anything. The ache in my head is like a mutating alien throbbing to get out.

"You stop trying to play Boy Scout, Chris. Stop trying to be a detective. Stop asking questions and snooping around. And stop

everything—and I mean everything—with your little girlfriend."
Something presses against my ear, and I realize it's the man's lips.
"Stop all of this or I will kill you, Chris. The same way I killed your
uncle. You got it?"

I nod and say "yes" or think I say "yes," because sometime shortly
after this I black out again.


## 71. WHISPERS IN THE DARK


I'm fifteen and riding in a convertible with my friends and my tunes
surrounding me.

Sophomore year is over and life is ahead of me and nothing
really matters. It doesn't matter that things at home are crumbling
or that my father's filling me with stories about heaven and hell or
that I'm starting to do things I shouldn't be doing or that I have
this sinking feeling every now and then that things are suddenly
going to get bad.

But on this night they can't and won't because the music's much
too loud to let it.

I can block it out with the volume.

The glowing skyline of Chicago in the distance speaks of
opportunity.

The bass throbbing against my gut speaks of the wild adult world
I want to join.

Yet the shadows still seem to follow even in the dead of night.

For some reason I'm thinking of this summer night when I wake up shivering in the darkness.

My head aches.

My hands feel numb. I find they're still tied behind me, yet they don't feel as tight as they were before. I wrangle around my legs and find that they're free. One of them stomps against the wall—a wall that's particularly soft.

*Feels like dirt.*

It not only feels like dirt, but smells like it too. If dirt has a smell.

I feel a sense of déjà vu.

I keep blinking and realize there's still something covering my eyes, something wrapped all around my head.

I pull, tug, try to bend and slip out of whatever's holding my arms behind my back.

*Breathe in and relax and figure this out, Chris.*

So I do that.

I calm down as much as I can. My heart doesn't exactly cooperate, but at least my mind starts to function.

I slide backward as far as I can, my fingers reaching out like a piano player jamming a tune. Leaning against the wall, I manage to guide myself up so I'm finally standing. Then I keep feeling the wall behind me, a dirt wall in a hole that I must be in.

*A hole that seems very familiar.*

Something hard and cold brushes against my knuckle and I touch it, realizing it's a rock. A rock with a sharp edge.

In a matter of a few minutes, I've worn out whatever bind is keeping my hands behind my back.

It's easy. Too easy, in fact. As if whoever tied me up deliberately made sure I could unfasten the rope. With my hands free, I tear off the cloth from my eyes.

It's still almost pitch black in here, but as I look upward I suddenly recognize this place.

And I wish that I had kept the bandana on.

*The cabin.*

It's the same square hole, with the faintest of light coming from the opening above me.

I was always going to come back and check it out, see where the dark opening led to.

A cold breeze seems to whisper at me in response.

I stare in its direction.

*Something's there.*

It's a crazy thought, and I know that I need to get out of here. But my arms are just starting to get some feeling in them, and my head is only slightly out of its foggy hole.

*Get out of here now, Chris.*

I massage the dirt walls to find that ladder again. I soon lock on to a railing and start to pull myself up.

That's when I hear the voice.

"Chrisssssssssssss."

I'm so freaked out that I grab onto the railing above me in the wrong way and then I find I'm not grabbing anything.

My fall back to the ground knocks the wind out of me.

I cough and stand and search for the railings again.

"I see you, Chrissssssssss."

The voice is low and soft and sick and evil.

And it sounds like it's five feet away.

My skin is crawling with bumps and my mind is tearing off in fear and I'm reaching and climbing and slipping and holding and in what seems like an hour I make my way up and out of that hole.

I scramble away from its opening like some tiny animal escaping the jaws of death. I knock over a chair and find myself tumbling again, my body landing on the dull edge of something that scrapes my side.

It's dark outside, but I can see the windows and slight gray opposed to the black of the hole.

I see the door and open it and scramble outside into the woods, sucking in air and gasping and probably looking like someone possessed.

All I know is that I need to get back to my house.

It's downhill.

I know I shouldn't be sprinting through the woods because I might trip and fall onto something really, really sharp, but it's better than whatever is behind me in that cabin.

*Underneath that cabin in that ungodly hole.*

I'm back home before I know it, and I'm in my living room for several minutes breathing in and out before I notice the blood on my shirt.

"Mom?" I call out several times.

But she's not here. Fortunately.

I don't have to explain something I can't.

Sooner or later it's going to hit me how much trouble I'm in.

## 72. WHAT DIFFERENCE DOES IT MAKE?

I'm listening to The Smiths and wondering if life can get any worse.

I don't want to find out.

I know what I have to do.

I make mental notes of the situation.

There's Mom. Trying to work her away around the sadness she's been left in.

There's Dad. Somewhere else far, far away with whatever God he believes he knows.

There's Jocelyn. This beautiful girl, inside and out, who somehow finds herself in all this trouble.

There's Gus and his friends who want to pound my face into the ground.

There's Newt, who somehow knows all the town's secrets though it's forgotten about him.

There's Billy Bob, who just escaped from the Ku Klux Klan to knock me out and tie me up and threaten me in the middle of a cabin in the woods.

I could go on but I don't want to.

All I want to do is rescue Jocelyn. But I've been trying, and things have gone from bad to worse.

"And I'm feeling very sick and ill today," the singer tells me.

*Yeah. Me, too.*

I know I've got to stop. With everything.

I don't want anything to happen to Jocelyn. Or Mom. Or me.

Whoever is watching is doing a good job.

And it could be anybody. Jocelyn's step-uncle or a teacher at school or that weird pastor or the weird, red-headed vagrant in town with his dog or my Aunt Alice.

I don't trust anybody anymore.

I know what I have to do. But I'm not going to like doing it.

*Take this out when you need it, Chris.*

I hear my father's voice as if he's whispering from the other room.

It takes me a minute to find it. It's in the same bag I tossed it into before leaving Illinois. A part of me wonders why I kept it to begin with.

*You might be surprised what you'll find inside.*

Maybe a teeny, tiny part of me believed Dad when he gave it to me. I wouldn't admit it to him or anybody else, but I can admit it to myself.

I hold the Bible in my hand.

*Maybe it can help somebody else, even if it can't help me.*

I know what I need to do.

I place the Bible on my desk, then turn up the music. I want to run away and bury myself in something somewhere far, far away from here.


"What's this?" Jocelyn looks at me with curious and worried eyes as she holds the Bible.

"It's a gift. A 'farewell gift'?"

It's shortly before history class, and I asked to talk with her briefly. She asked in a whisper if everything was okay, and I lied. I don't want her to know about yesterday. I don't want her to know about anything regarding me.

"What do you mean, 'farewell gift?'"

"You know," I say.

"Chris—"

I look around to see if anybody is spying on us. But how would I know? It could be anybody.

"I can't."

"You can't what?" Jocelyn asks, angry now.

"I can't be around you anymore."

"We already agreed to that. We said—"

"No," I interrupt. "I mean—anything. I can't."

"What happened?"

"Nothing."

"You're lying to me."

"Nothing happened."

"Chris, talk to me."

"No. They're watching."

"I know," she says through clenched teeth. "I've said that to you."

"But I just—I can't do anything."

"What happened? I know something happened."

I shake my head, making sure that the spies who lurk know that I'm making it very clear.

No means *no*.

Even if it also means breaking my heart.

"What's this for?" Jocelyn asks.

"My father gave it to me. I thought maybe it could help you."

"Because you can't?"

"Don't—"

"I can get a Bible anywhere. Where am I supposed to find another you?"

"Please don't be angry."

"Angry? I'm not angry. I'm—I'm completely baffled. I'm disappointed."

*I can't tell you any more because I don't want you hurt like my mother or like me.*

I want to tell her but I can't.

She can't know.

"Chris?"

"I'm sorry," is all I can say.

And I am.

I'm sorry that I can't do more or say more.

That doesn't mean I've given up trying to help her.

It just means she can't know about it.

I love this girl, and I know I will do anything to help her.

Anything.

Even if it means momentarily hurting her.

## 73. RUNNING

Nobody knows. Nobody's got a clue. That's the toughest part, at least to me. I want at least a handful of people to have an idea. To have some kind of knowledge.

About me.

Jocelyn started to, and that's the worst part of this.

That the very one person, the single soul that I was opening up to, now has to be the person I walk past in these hallways. The person who glances with resentment. The person who becomes a stranger like the rest of them. Like the rest of the nameless, faceless, careless fools I'm stuck around.

The rest of the week blurs by as November turns to December. Twice Jocelyn gives me letters, but I reject them. I feel like a parent grabbing a child's arm and hurting him to avoid his running into the path of an oncoming car.

I don't want to hurt Jocelyn, but I don't know what else to do.

If Stuart and Lucy and Harold all disappeared around Christmas, I only have a few weeks to find out what's going on. To try to make some sense of it and then to tell somebody who can do something about it.

I keep thinking of Sheriff Wells, of the card he gave me with his cell number on it.

*Anything funny happens—anything—you call me, okay?*

Being knocked unconscious and bound and gagged only to awaken in the bottom of a hole in the middle of the woods—yeah, that's pretty funny.

*Funny as in hellish.*

I know that Jocelyn won't say anything. And I can't break her trust, either.

Yet if what she says is true …

So I keep low and stay out of everybody's hair and try to figure out what to do next.

I just wish I had a clue.

I think I can trust Sheriff Wells.

I just need to gather more information to show him.

Time is running out on me.

More importantly, it's running out on Jocelyn.

On Thursday it seems that someone else feels the same way.

I find a note in my locker, like the others, folded and taped to the inside.

I half expect it to be from Jocelyn and am sad that it's not.

It's short and simple.

> Start at the top. But be careful.
>
> A friend

I want to meet this friend, since it's obvious I have so few.

It takes me a while to figure out what the letter means.

Start at the top.

Who controls most of this town? Who is the head honcho around here?

*Staunch.*

Start with him.

But start by doing what?

*He's right down the road, and you've already managed to spy on him once.*

I'll start with him. And I'll start tonight.

## 74. Eyes in the Woods

You know how you get cold sometimes and start shivering and can't stop? That's what I'm doing now as the breeze whips snow-flakes into the spot I'm hiding in. I can barely see the glow of lights coming from the Staunch mansion. It's ludicrous—me shaking and trying to spot something in the dark. It's stupid. *I'm* stupid. I know I should go home.

Because what exactly am I going to see outside? On a dark night?

*A dark and stormy night,* a voice reminds me.

Sometimes I rush headfirst into something before realizing that it's probably not the best. I've always been like this. Call it impatience or zeal or stupidity. I don't know what to call it except my personality.

This isn't helping anybody.

I head back the way I came, down the edge of the creek. The water is still moving with ice edging its banks. My eyes have adjusted to the darkness, but because of the clouds it's dark, hard to move quickly.

I've gone maybe a hundred yards or so when I hear something in the woods.

I curse out loud, thinking of that dog. That thing that resembled a dog.

*That wasn't a dog and I wouldn't tell that to anybody else but I know that thing wasn't a dog.*

I hear a shuffling sound. The sound of something moving in the forest. Something too light to be human, but too heavy to be a chipmunk.

My legs start moving quicker.

And of course I slip and plunge one leg into ankle-deep water.

It's more annoying than anything else. The water is freezing, and now my foot is too. As I get back onto dry land, I hear another noise.

This time I see something.

On the ledge in front of me, which drops abruptly into the creek, I see eyes.

Bloodred eyes.

Even in the murky shadows I can make out its shape.

This thing isn't a dog.

It looks like a coyote—*that's kinda big for a coyote.*

It's got wide, pointy ears, kinda like a German shepherd. The body is big too, but this thing isn't a dog.

*It's more like a wolf.*

It's standing perhaps ten feet above me, directly in front of me. If it wanted to it could leap on top of me and have a nice, juicy dinner.

I freeze.

I see its black nose, its lighter colored mane, the whiteness around its mouth, the teeth that seem to smile and brag about being so sharp.

It's got long legs that seem to stand at attention.

It doesn't growl—that's what dogs do, and this thing isn't a dog. It doesn't even sneer.

It just stands and stares.

I don't back down, but I don't dare move forward, either.

I'm not sure what the rule book says about encountering wolves in the woods. If I had an iPhone I could Google the info along with taking a snapshot and loading it onto Twitter and sharing it with the world.

But I'm in the middle of nowhere with nothing but my shivering skin.

The eyes bear down on me. Challenging me. Daring me.

*Is it warning me? Warning me to stay away?*

I don't know. I'm too scared to know if it's just curious or ready to attack.

It suddenly turns and dashes away into the darkness.

I stand there for a long time, reminding myself again how stupid I am, telling myself I've gotta stop roaming these woods like someone who belongs in them.

## 75. THEFT, AND WANDERING AROUND LOST

Friday: Three different times I walk away from Jocelyn, leaving her without saying a word.

Saturday: I ignore her one-line email. I don't answer it when she asks why. I can't and won't. I don't want Big Brother seeing what I have to say.

Saturday night: After trying to go to sleep, I dream of her. I wake up after finding her in a grave.

Sunday: I think about riding my bike to her house. Then I think that somebody might be watching like they always are. So I go into the town instead.

# 76. SECRET MEETING

I suddenly notice something that's been scratching at the surface of my thoughts, waiting to get out.

There's no sign of Christmas around.

No Christmas lights on any Christmas trees. No signs announcing Christmas sales or images of Santa and his reindeer.

As I walk through Solitary, which is slightly draped in a thin layer of snow, I realize that there's no evidence of Christmas coming in this town. Neither fun, gift-giving Santa Christmas nor faithful, grace-giving Jesus Christmas. Either way, Solitary seems to have missed the memo.

It's December 5. Back home they start advertising for Christmas by late September. Well, at least by November. By now Christmas would be draped over everything.

Here there's nothing.

This has got to be the strangest thing I've seen here yet.

Even with the slight accumulation of snow I've managed easily to ride my bike into town. Mom said to come by the restaurant this afternoon for an early dinner. It's about four thirty, yet it feels more like six. The town is busy, with cars parked all along the main buildings and across the street next to the bluff that separates the town from the train tracks. When I enter Brennan's Grill and Tavern, I see a packed house and my mother looking busy.

"Hey, Chris," she says as she dashes by me carrying some menus. When she comes back she gives me a hug. "Roads bad?"

"Not really."

"It's a lot more crowded than I thought it'd be. You want to give me another hour or so?"

I nod. "I'll just go check out some of the stores. If they're still open."

"The library is."

"Yeah, I can hang out there for a while."

A few minutes later I enter the mostly empty library and wander the aisles. I sense someone following me, and glance over my shoulder.

Déjà vu.

Except this time it's not in the bookstore but rather the library.

Jocelyn puts a finger over her lips and urges me to follow.

At the back of the library is a set of doors. We enter the last one on the right. A stark fluorescent light crackles to life, revealing a room where stacks of books either coming or going are piled like a child's set of building blocks. The light helps the room resemble a jail cell. Or maybe one of those rooms where authorities grill you after you've been arrested for manslaughter.

"What are we doing?" I ask her as she shuts the door.

"Listen to me, okay?" She tugs at my arm.

For a moment I wonder if she's going to hit me, her expression is so intense.

"Nobody is here, okay? Look at this room. It's for storage. Nobody is here and nobody is watching. They don't have this room bugged."

"Jocelyn—look...."

Then she buries her face into my chest and holds on to me.

We hold one another for a long time without saying anything.

I can feel her heart beating against mine. I want to kiss her soft lips and tell her it's okay and let her know that she's safe with me.

I want to do this and so much more.

"What is going on with you?" she eventually asks as she moves away and stares up at me.

"I don't—"

"No, you tell me, and you tell me right this instant."

"The other day at school somebody did the same thing to me that they did to my mother. They doped me or drugged me or something. I woke and found myself tied up in a cabin in the woods. They warned me—a voice warned me to stay away from you. To stop snooping around."

"Oh, Chris."

"I couldn't tell you. I couldn't do anything. They're watching anything I do. Everything I do. I don't trust anyone. And I don't want you getting hurt."

She hugs me again, and I can feel her shiver.

"I keep thinking—we've gotta be able to tell someone."

"No," she says.

"I know. I haven't. I haven't even told my mother. But this is crazy. What happens when—what happens if they take you, and they take you for good?"

"There's still time."

"Still time for what?" I ask.

"Maybe because of everything that's happened—maybe they're too afraid of doing something to attract attention."

"Who are we talking about here?"

"I don't know," Jocelyn says.

I tell her about the last note I received in my locker. "You didn't write that, did you?"

"No."

"What's it mean? You think they're talking about Staunch?"

"Maybe," Jocelyn says. "Maybe it's just a way to keep you from looking elsewhere."

"We've gotta tell someone."

"I've tried that before. Twice. Both times it backfired."

"Who did you tell?"

Her eyes pull me in. Her skin is so clear and so soft. I want to scoop her up and slip away, far away from this place.

"Sometimes I think my aunt is with them," she says.

"Why?"

"I told her about—about a few things. Not everything. She said I was overreacting, that Stuart was just a troubled boy who disappeared. But ever since, it seems like she's been more careful around me. Like—I don't know. Almost like she's been avoiding me."

The world seems to be spinning too fast, the reality too sharp to fully touch and comprehend.

"What if we left this place?"

"What do you mean?" Jocelyn asks.

"I mean—leave. Pack our bags and go."

"Chris …"

"I'm serious. After school gets out. Just go."

"Go where?"

"I don't know. Does it matter? Somewhere outside of this place. If someone comes hunting for us, we can get help. This isn't a *Terminator* movie. This is reality."

"I don't think it's that easy."

"Sure it is. You take your Jeep. We do it the day school gets out."

"That's crazy."

"This whole thing is crazy."

"I don't know...."

I brush my hand against her silken cheek and then I kiss her.

For a moment, the spinning stops.

For a moment, the world seems to be at ease.

For a brief, beautiful moment, the world is good and the world makes sense.

"Chris ..." she says.

"We can go back to Chicago. We can go to my father. Not that I want to, but it's a place to go. I know we'll be safe there."

"What about your mother?"

In my excitement and zeal and passion, I'm forgetting the obvious. She can see it on my face.

"You going to take your mom with us?"

"That might be a problem," I say.

"We can't just run away and leave her."

"Then what do we do?"

"I don't know."

"There's gotta be someone we can trust. What about Sheriff Wells? When he was at our house—I don't know. He seemed trustworthy."

Jocelyn looks skeptical. "I don't know. You have to be careful."

"Why?"

"Because—because I don't want something happening to you."

"Why are you so worried about me and yet you've almost given up on yourself?"

She shakes her head and looks away. "I better leave," she says. "You stay here for a few minutes to let me slip out."

"Where do we—how should we talk next?"

She smiles, for the first time in this conversation. God, is it a wondrous smile.

*Guys would go to the ends of the earth for a smile like that.*

"There's a place I haven't shown you yet."

"What? Behind the falls? At an abandoned church?"

"No," she says, still smiling. "Another place."

"What's so special about this place?'

"Nobody knows it exists. Or at least nobody cares that it does."

I shake my head. "Every single thing has to be some big mystery, doesn't it?"

She reaches over and touches my chest right above my heart, then dazzles me with her glance. "Not everything, Chris."

With those words, she leaves.

Just like that.

I wait another ten minutes, then leave the library.

I ignore the scowls of the ladies behind the desk.


## 77. THE SURPRISE


It's quiet. A little too quiet for the locker room this time of the day. It's like everybody's been sent home.

*Or everybody else has been told to get out.*

When I hear the swinging door to the room blast open, I know my time is due.

I quickly claw my long-sleeved T-shirt over my head, then turn to see who made the noise.

Gus is standing there, a baseball bat in his hand, Burt and Riley behind him.

There's no Oli.

*Surely Oli's around somewhere.*

"You ever been hit by a bat?" Gus asks.

I swallow and bend over to slip on my tennis shoe. "Can't say I have," I say, quickly tying the laces.

"You know what one of these can do to your side? To your back? Nobody will even have to know. You can take out a rib pretty easily."

His face, his eyes, his walk—everything is amped up. Like he's on something. Maybe he's just flying on adrenaline and pent-up anger. All I know is that this is real and that bat is real and I'm not going to be so lucky this time.

A map of the room plays out in my head. There's a long row of lockers that feeds into the bathroom. No exit out that way. To my right is the entrance to the room, which Gus and his boys are blocking. To my left is the small hallway leading to the gym and field.

Something tells me that door is blocked too.

Gus curses at me. "You know something, I don't care if I get suspended. Not for this. You've been a pain ever since you stepped foot in this school. I'm sick of you making me look stupid."

He steps closer.

Talking isn't going to do anything. I know I have to run.

I nod, smile, then bend over and pick up somebody's bag with some football cleats in it.

"Look, man," I start to say, then whip the bag toward Gus as I sprint to my left and head to the hallway.

I'm sure he'll just swat the bag away like an annoying insect, but I don't look back to see.

The small hall makes a ninety-degree turn that leads to the door.

I slip and pound against the cement wall as I turn the corner.

To see Oli.

He's standing there, blocking the closed door, looking irritated and ready.

And then …

"Man, you gotta be a little smarter, Chris," he says in a whisper that I hear but don't understand.

*Why's he whispering, and why's he opening the door?*

"Keep your mouth shut about this, okay? You got it?"

The door is opened and I don't get it, but I nod and I sprint through it toward the gymnasium.

The door shuts behind me.

As I run through the gym, I try to think how this happened.

Oli just opened the door.

He just let me go.

I think back to the other times they've tried to grab me.

Once was in the bathroom, where I caught Oli off guard and tore out of the stall. The other was in this same locker room, where I managed to get by the big guy.

I replay the scenes in my head, now wondering if I was really so crafty or if Oli might have let me go each time.

*I can outrun Gus, and those other two guys are wimps, but Oli's the real deal.*

As I reach the hallway to the high school, I wonder if I might have a secret ally

# 78. MIDNIGHT

It's not like I'm unaware of my lack of connection. Even here at this high school in the middle of nowhere, I see kids walking around with their phones, typing and texting and connecting. It's no different from back home. Kids are kids. The fact that I finally just got Internet at home doesn't escape me.

My problem is that the more I feel I connect, the more trouble I get in.

Connection now comes the old-fashioned way. Just like it has all along since I've been here.

The sheet of paper, the handwritten note.

Good old-fashioned communication.

Nondetectable communication.

Rachel comes up to me on Wednesday as I'm walking away from lunch and slips me a note.

"How are you doing?" she asks.

Since I've been banned from Jocelyn by someone or some people I don't even know, I haven't had much connection with Rachel or Poe either.

"Fine."

"That's good to hear."

"I can guess who this is from."

She shakes her head. "I don't know what you're talking about. Just wanted to say hi. I miss having you around at lunch."

"Yeah, me too."

"Crazy place, huh?" Rachel says.

"Yep."

"Don't let it get you down."

"How's Lee?"

"He's not."

I nod.

"Watch your back," Rachel says in a matter that I can't tell is joking or serious.

I am watching my back. Every moment of every day.

I take the note into the bathroom, making sure Gus or his buddies aren't around to follow me, then read it.

The only thing on it are directions.

That and a time. Five p.m. today.

The intrigue continues.

The old railroad signal stands like a rusty relic from the past, one eye staring out under a round tube, unused for many years now. This is where I'm supposed to stop and head into the woods.

I glance at my watch and can barely make out that it's five thirty. The sun is already far below the trees, and I know that any daylight will soon be gone. I didn't realize how long it would take me to get here. I'm walking with my backpack over my shoulder.

I hope Jocelyn will still be there.

I head into woods that instantly seem to get darker. In her note, she says to simply turn right at the railroad signal. That I can't miss it. I walk as straight as possible.

*What can't I miss? A big hole in the middle of the earth? A dark, haunted prison? How about a field full of the walking dead, all coming at me?*

But ten minutes later, if that, the woods open up, and I see a large, square, two-story building.

It's a big barn in the middle of nowhere.

A light flickers inside a window (or the empty hole that used to be a window).

Either Jocelyn is there or I'm about to be really freaked out.

As I get closer, I see that the large mouth of an opening no longer has a door. I enter and feel chilled and look for the source of the light.

"Chris?" a hushed voice calls out.

A beam from a flashlight causes me to squint and hold up my hand. The light goes back out.

"Come here," she says.

I walk past several stalls that probably held horses or cattle at one point. There's only dirt on the ground as I walk through cobwebs and brush them off my face. I reach the open door where the light came from.

It pops on again, and I see her face. Hovering in the darkness, a white angelic portrait of perfection.

"You're late," she says.

"I didn't realize how long it would take."

"I'm sorry—it's a long haul, walking."

"What are we doing here?" I ask.

"Come here. Look."

I stand by her and smell her sweet strawberry smell. The flashlight points at a corner in the stall. I see a box of some kind on its side—then something black and furry pops its head out.

"What is that?" I ask. For some reason I think of one of those creatures from *Return of the Jedi*, an Ewok.

"It's a puppy."

"What?" I ask, laughing and kneeling down to see it.

Sure enough, the black and white ball of fur is a puppy. I pick it up, and it reaches my face and starts to lick me.

"Where'd you find him?"

"It's a her, actually. A neighbor gave it to me. Wade threatened to kill her—and I've seen him run over dogs. I know he'd do it. So I brought her out here."

"What is this place? How'd you find it?"

"Just an old barn that hasn't been used in years. Probably because the trains don't run through town anymore. You probably didn't see it, but there's a road right behind the barn. Kinda hard to get to—you have to use four-wheel drive—but it only takes about ten minutes from downtown."

I'm petting the puppy as I look around.

"Nobody is watching this place," Jocelyn continues. "I like to imagine that it's mine."

"Not sure what it looks like in the daytime, but it sure doesn't seem very homey."

"You ever see *It's a Wonderful Life?*"

"Yeah, think so. Bits at least."

"Bits? Come on."

"It's an old movie," I tell her.

"And what's that mean? There's the scene where they're looking at this old house, and Donna Reed makes a wish to be living there one day. I've done that with this old place."

"What's the puppy's name?" I ask.

"Midnight."

I can feel Midnight licking my cheek again. She's so light, like I'm holding a fur glove in my hand.

"So she just stays here? You don't worry about her?"

"Nah. This stall opens up to another—I close the doors, but she's got plenty of room to run around. That keeps out any animals that might look at her like an evening meal."

"More like an appetizer."

Jocelyn chuckles. "I come here once a day to check on her and just hang out. I like to imagine what it would be like to live here. This place, this freedom, being able to call it my life." She takes the puppy from my hands. "Sometimes I can't wait to see Midnight. Sometimes that's what gets me through the day."

"Sounds poetic," I say.

"It's a lot more than that. It's hope. It's a wonderful thing, hope."

"I love you."

The words seem to come out of nowhere, and I half wonder who said them.

She looks at me, and in the beam of the light shining down on the ground, her face is accented and shadowed and glorious. She gives me her usual sweet, sad smile.

"Sorry, that just—that just came out."

"That's the best kind, then."

Jocelyn puts Midnight back on the blanket in the box and takes my hand. She closes the door to the stall and then leads me to the back of the barn. She tells me to hold the light as she climbs an old wooden ladder, then beckons me to follow.

Sometimes I feel like Midnight must feel, following this girl everywhere she goes.

Soon we're sitting on the ledge of an opening at the top of the barn where there used to be either a large door or window. I can still see the edges of the smoldering sun in the distant horizon.

She leans against me and holds my hand. "I'm not scared anymore, Chris."

"About what?"

"About anything."

"Why not?"

"Because I don't have a reason to be."

"That's good, right?" I say, not sure why she doesn't have a reason to be but not wanting to break the mood.

For a long time we sit there, Jocelyn pressed up against me with the rest of the world far away.

"I meant what I said," I tell her as I gaze into the dark forest in front of us.

"I know you did."

Just as I'm wondering if she feels the same way—if she's going to tell me how she feels—Jocelyn answers my wandering thoughts.

"You can't imagine what your kindness has meant, Chris."

"I'm not being kind. I'm just—I'm just wanting to be with you."

"I know. Wanting to be with me versus wanting me—there's a difference, you know."

"I'm not saying that I don't want you," I say.

"I know. I'm not an idiot."

"Yeah."

"You're a good guy, Chris. Don't ever forget that."

She moves her head to look up at mine. I slowly move down to kiss her.

We stay there for a long time.

## 79. Hiding in the Darkness

The howling outside the house sounds like it comes from some possessed animal. A werewolf or something. I hear it and scramble out of bed, noting my alarm clock reading two in the morning. I look out my window but see nothing but darkness. There's a faint tapping of hard snow as if it's trying to get inside for warmth.

A storm's coming. I don't need a forecaster to tell me that.

I hear the scream again, and this time it jerks me completely awake. I grab for any kind of clothes I can find on the floor and tear down the stairs.

Forget werewolves.

I know that sound, and I know I have to get outside.

My hands shake as I slip on my winter coat and try to zip it but can't. I put on the shoes I left by the front door and don't find it surprising that the door is already opened a crack.

I think about the muddy prints I saw on the deck. About the eyes that watch me. That watch us.

That watch my mother, who's outside right now, who's having a nightmare and screaming.

*If that's why she's screaming.*

I turn on the outside light and step onto the deck. Wind whips against my face and neck. I round the deck and head to the back of the woods.

*Should've brought a flashlight.*

But sometimes it's better to stay in the dark. Sometimes it's better not to know exactly what you're going to find.

The screech comes again. It's directly in front of me.

Then I see it. A ghost in the middle of the woods. A specter floating and haunting these woods.

It's Mom, wearing nothing more than a long white nightgown.

"Mom," I call out, but my voice seems to wilt in the wind and the woods.

She's just standing there, her hands over her eyes.

I wonder if I'm the one dreaming.

*This can't be real, can it?*

"Mom," I say as I reach her.

I see her hands move and her eyes look out at me.

Then they grow larger.

The scream she lets out scares me.

I reach her just as her eyes are rolling back in their sockets and her body is starting to collapse.

My mother balls her hand to try and stop the shaking. She's got a couple of blankets over her, a cup of hot tea in the other hand, a face pale and distressed.

I'm sitting across from her like a parent with his child.

I'm not ready for this kind of responsibility.

I need to go out to a party and drive a car into a tree or something.

Mom sighs, takes a sip of tea.

So far we haven't exactly spoken.

"I don't know what to say," she says as if reading my mind.

"It's okay."

"I just—I keep things from you because I don't want to alarm you. It was so much easier when all of us were together."

I nod. She doesn't need to say anymore. Three is better than two any day.

"I've been having nightmares. Ever since coming here. That's why I've been acting so crazy. I don't know what to do."

I see her eyes tear up, and I feel absolutely and positively helpless.

My body seizes up, even though it wants to go around the table and put my arms around her.

That's not the cool thing to do. But more than that, I don't want to show how utterly sad and scared I am.

"I don't know what to do," she says again.

"What are you dreaming about?" I can't help but ask.

She shakes her head, looks away.

"Mom?"

"Nothing. Just—nothing good."

She sips her coffee and looks out the dark window.

Part of me wonders what haunts her.

Yet another part of me prefers not to know.

Like I said, sometimes it's better to stay in the dark.

That way you won't know what's hiding inside it.

# 80. THE VOICE THAT NEEDS

I'm thinking of her when she calls.

It's Saturday afternoon, a few days after the incident with my mom. She's in the laundry room, not working today. It's snowing again, just like it's been doing on and off for the last few days.

When I hear Jocelyn's voice, I just know.

I know it's time.

I know that something's up and that something's wrong.

All by the way she says "Chris."

"Hey."

Panic streaks through her voice. "You have to come. I'm scared—he won't let me leave—"

"What—whoa—hold on. What—who are you talking about?"

"Wade. My aunt's gone, and he's been drinking all day. He went out to his truck for something, but I know he'll be back and—"

"You can't get to your Jeep?"

"He took my keys, Chris. He said my days of teasing him were done, that he was finally going to do something about it, about me."

I think of what Newt told me, about what guys said about Jocelyn and Wade at school.

"Jocelyn—just wait, okay? I'll be there."

"Chris—"

"Listen to me. Everything's going to be okay. My mom is home, and I'll get there right away."

I pause for a minute.

"Jocelyn?"

I don't hear anything. I repeat her name and realize the other end is dead.

I curse and hang up the phone and start to run to the laundry room to ask my mom if I can borrow the car.

Then I realize that's crazy.

*She's not going to let me borrow the car when I don't have my license and can barely drive.*

Instead I sprint up the stairs.

I take the gun out of hiding.

I slip it in the back of my pants and suddenly worry about it going off and shearing a portion of my backside.

I walk a little more slowly down the stairs. I yell out to my mom that I'm heading out, then I take her keys with me.

The drive—if what I'm doing can actually be considered driving—seems eternal. It's like a motion picture of memories hits the windshield as I'm heading to Jocelyn's as fast as I can.

As many friends as I had back home, I never had someone that I cared about this much.

*That I loved.*

Never someone I felt as open and honest around.

So now I find her, and she's a troubled soul. A troubled soul in a troubled life. And I'm heading there now, driving toward trouble.

The gun resting on the passenger seat is heading for trouble too.

I think of everything that's happened since I've come to Solitary. All the warnings and the threats and the dark signs and the omens and the nightmares.

I wonder why I'm here, and if there's some gargantuan conspiracy against me. Or against Jocelyn and me. Or against my mother.

Or maybe against all of us.

Light snow is falling, and I can feel the slippery road underneath making it more difficult to speed.

I grab the steering wheel like a man trying to strangle an intruder.

When I pull into the long drive, I go as fast as I dare and park behind the two cars there.

For a long second—a very long second—I sit there and look at the house and then at the handgun.

*What are you doing, Chris?*

Then I take the gun and climb out of the car, ignoring the voice of reason and heading toward the voice that needs me.

# 81. CAPABLE

These are the things you don't expect will happen to you when you're sixteen years old.

Stepping up to the house of the girl you love holding a heavy gun in your hand.

Thinking of knocking, then instead trying the handle and finding it open.

Walking into a house uninvited, scared of what you'll find and pumped full of fearful adrenaline.

Hearing screams from the back, screams that you know belong to Jocelyn, screams that sound midway through something gone bad.

Tearing through a living room toward a hallway and then toward a slightly opened doorway where the screams are coming from.

You would shake if you weren't so determined. You would stall if you weren't so enraged.

Your foot kicks open the door, and the scene isn't surprising, but it's shocking nevertheless.

You see a figure clutching at her chest with bare arms, her shirt open and torn, her hair wild, her eyes tear filled, hate filled.

Jocelyn is screaming. Her jeans look like they have blood splattered on them. Her neck and shoulders bear the marks of nails scraping against the flesh.

You don't need to know any more.

Inside the bedroom with its large king-sized bed, the man with his back to you is shirtless, wearing only boots and dirty jeans.

A tattoo of a black-winged vulture covers his back.

And as the door slams against the side of the wall, he turns around.

Glowing embers stare back at you. Blood is smeared under one nostril and against his cheek. His fists curl.

These are the things you don't think will happen to you when you're sixteen years old.

But age and sense and peace and love don't exist in a place like this.


"Get away from her," I say.

The voice coming out surprises me, but I don't have time to stand and evaluate it and wonder how I feel about it.

"You really gonna use that?" Wade asks, his mouth and lips sickly wet.

I'm standing maybe ten feet away from him, pointing the gun at his head. "Don't make me."

He laughs at me and curses as Jocelyn screams out at me to stop.

"Don't make me laugh, little boy."

He takes a step, and I think for a split second and decide to go for it.

I press down on the trigger.

The gun is aimed at the wall and takes out a chunk of a dresser.

Jocelyn screams again; Wade curses and holds his head.

"Jocelyn, get out of here," I say.

Her shirt is ripped, hanging open, and I feel embarrassed so I look away.

"She's not going anywhere."

I point the gun back at him. "I don't think this is the first time you've hurt her, but I swear on my life, it's the last."

"You better swear on your life because it ain't going to be around much longer."

Jocelyn moves past Wade, and he puts out an arm, sending her back into the wall. She crumbles to the floor.

I aim and fire the gun again. It roars to life. A bullet hits the edge of the bed.

I fire a third time, and this bullet finds its way to Wade's lower leg.

He howls and drops like a poached animal as Jocelyn stands up and runs out of the room.

I look at the writhing figure on the floor and want to say something brilliant, something a tough guy might say in a movie. But I have nothing. I'm scared of him attacking me, scared of him dying, scared of what's going to happen to me.

We exchange a glance. Even though I'm scared, I don't back down.

He sees it in my eyes.

He knows what I'm capable of doing.

## 82. THE RIGHT THING

"Did he hurt you?"

"No."

She's wearing a coat and holding her arms across her chest as if she's still cold. I'm blasting the heat as I drive down the snowy road.

"Did he … did he rape you?" I ask.

"No!" she says, louder, but she looks at me as though she's furious with me. "I'm not some delicate little flower that you need to save, Chris."

"Jocelyn, I didn't—"

"If you want someone that's pure and untouched, you best look somewhere else."

I shove the brake and send both of us into the dashboard. The car stalls at the edge of the road.

"Why are you yelling at me?" I say, my own voice none too soft. "You called me, and it looked like I got there just before something bad happened, so don't give me any attitude."

Jocelyn closes her eyes, and a sob leaks out of her.

I hold her then while she cries, and tell her I'm sorry and that it's going to be okay.

"We're going to go back to my house. Okay? He's never going to touch you again."

"I'm just—"

"Don't, Jocelyn. You don't have to explain. You don't have to say anything."

"It's just so …" She's gasping for breaths between her cries. "I'm—I didn't want you to see—to know—"

"It doesn't matter. Nothing matters. The only thing that matters is that we get you to a safe place and then we notify the cops."

"Chris—I—"

"Shhh."

"I'm—I didn't want to pull you into this, but I didn't know what else to do."

"You did the right thing."

I feel her haggard breathing against mine, and I know that I did the right thing too.

When we get home I'm going to tell my mother everything.

I need some help with all of this.

## 83. STRANGERS WHO WATCH

My mom just shakes her head.

"What?" I ask.

This is the understatement of the year.

I just took off with her car, without a license and without telling her, and ended up shooting a guy in the leg just as he was attacking Jocelyn.

*Yeah, so what?*

I can tell she doesn't even know where to begin. I wouldn't if I were her.

*Try walking in my shoes, Mom. There's a lot more I still haven't told you.*

"Chris ..." she says, then stops.

She looks tired.

"I didn't want you to know—I didn't want to involve you, Mom. But sooner or later—I don't know."

It's a little past seven, and Jocelyn is sleeping in the next room, knocked out by some pills my mom gave her. When we first got home my mom started to launch into me till she saw Jocelyn by my side and I explained what happened.

Her first response, after taking Jocelyn in her arms, was to tell me to get the phone so she could call the police. But Jocelyn convinced her not to.

I'm not sure if it's because she's humiliated or trying to protect herself. Or trying to protect us.

I didn't tell Mom about the other stuff. I'm not sure how to begin.

"Where did you find the gun again?" she asks.

"In the closet upstairs."

"This is the second incident involving a gun, Chris."

"I had nothing to do with the one at school."

"And yet you shot a man tonight."

"What was I supposed to do?"

"You tell me, that's what you do." I can hear the desperation and anger in her voice. "You need to tell me things."

"She was in trouble, and I didn't know else what to do."

"You come to me. Now *you're* in trouble."

"He was going to hurt her, Mom. ... He would have raped her."

Mom shakes her head, then rubs her temple. Her hair is messy, bits of gray showing in the dirty blonde locks. The bags under her eyes seem dark and heavy.

"I should call your father."

"What?"

"He'd know what to do."

"Mom, you can't."

"Who else should I call?"

"Don't. Don't involve him. It's none of his business."

She shakes her head again. "What'd you do with the gun?"

"I tossed it in the woods on the way home."

She nods, believing the lie.

"We have to tell somebody," she says.

"What's Wade going to do? Go to the cops and say he got shot while trying to rape his girlfriend's niece?"

"Her aunt needs to know."

"Her aunt is gone until Sunday."

"She needs to know. I would want to know."

"Let Jocelyn tell her," I say. "Tomorrow."

Mom sighs. "Why does all of this keep happening to us?"

"I don't know."

"I just keep thinking—keep hoping—but it just keeps getting worse."

"Things could've been a lot worse today."

"I'm not angry with you, Chris. But you have to tell me what's going on. Especially now that your father is out of the picture."

"It needs to stay that way, too."

"Chris."

"We can take care of ourselves."

Mom smiles, but I know that she doesn't believe my statement. I don't think I do either.

An hour later, feeling restless and nervous and curious, I slip into my mom's bedroom and hear Jocelyn's gentle breaths as she sleeps.

I kneel on the edge of the bed. A fraction of light from the family room slips in, allowing me to just make out the profile of her head on its pillow.

Is it all random, how people meet and befriend one another and fall in love?

Is life completely random, or is there some big, fat purpose behind it all?

If God does exist, how can we explain all the truly horrific things that happen day after day after day?

Jocelyn stirs, and I wish I could hold her.

I dream of a time when I can be close to her.

I'm thankful nothing worse happened to her today. Thankful she called. Thankful that she allowed me in her life to help her.

*I'm never going to let anything happen to you, Jocelyn. I'll die before I let anybody hurt you.*

I lay a hand on the shoulder underneath the blanket. I hear her stir and say something, but I can't make it out.

Maybe my life and this move and the way things turned out with my parents were all meant for me to come across Jocelyn's path and help her. Maybe it was all meant to save her.

*So who's going to save me?*

I hear the restless wind outside and can't help shivering.

I think of the little puppy Midnight tucked away in the barn and think that maybe, just maybe, it's better to be hidden and secure in an unknown place rather than trapped by the eyes and ears of strangers who watch.

Strangers who wait.

Strangers who surely know what's happening.

## 84. DANGEROUS PEOPLE

It'd be nice to think that waking up in the same house as Jocelyn was romantic. But after a night of restless tossing, I come downstairs to find my mother and Jocelyn already awake.

So much for bringing her breakfast in bed.

It feels like summer camp, having Jocelyn here, seeing her raw beauty this early in the morning. It also feels natural, like she belongs here with us, like she is safe and secure and happy.

For a while this morning we believe it.

But that's before the cops come knocking on our door.

Jocelyn had to call her aunt. There was never a question about that. What she told her I didn't ask, but I got the feeling that she didn't mention anything about the shooting.

Yet she told her aunt enough.

About two o'clock Sunday afternoon we hear a car come up our drive. Mom opens the door to find a dark-haired woman wearing a strange combination of clothes—a long flowery dress and black leather boots and an overcoat that looks like it came from an apocalyptic movie—and Sheriff Wells standing behind her. When I see the sheriff I start to panic.

*I'm going to go to jail and will never see Jocelyn or my mom again.*

Mom doesn't sound like she's panicking. At least not on the outside. "Can I help you?"

"Where is she?" the woman says in an accent that seems to want to cover up her Southern roots.

"Are you Jocelyn's aunt?"

"Where is she?" the woman demands.

"Helen—it's fine, I'm in here."

My mother lets them in and closes the door behind them. I might as well hold out my hands and let the sheriff cuff me.

I can see a very faint resemblance between Jocelyn and her aunt—the long, dark hair, though Jocelyn's looks like a model's and her aunt's looks like a dwelling for a pack of wild birds. The eyes, too, though Aunt Helen has a hardened look about her, a look that's also missing something.

*She looks kinda crazy.*

I'd never say this out loud or to Jocelyn, but it's the truth.

I guess anybody willing to shack up with good ole Wade must be a little crazy.

"I called the law immediately," Helen says, making me slightly pause on her usage of the word *law*. "We went to the house right away."

"And?" Jocelyn asks for all of us.

"Place was deserted," Sheriff Wells says. "Looks like your uncle—"

"Step-uncle, though not technically," Helen asserts quickly.

"Well, whatever he is, looks like he's gone. Want to tell us exactly what happened?" the sheriff says.

"My aunt was gone on one of her excursions—"

"I collect antiques, dear."

"Yeah. And she left me with Wade. He was drinking all night and day. Kept talking about how cozy it was, just the two of us there alone. It's not … not the first time he's come after me."

Her aunt looked as though she wanted to argue, but Jocelyn wasn't finished. "He took the keys to my Jeep so I couldn't leave. But when he went outside to his truck for something, I called Chris, and he came to my rescue."

Sheriff Wells turned to me. "And what did you do, son?"

"I got there and just—I just told him to stop."

Both the sheriff and Aunt Helen stare at me, waiting for more.

"I told him I'd called the cops and they'd be coming any second. That freaked him out."

"And that was all?"

For some reason Wells looks at me like I'm lying. Which, of course, I am.

"Yeah, that was it."

"So mind me asking where the two bullets came from? Along with the blood in the bedroom?"

"It was me," Jocelyn shouts out. "I did it."

"No, she didn't. She didn't do anything."

"What really happened?" the sheriff asks.

I swallow and look at Jocelyn.

Then I tell them the truth. Everything.

Well, almost everything.

"And you just tossed the gun out the car window?"

"Yeah," I say.

"Where?"

"I don't know. Somewhere in the woods—somewhere between there and here."

Wells stares at my mother for a while and seems to be thinking.

"That fool of a man—I told him to stop it—I told him he better get his mind back in the right place." Aunt Helen sits next to Jocelyn and looks her over. "He's gone, now, and he's probably gone for good."

"Look, why don't you ladies go out while I talk to Chris and his mother, okay?"

Jocelyn looks at me with a fearful glance, one that seems to say, *Don't leave me. Don't let me go.*

"Can I—" I start to ask.

"I just need a few moments," the sheriff says.

I nod as Jocelyn follows her aunt outside.

I hear the sheriff sigh and watch as he rubs his hand through thinning hair.

"Look. I know Wade—he's up to no good. He's had some run-ins with the police before. I know his kind. I wouldn't shed a tear if you'd killed the guy. He's probably already down to Florida by now, drunk out of his mind and probably needing a change of pants after you almost killed him. I doubt he'll be back."

I'm waiting to hear the verdict, waiting to hear the trouble I'm in.

"You keep your original story and that'll be the end of it. I'll have Jocelyn file an official complaint and that will be it. No gun and no shooting and no missing handgun. Got it?"

I nod.

"Thank you," Mom says.

"Listen to me. Both of you. Wade is a lowlife. And there's no guarantee he won't come back. You two are alone in this cabin, and I can't be driving by every moment of every day. You sure you got rid of that handgun?"

I nod and breathe in and don't blink, but I doubt the sheriff believes me.

"Well, if you did, if you really did, then you guys might think about getting some more protection. Mrs. Buckley, there are some dangerous people out there in this world, even around Solitary."

"You don't think that this has anything to do with what happened to me at the restaurant?"

The sheriff shakes his head. "That's what I don't like. You two are attractin' trouble, and I just—well, you might just want to think twice about Solitary."

"What about Solitary?"

"Being here."

"We're not going anywhere, Mr. Wells."

"I hear you. I know. I'm just sayin'."

"What exactly *are* you saying?"

I wait for a response, but the sheriff just nods. "Nothing. Except be careful."

"We're being careful. My son just happened to be called to help out a young girl in a precarious situation."

"I know. It's just—well, it seems like there are more and more of these—what'd you call 'em?—percarious situations."

"Precarious," Mom answers.

I look at the sheriff and wonder.

*Can I trust him?*

I wonder if I can tell him what's going on with Jocelyn. What's happening with her and what she suspects about this place.

"You folks gotta be careful, that's all I'm sayin'. I don't want to have to come back here if anything happens, got that?"

"I understand," Mom says.

The stern face looks at me, as if waiting for me to tell him more.

*Don't, Chris. Not yet. Not now.*

We walk outside and see Aunt Helen standing next to the police car with Jocelyn.

"I'll take them home," Sheriff Wells says. "I need to get a statement from Jocelyn."

I feel like I'm at the edge of an ocean watching Jocelyn getting into a boat heading into the stormy sea.

She hugs me and tells me it will be okay and she will call me later.

I want to ask what we do from here and where do we go and what happens next, but I know she doesn't have a clue anymore than I do.

As we hold one another, I can feel a trembling.

I can't tell if it's me or Jocelyn.

Or both of us.

"I'll be fine," she says.

But I don't believe it.

As the car backs down our driveway, I watch it leave and I wonder when I'll see her again.

I stare down at the woods below us, hearing the burble of the creek.

I watch for a while, as if I'm waiting to see someone come out of those woods.

I know someone is watching me. I just can't see him.

Someone's there.

*If you are, then you'll know that I'm not scared.*

That's what I think, but deep down, I'm terrified.

I'm terrified of losing her.

# 85. NERVOUS LAUGHTER

It's always strange how life moves on after something dramatic or even tragic. But it doesn't have a choice. The world keeps spinning and the story keeps going whether you like it or not.

The following week is uneventful, and in many ways, things go back to the way they were before the warnings and the drama occurred.

For whatever reason—I don't think it's even a conscious

decision—I'm back to talking to Jocelyn in the halls, eating with her and the girls at lunch. I invite Newt to join us, but he doesn't. Jocelyn scares him.

The thing is this: I'm not disguising my friendship with her anymore.

It's as if both of us know that I shot someone in her defense.

As if both of us are thinking, *If it happened once, it will happen again.*

I can't say that I'm feeling bolder or stronger since the incident. In fact, every day I half expect to see a bloody Wade step into my path like some sick and foul-smelling zombie.

Yet the teachers drone on and the dirty snow sticks on your jeans and the cafeteria food all begins to taste the same—this is how I believe the world moves on. You get lulled in by the action of one period after another, of the days being shorter and your mom's shifts being longer. Of exams coming before Christmas break. Of homework that takes your mind to another time and place. Of life that moves faster than you can or ever will.

The week passes, and it seems like things are better.

Then Friday comes and ruins all that wonderful, boring momentum.


I'm on the side of a road—I'm not really sure exactly where—and I'm running.

Why am I here? Why am I running?

These are good questions.

If my hands weren't covered in blood, I'd probably answer them too.

But soon enough, when things don't exactly add up—like how I can just keep sprinting without actually slowing down and hurting and sucking wind—or how I'm not even sweating—or how I'm wearing the sweetest Nike shoes ever when I don't own anything by Nike—when all of these things suddenly seem to not make sense, I understand why.

That's when I open my eyes and wake up.

What was I doing on the side of the road, blood on my hands, running? It's not a good way to start a day. Even if that day is the last day for the school week.

I see him on my way to school that morning.

See him standing at the edge of my driveway.

The big redheaded man in the trench coat, the one I saw in town right after we moved here. I see him standing down there as my mom backs the car up to drive me to school.

"Who's that?"

"I don't know," I say. "Slow down."

The man stands there for a moment, his big German shepherd at his side, almost deliberately blocking our path. He looks like a ghost in the early morning fog.

I glance at my mom in surprise and shock, then turn back around to find the end of the driveway clear.

"Where'd he go?"

"He just disappeared."

And he did. Just like that, the figure is gone.

I think about those large tracks on our deck and suddenly figure out who they belong to.

But what's this creepy guy doing around our house? Does he live close by? Is he spying on us for someone else?

"That's strange," my mom says.

I can only agree with her. It's becoming a cliché to say something is strange around here. *Everything* is strange.

Strange and unexplained.


"Still no sign of him?"

Jocelyn shakes her head. We're talking about Wade, her step-uncle, who disappeared with a slug in his calf. "I don't think we will either."

"How's your aunt doing?"

Jocelyn rolls her eyes but doesn't answer. I can't tell if it's just because she thinks her aunt is flaky, or if there's something else.

*It's so hard to read you, even though I feel I know so much about you.*

Maybe that's just how it is with other people. Specifically other girls. Or maybe the entire female population. I don't know.

We round the hall on our way to history when we see them.

The creepy vibe just keeps continuing.

Pastor Jeremiah Marsh stands at the end of the lockers next to an open doorway, his hands stretched out as if he's making an important point. He's talking to Mr. Meiners, who looks at him in a grim manner, as if he's being told someone in his family just died.

As we pass them by, both men look at us and stop talking.

"Chris, Jocelyn," the pastor says to us, nodding.

We mumble hellos as we pass them.

"What do you think that's about?" I ask Jocelyn.

"I can only imagine."

"Imagine what?"

"I have a vivid imagination," she says. "You have to remember that."

"How do they know each other?"

"Everybody in this town knows everybody else. Especially all those living inside of Solitary."

"But Mr. Meiners—does he go to that church?"

"I don't know," she says sharply, as if to say, "Drop it."

I don't pursue the question any more.

Surely it's nothing. Surely the pastor is just visiting the school for some reason.

*Please don't call me Shirley.*

I want to laugh out loud and squeeze the insanity from my brain cells. I can probably fill a bucket from it.

"What's that smirk on your face for?" Jocelyn asks as we arrive to class.

"I don't know. I really don't. Sometimes I just—it seems like all I can do is laugh."

"It's better than crying."


# 86. BREATH OF HEAVEN


My mom contradicts herself. I guess all of us do. But when you're an adult you gotta be careful because kids are watching, you know?

I'm old enough that I no longer get so confused. I'm kinda over all of it. But still I have to find it funny—or perhaps ironic—to see my mother's actions.

She celebrates Christmas, and not just in a small way either. With all of her anger at my father for his newfound faith—maybe I should call it a righteous anger, now wouldn't *that* be ironic—she still seems to almost believe in the whole child-in-a-manger thing. Guess that's okay. Yeah, Jesus was born in a manger in a town called Bethlehem. That's a safe thing to believe in. I mean, if you don't, then you can't have all those great Christmas carols, including my favorite, "We Three Kings."

It's the other part, the Easter part, that Mom has a problem with.

She's okay with the birth, just not the death. And especially not the resurrection.

As for me, like I said, I'm over it. I'm indifferent.

The only thing that concerns me is Jocelyn celebrating this day with us.

And as for Jocelyn, well—she takes Christmas *very* seriously.

Christmas Day comes, and with it comes snow, and with that comes safety. I don't know why, but I know that nothing's going to happen on this day. Maybe because it's supposed to be sacred or maybe because the strangers outside are too busy to watch. I don't know. All I know is that Jocelyn is planning on coming over later to celebrate Christmas Day with a party of three.

Mom has already told me that we won't be celebrating with our aunt. Something tells me that Aunt Alice won't exactly be celebrating Christmas.

*She'll be too busy sticking needles in her voodoo dolls.*

I'm sure Mom would tell me to knock it off if she could hear my thoughts.

I hear the song in the background. Christmas music is okay and it pipes out loud: one of those solemn, contemporary Christmas tunes, one I've heard a bunch of times before.

Glancing out the window, seeing the thick flakes dancing around as I watch the driveway for Jocelyn, I feel depressed. Listening to The Smiths or Interpol or something like that should be depressing, but Christmas music? But this song is sad. Like I need any more sadness in my life.

I remember this one since it's on this CD my mother plays every year. The lyrics stand out. *In a world as cold as stone,* the woman sings. *Must I walk this path alone?*

I can relate. Not the "breath of heaven" part, but the walking alone part.

The wind outside blows as the woman sings of hope, almost like a prayer.

It's nice to think that someone is up there listening to a prayer such as this in the middle of the darkness, but I don't buy it.

Just like there's no Santa and his reindeer in the North Pole, the same goes for the little baby Jesus coming to the world to save us all.

I haven't been saved, and don't see salvation coming any time soon.

*Help me,* the song goes.

*Yeah.*

*Help me.*

*Hold me together.*

A nice thought.

But we're all alone down here, and no song can ever change that.

I see the Jeep pull up and watch Jocelyn step out.

She takes my breath away. That's all I know and all I care about.

She can help me and hold me together. And I can do the same for her.

"I don't want to leave."

"Then don't."

Jocelyn is lying on the couch with her legs over my lap, a blanket covering both of us. We're stuffed and warm and comfortable, and life is good.

"I have to," she says. "My aunt wants me home."

"How about tomorrow? Mom would you let stay over."

"I don't want to leave my aunt alone. I already spent most of Christmas with you."

"I'm greedy."

My eyes don't move off of her. Sometimes it seems like I could study her all day and all night long.

"Thank you for today."

The gifts are scattered around the room. Mom and I got several things for Jocelyn. Nothing huge, like an iPhone or a diamond ring, but small, nice gifts. Mom has been in her room for the past hour, giving us some space.

I gave Jocelyn a couple more things then, when Mom went to

take a nap. One of those was a mix CD with songs all designated to mean something between us. The other was a little booklet I made up that had an assortment of pictures and descriptions (most printed off the Internet) of Chicago. The title of the book was quite subtle: *A Place We Will Escape to One Day.*

I told Jocelyn I was serious, that I wanted to take her to Chicago one day, that maybe we could do it sometime in the new year. I'd tell Mom we were visiting my father, but we wouldn't have to do that. Jocelyn had smiled and kissed me and thanked me for the thoughtful gifts.

It's already nine, and I know she has to leave. She still hasn't given me her present.

"Did you really get me something?" I ask.

"I did."

"Are you going to give it to me before you leave?"

"It *is* a Christmas gift."

"Then let me see."

"I didn't have time to wrap it." She produces a small box that fits in my palm.

"If this is a ring, don't you think it's a little soon to be talking marriage?" I ask with a smile.

"Just open it."

I open the box and see a round, brown strip of leather. A wrist band.

"Cool," I say.

Jocelyn smiles, taking the band and putting it on my right hand. She ties it carefully.

"My mother gave this to my father when they were dating. She got it on a mission trip. She told him that she wasn't ready to give him anything else, but she still wanted something round that stuck to him. Something that he never took off that would remind him that they belonged to each other."

Suddenly what I'm wearing seems priceless.

"I can't wear this," I tell her.

"It's my gift to you."

"Jocelyn—"

"I wouldn't give it to you if I didn't mean it."

I lean over and put my hand to the side of her face, then kiss her lips.

When I pull away, I remain close to her face.

"I love you," I tell her.

"I know. Thank you for today."

"We can do this tomorrow if you want. And the next day. And the next."

There it is again, the sad smile, the melancholy glance. She lets out a sigh and tells me she needs to go.

I look at the leather bracelet as we get up.

"What are you thinking?" she asks.

"This feels right."

"I know. I always wondered—but I won't. Not anymore."

"Wondered about what?"

"If someone would come along—someone that fit me—someone that belonged with me. I'll never have to wonder anymore."

I hold her for a long time before she opens the door and walks out into the cold darkness.

I watch her car drive off into the night.

# 87. DECEMBER 26

The day after Christmas, I turn on my computer and find an email from Jocelyn.

> DEAR CHRIS:
> I'VE MADE A MISTAKE.
> THIS ISN'T GOING TO WORK OUT.
> I NEED SOME SPACE. PLEASE, CHRIS—JUST GIVE
> ME SOME TIME TO THINK THINGS OVER.
> JOCELYN

I stare at the message like it's in a foreign language.

This is the same girl who just said "I'll never have to wonder anymore."

The same girl who just spent Christmas with me, much of it side by side and in one another's arms.

*Mistake?*

*Isn't going to work out?*

*Space?*

*Time?*

I want to think it's a joke, but nothing about it sounds like a joke. I email her back.

> WHAT'S GOING ON?

And then a few minutes later I email again.

JOCELYN—WHAT'S WRONG? WHAT'S

HAPPENING?

Then, after not getting a response, I get the phone and call her.

I just get their answering machine and hear her aunt's voice. I leave a message.

I leave two more that morning.

Nothing.

The day passes and I hear nothing.

It's only in the afternoon that I start to worry and wonder.

Mom is at work, and it's snowing. I know the roads are bad.

All I can do is sit in this house and worry and wonder.

A thousand voices tell me something, but none of them enough. All of them are insufficient.

By the time night comes I can't take anymore.

I go below our deck where my bike is stored and find the tires shredded like fragments from a bomb blast. They're not only flat, they're slashed. Beyond repair.

Wind whips my body as I look into the wilderness and wonder who did this.

I go back inside and wait to hear from Jocelyn.

Wait to understand what's going on.

## 88. DECEMBER 27

So I wait.

## 89. DECEMBER 28

And I wait.

## 90. LOVESICK

Finally, the Wednesday after Christmas, after several days have passed and I've heard nothing more from Jocelyn since her cryptic and baffling email, I have my mother drive me to her house. I have her wait at the end of the driveway so she doesn't have to see any drama unfold. Yet as I approach the house, I suddenly know that nobody is there.

There's no car. The snow on the driveway looks several inches thick and untouched. No lights are on and there aren't any footprints in the snow.

The house looks abandoned.

I knock on the door several times then try opening it. Part of me wants to kick it in (if I could actually manage to do that), yet I know there's no need to.

Nobody's been around here for some time now.

I wonder where Jocelyn and her aunt might have gone.

*What about Wade? What if he came back and forced them to go somewhere?*

I know what I need to do.

I run back to my mom and tell her to stop in town on the way home.

I need to see the sheriff.


"Just slow down a second."

The deputy I'm talking to, Kevin Ross, chews gum robotically and rubs his nose as if he's bored. I stop talking and compose myself.

"Is the sheriff around?" I ask again.

"I already told you he's out."

"When's he going to be back?"

"When he gets back."

This guy doesn't like me, I already know that. He looks like the kind of guy who has an attitude simply because he gets to carry a gun around all day long.

"So Jocelyn Evans sent you a Dear John note—"

"She sent me an email," I say.

"And what did it say?"

"It was just short."

"What did it say?" the deputy barks out at me.

"That she made a mistake. That she needed some space."

"A mistake with you?"

I nod.

"So this space she's talking about—what does that mean to you?"

"I'm worried something happened to her."

"Because she broke up with you?"

"She didn't break up."

"Oh, no?" There's a smug grin on his face that I'd so like to wipe off with a hammer.

"She's just confused."

"Uh huh. So giving her a little space is going to her home and checking up on her?"

"Can I talk to the sheriff?"

The guy grabs my wrist and squeezes it so hard I start to see tiny stars. He shoves his face in mine, and I can smell onions on his breath.

"You listen to me. You leave that girl alone, you hear me? She's fine."

I wince and tug at my hand and he releases it.

"Her uncle—her step-uncle—"

"Yeah, yeah, I know about Wade," Kevin says. "Sheriff told me about the little altercation."

"I'm just worried that he might have done something."

"The sheriff told Helen that if they go anywhere or do anything, or if anything—anything—happens, to let him know. So she did."

"She did what?"

"Maybe it's not your business."

"I'm just worried about something happening to Jocelyn."

"Her aunt told Wells that they were going on a little trip. Called the morning after Christmas. Something happened. I don't know. Whatever you said or did musta left an impression. Because her aunt's gone bye-bye."

"Where?"

"Somewhere warm."

His smile mocks me.

"Did they say anything—"

"Enough of this," he snaps. "I have other things to do with my time than listen to some lovesick little boy. Enough. You got it?"

I nod.

"And you listen to me," Kevin says, his long, skinny finger pointing at me. "You come in here asking more questions or needing the sheriff or any of that, you're going to find trouble. You got that?"

I nod again and then stand up.

My wrist still hurts.

I leave the station and wish I were back in Illinois.

Alongside Jocelyn.

## 91. NOT A CLUE

Maybe there's truth in it.

Maybe every single thing related to Jocelyn doesn't have to be some deep, dark conspiracy.

After talking to the deputy, the overgrown brat of a boy who acts like he's still in high school, I decide to touch base with Poe and Rachel.

Poe is her normal aloof self on the phone, short and distant and claiming no knowledge of Jocelyn's whereabouts.

"She's been too busy lately to fill me in on her wonderful life," Poe says to me.

*Where'd that come from?*

Before saying good-bye I tell her to let me know if she hears from Jocelyn.

"I'll be *sure* to do that."

Which means that she won't give it another thought.

*What's up with girls? I mean, really?*

It takes a couple of phone calls to locate Rachel. I get her on her cell and she sounds out of breath. Says she's out of state at some outdoor mall shopping. She basically says the same thing as Poe, but in a nicer way.

Maybe Jocelyn's aunt did decide they should leave.

*But where'd that email come from?*

I don't believe it was from Jocelyn.

I don't believe that for a second.

Girls can be girls, sure. But not after Christmas Day. Not after everything that was said and done.

I see the leather band around my wrist. I make a fist, then release it. I do this a dozen more times.

Then I touch the band as if it's Jocelyn's hair.

*Where are you?*


Two days before New Year's Eve, the phone rings.

I jump up from the couch and the boring reality show I'm watching to grab the phone.

*It's her. She's going to tell me she's fine and she's in Florida and she just freaked out a bit like people do.*

"Hello?"

Hoping, praying, wanting, needing Jocelyn.

"Chris."

It's a female voice, but not Jocelyn. This voice sounds older. Lower. Even though she whispered, I know it's not Jocelyn.

"Yes?"

"Don't give up."

"Excuse me?"

"It's not too late to save her."

"Who is this?" I ask.

But then the phone clicks off.

"Who was that?" my mom asks from her room.

I stand with the phone in my hand, feeling the room start to turn like a ride at an amusement park.

"Just a telemarketer," I say.

*And, oh yeah, they're selling terror and insanity free of charge.*

I don't have a clue what I'm supposed to do now.

## 92. THE MOVIE STAR

I'm standing at the edge of a bridge that goes over the train tracks. It's not far up from the main strip of Solitary. My hands are in the pockets of my winter jacket. My cap is helping to keep me a little warmer. It's a brutally cold day, the last day of the year. The weather reminds me of Chicago. The sky is clear and getting dimmer. The cutting wind reminds me it's only going to get colder.

I'm waiting for someone or something. I don't know what. Maybe this was a ploy to get me to come here. Why, I don't know.

All I know is the handwritten message I received yesterday.

> Go to the east end of the Sommerville Bridge at 5:00 p.m. tomorrow, December 31. Wait there.
> Her life depends on it.

The message came via regular mail. The envelope was stamped and addressed to me. Mom gave it to me, assuming it might be from Jocelyn.

There was no name on it, however. No return address.

Nothing except the postmark where it was sent from.

Solitary.

Of course.

*The madness exists only in this little strange town. They're pumping something into the water that's making everybody crazy.*

I can't keep still, bouncing up and down and moving to keep the blood flowing.

This evening is quiet.

*Too quiet.*

I stare down the hill toward Solitary. It looks peaceful and innocent, like a little girl on the edge of the road with pigtails and a
lollipop, smiling.

*Why do I get this sick image of the little girl shoving the end of her
lollipop in my eye?*

The revving of an engine startles me and sends me to the side of the
road. The sound came across the bridge from the west side. It's a silver
SUV with tinted windows. Its lights are on, but I can't see who's driving.

It stops, and the passenger door opens.

"Get in," a voice orders.

A female voice.

The same one who called the other day.

I do as I'm told.

It helps that the pistol is in my jacket pocket. I keep my hand
buried inside it, holding on to the gun.

Just in case.

I have barely shut the door when the woman races down the
road and takes a sharp left, turning away from the town's main street.

The woman sitting across from me driving the Mercedes SUV—
the *new* Mercedes SUV, by the smell of it—looks like a movie star.
She's wearing a white winter cap, her long blonde hair falling out of
it past her shoulder. A white scarf is draped around her neck, falling
onto a long overcoat. Underneath the cap are shades that seem to
cover half her face.

She doesn't look at me, but stays focused on the road.

"What is this?" I finally say as I sway with the turns.

"Just hold on."

We drive for ten or fifteen minutes. The road we're on is familiar for a moment, but then she takes a turn or two that make me lost. She drives in silence, as fast as she can. The only thing I can see her doing is looking up in the mirror to see if anybody is behind us.

Soon we slow down and turn down a street that comes to a dead end in the middle of the woods.

She puts the car in neutral, then turns and faces me. "Listen to me," she says, her eyes hidden away like those of a rock star behind sunglasses. "You don't have much time."

"Much time for what?"

"Jocelyn's life is in danger."

"Where is she? Who are you?"

"It doesn't matter who I am."

The woman looks older, but I can't tell how much older. She looks tall and slender, her face white as a vampire.

"What matters is that you do what I tell you to do. If they think others are around, they might be scared and back out."

"They?" I ask. "Who are you talking about?"

"Chris, listen. There are things at work here that you can't begin to fathom—trust me on that."

"Who are you?"

"I was a friend of your uncle," she says.

I stare at her, speechless.

"Robert Kinner. Your mother's brother."

"Do you know where he is?"

She shakes her head, remaining silent for a moment.

"Is he involved in this?"

"Listen—I drove us out here so that we wouldn't be followed. But they're watching everyone they can."

"Who?"

"The ring. The leaders. There's no name. They just are."

"What do they want?"

"They want secrecy," the woman says. "That's all they care about. To keep their secrets from the rest of the world."

A part of me should probably be freaking out right now. I should probably open the handle to this door and sprint out shouting "Help!" For some reason, however, I'm relatively relaxed.

*As relaxed as someone with his hand on a gun might be.*

"You need to get their attention somehow. But you also need to not get caught. Just listen. I'm going to leave you here, and you need to walk a mile downhill. Through the woods. A straight shot. No turns, nothing. Just head directly downhill and you'll see it."

"See what?"

"An open area in the woods. Used to be a campground. Now it's used for other things."

"Other things?"

"You have to be careful not to be seen. But you must try to get their attention. It won't be a very large group. They always meet like this before the ceremony. Their own version of a prayer meeting. Make sure they know they're being watched, then get away from them. Get away, and maybe—just maybe—it will work."

"What ceremony? What will work?"

"I want you to scare them."

I didn't pretend to understand. There was only one thing I wanted to know. "Where's Jocelyn?"

"She's there."

"She's with them?"

"Yes. Trust me."

"Why are you telling me this?"

"Because of—because of who you are. Because of who your uncle was."

"I don't—"

My voice trails off because I don't know what to say.

She reaches across me and opens the handle to my door. I climb out and then shut it. The window rolls down as those large sunglasses face me.

"Don't underestimate yourself, Chris. You'll be surprised what you're capable of doing." She shifts the car back into drive and tears down the gravel road.

## 93. SWALLOWED WHOLE

It's dark now.

I'm walking through the woods, carrying the gun now, making sure that I don't trip over something and accidentally shoot myself. The safety is on, but still—I don't like guns. Never have and never will. I'm beginning not to like other things, like the forest and shadows and hills and nighttime.

I replay what happened over and over again. The woman in

the white cap and scarf and sunglasses telling me what to do in the middle of nowhere. Telling me she knew my uncle. Telling me that I need to save Jocelyn.

*Save her from what?*

I know the answer to that, but don't want to utter it. I don't want to think it. Saying it or thinking it might mean that it could actually happen.

And all of this—every little bit of this—feels both like a nightmare and a dream coming true.

Jocelyn is the dream.

What's happening to her is the nightmare.

I'm stuck in the middle, just some stupid sixteen-year-old kid thinking that I know better and I can be better, but really just completely terrified.

I do as I'm told and walk down the hill. I'm walking for about ten minutes, maybe longer, when I see flickers of light.

The forest begins to thin, and I soon reach the edge of the trees. They open up to a clearing the size of half a soccer field. I look out and then wonder if what I'm looking at is real.

I see maybe half a dozen people—maybe more—wearing dark robes. At first I think they're black robes, but as my eyes adjust, I see that they're red.

*Of course they're red.*

They remind me of the robes I've seen on pictures of the Ku Klux Klan, with hoods that have slits for eyes.

There are lights scattered around this area, small lanterns hanging on beams. The people all stand facing the same way, as if they're waiting on someone. I don't hear a thing, and that in itself creeps me out.

Just a bunch of people standing there in dark robes in the middle of the dark night.

Then I see another figure—this one in white.

*Is this some kind of Klan group, a variation on it? Some crazy hillbillies up to weirdness?*

I still can't hear anything, but it seems like the figure in white—hood and all—is addressing the group. There're eight of them.

I shiver, feeling heaviness. Feeling despair. Feeling light-headed and cold and burning at the same time.

*Where's Jocelyn, and what does she have to do with this?*

I watch for a few minutes.

The person in white is talking—I know this. But I can't hear anything. I'm not close enough.

*Get out of here, Chris.*

I don't need someone to tell me that there are weird things in the world. I have the Internet for that.

But in front of me—in my face, in my lap, in my hands—all of this feels out of my control.

I try and figure out what I'm supposed to do.

*Get their attention. Scare them.*

That's what she said. Get their attention and then get out of here. Easier said than done.

*I can outrun a bunch of freaks in robes, no problem.*

I consider throwing something out there. Then I think of maybe firing a shot in the air—I have several bullets left. That would get their attention. That would make them think twice about having their weird little—

"Hey!"

The voice shakes me, causing me to jerk and slam the side of my stomach into a broken tree branch. It scrapes and punctures my skin.

"What are you doing here!" the voice shouts. "Hey! Someone's over here hiding out! What are you doing?"

I see the outline of a robed figure standing only a few feet away from me.

The group at the center of the field are turning, some of them running toward us.

Then he's on me.

A hand takes me by the throat and tightens, and I take both hands, including the one holding the gun, and flail them toward the figure's head.

Somehow I get the hood off.

I see a face I don't recognize.

A face with a sparse beard and mustache, the face of a kid who's gotta be my age, maybe older.

He lessens his grip.

Then he plants an elbow in my gut.

The gun goes off, and the guy howls as he lets go of me and reaches for his side. He curses as I look down as if the gunshot came from someone else.

I didn't mean to shoot it.

It just went off.

I want to say this to him, but then he launches himself at me and grabs my hands and tries to get the gun away from me.

We roll around in the ground, and his robe gets caught on a branch. I slip out of his hands and kick him somewhere on his body as I take off running back from where I came from, away from the field and this guy I just shot and the others who are coming.

I can hear voices.

Shouts.

I tear through the woods, the trees, branches hitting me, the night shaking all around, the shadows smothering, the air I'm trying to breathe getting thinner and thinner.

I don't turn around.

I don't dare drop the pistol.

I think I still hear voices, but maybe they're just in my head.

I hear my own breathing—sucking, panting, ragged, harried— as I bolt over a log, pound a shoulder into a limb, get swatted by a branch.

I run for an eternity.

I run so fast I can't think.

The only thing that stops me is something jutting out from the snow-and-leaf covered forest floor.

I fly for a moment and land in something soft and cold.

Thankfully the gun in my hand doesn't go off again.

My heart beats so fast I feel like it's exploding in my mouth.

My ears ring. My body shakes.

I listen for any movement, but don't hear anything.

I wait. For an hour or more. I don't know for sure.

I feel dizzy and electric.

Part of me wants to close my eyes and close them for a good long time.

For a moment I keep them open, wide open, waiting, watching.

The stillness covers and coats and swallows.

I'm fighting the darkness, and soon I can't help it. I drift off.

# 94. THE REMINDER

Sometime later—I don't know how much later—my eyes open. It takes me a while to regain my senses and remember where I am.

*I have no idea where I'm at.*

After a bit I start moving again.

I walk carefully through the woods, my side hurting. It doesn't just ache like it got hit. It throbs as if the cut is deep. I know that it's bleeding.

I have no idea where I am—I could be in South Carolina as far as I know. I just know that I'm far away from that open field with the disturbed folks playing Halloween.

The first thing I'll do when I come to a town is find somebody—anybody—who will listen to me.

I'm going to tell them to take me to the nearest police station where I'm going to tell everything.

This is insane.

Enough's enough.

If they won't listen, someone will.

I'll send an email to the entire world and get someone to respond.

This little backside that nobody knows about needs to get revealed. The world needs to know.

There are some sickos here and they need help.

Jocelyn—if she's a part of this in any way—needs help.

I need help.

And then, as if my unspoken prayers were answered by an unseen god, the forest opens to a clearing, and I see a house.

Jocelyn's house.

"You gotta be kidding," I say aloud.

No way.

I laugh, and it hurts.

I don't see anybody around—still no lights on, no car parked outside. It's just like I saw it a couple of days ago.

I'm going to break down a door and see if I find anything. Then if I don't, I'm going to call the cops and tell them I need help.

When I get to the door, I'm glad I try the handle again.

This time the door opens with ease.

As if someone wants me to go inside.


I move slowly, quietly, as if someone's here. I'm almost surprised when I find a switch and flick on the lights and see that there's still power.

The house looks the same. Nothing unusual.

"Hello?"

I call out several times but don't hear anything.

*What if Jocelyn's in the back? What if she's in her bedroom and she's all rig—*

I shut up the voice. I'm holding the gun in my right hand and I'm ready. The safety is off and the gun's ready. Ready to at least show someone that I'm ready.

*Ready to pretend like I'm ready because I'm not ready and I'll never be ready.*

I find a phone and pick it up with my other hand.

There's no tone.

Either someone didn't pay their phone bill, or someone cut out the phone line all together.

"Jocelyn?" I call out as I walk back to the bedrooms.

Maybe Wade is here, waiting.

*And maybe you're stupid for coming back.*

I know now the reason filmmakers make people do stupid things in movies. Because in real life, people *do* stupid things. People run ahead when they really should run away. People open the door when it should always, always remain shut. People enter the room when they really should exit the building.

My breathing is haggard like an old man's. I'm really scared and suddenly realize my whole body is shaking. My back and my forehead are sweaty, yet my hands and face are still numb from the cold outside.

I turn on the light and see Jocelyn's bedroom.

This is the first time I've ever been inside it.

It looks pretty basic. No pictures on the walls, no theme going on. I open a sliding closet door and see her clothes hanging there. Same for the drawers in her dresser.

Everything's here. Nothing looks like she's gone on some long trip.

If I had time I'd search carefully for clues. But I don't.

There's a small desk alongside the wall; her laptop sits on it. I open it to see if there's anything inside it. Maybe to see if I can access her email.

After a few minutes of trying, I see that they don't have Internet, either.

I look at her emails and find a lone message that doesn't have a recipient. It's a message that looks ready to send.

I click on it and see my name at the top.

> CHRIS:
> IT'S GOING TO HAPPEN BEFORE THE NEW YEAR.
> THIS IS ALL I KNOW.
> THE PLAN IS FOR IT TO BE AT THE PLACE I TOLD
>     YOU ABOUT.
> THE DEVIL IS STRONG HERE.
> DON'T DOUBT THIS.
> DON'T DOUBT THAT HE'S REAL.

There's nothing else. No name, no sign-off, nothing.

I read it again.

*The place I told you about.*

I think about this for a moment and then remember.

So much has happened in these last couple of months, in these last few weeks.

Sometimes a kiss can cover up a gravestone.

Sometimes a friendship can overcome temptation.

Sometimes an embrace can overshadow the hurt.

I remember where she took me that one day, the place beyond her house in the woods at the top of the mountain.

Her bedside clock says it's ten.

I try to make sense of the time, but nothing makes sense.

Nothing.

I just know that I need to get up on that mountain.

Maybe, just maybe, it's all in Jocelyn's mind.

Maybe I did enough—like the woman in shades told me to do—to scare the people in the robes off.

I shut off Jocelyn's computer, turn around, and head out of her room when something else on her desk catches my attention.

It's a photo. A slightly off-colored printout of a photo of the two of us.

The photo that was taken on Christmas Day by my mom.

Jocelyn looks happy and at peace. She looks like love.

I fold up the photo and put it in my pocket, then I scramble out of the house and back into the dark pit of night.

## 95. STRONGER THAN THE NIGHT

I run through the dark woods.

And I see her smile.

A branch swats me in the face. A limb tears my coat and cuts my arm. My foot pounds against something hard on the forest floor. The wound in my side from the tree branch still throbs, wet with blood. I know my hands are stained with it—some my own and some not.

I hear her laugh.

I'm sprinting uphill, sucking in air, sweating. It doesn't feel like December. It doesn't feel like New Year's Eve.

Then again, nothing feels right. Nothing has felt right since coming to this godforsaken place.

*The Devil is strong here,* her voice tells me. *Don't doubt this.*

I feel her hand in mine, gripping, shaking.

She said this would happen, but I still find myself in disbelief, hoping I'll wake up, hoping the cold is just from the night air in my tiny cabin bedroom.

I want to look at my watch, but I don't dare.

Every moment is precious. Every second counts.

Endless trees seem to hover in the dead of night, guarding what is just beyond. Wind whips their skeletal limbs, whips my face.

Three months ago, I didn't know her.

Three months ago, I didn't know anyone like her even existed.

Three months ago, I didn't have the faintest idea what the word *love* meant.

But as I run, I know this: I'm willing to give my life for this girl.

I'm sixteen with what I hope will be a long life ahead of me, but I'm willing to give it up, to give anything to let her live, to let her make it through this night.

"Please, God," I call out.

But God is a stranger to this place. And to my heart.

I recall her words.

"I believe."

But I don't. I never wanted to—not then, and not now.

A light cuts through the woods.

I'm close.

The gun is still lodged in my hand.

I know I'll use it again. I don't care.

All I care about is getting to her.

The wind howls in anger.

There are forces at work stronger than the darkness. Stronger than the wind. Stronger than the night.

I know this now: There is evil in the world.

And in this place.

The glow gets brighter, illuminating the towering trees around me.

I don't slow down.

I'm almost at the top.

I'm ready to kill.

I'm ready to die.

I'm ready to rescue her.

My searing legs finally reach the top of the hill where the fire rages, where the winds whip, where the night sky explodes above me.

And then I see Jocelyn.


## 96. FINALITY


*My bride waits in the glowing circle, waiting for me to rescue her and reclaim her as my own.*

Everything up to this moment has been manageable. It hasn't all made sense, but I've been able to get through it. My mother's nightmares and the sound of the wind at night and the strange tracks on the deck. The secrets and guilt that Jocelyn has carried. Her past, her present. The town secrets and the darkness and the strange premonitions.

All of this has seemed manageable.

*Maybe I've just deluded myself and convinced myself of a lie.*

But now, standing at the edge of the woods, seeing Jocelyn, I know that it's all changed.

Nothing is manageable.

I spot her a mile away.

She is a vision in white. The fires that surround her make her glow.

They also make the figures in red stand out like blood on a dove.

Everything changes—I change.

I don't feel my feet running toward the circle of stones. I don't feel my heart thumping and my breath stopping and my pulse racing as I sprint across the field.

I don't hear my voice screaming out her name.

I no longer care about anything.

There's no fear holding me back.

There's no shadow causing me to slow down.

I reach Jocelyn and feel her and know.

She's gone.

She knew this would happen all along, but I gave her the worst thing one could have in this sick and twisted world.

I gave her hope.

I don't hear my voice screaming out because the wind swallows it whole.

I don't feel the tears streaming down my cheeks.

I no longer have any idea where the gun is. I dropped it in my terror and rage.

I'm at the base of a large stone rock holding her cold, lifeless body. All around her are dry chunks of wood, all lined up as if they're part of bonfire.

Jocelyn is here, tied to this big boulder, wearing a white dress like a bride.

Her throat and wrists slashed.

Slashed some time ago.

I want to throw up, but I can't.

I want to slash my own throat and wrists, but I can't manage to even look out of my blurry, messy eyes.

I shake. And convulse.

I'm screaming.

A hand touches me. Somewhere.

I would like to think I still held my gun, but I don't. I'd like to think I'd break out fighting and beat the whole lot of them, but I'm weak and worthless.

I crumble to the ground right beneath where Jocelyn's body is tied.

"Chris," a voice says.

I feel snot and tears and sweat all clumping on my face.

I'm shivering like a pathetic dog.

"Chris, look at me."

The voice is familiar.

I look up and see the figure hidden in white. Behind him stand figures in red, all holding burning torches. Figures I ignored as I rushed to Jocelyn. Twenty or thirty in all, maybe more.

"Listen to my words carefully, boy. Listen and remember."

I can't stop shaking.

Something in me is gone. Something in me—a very vital part of living and breathing—has simply disappeared.

"Listen right here. We don't need you. You leave, and we'll forget you. Do you understand? We'll let you go because we don't need you. This has nothing to do with you, Chris Buckley. Never has."

I hear something that sounds like a wounded, dying animal.

Sobs. Gasping, ghastly sobs.

They come from me.

"We can do this to your mother, Chris. To your father. We can do this to anybody who means anything to you. But not to you. You will be forced to live through it. Hell is not dying, Chris. It's knowing. It's knowing and living."

I sink to the ground and put my head down and want to die.

A hand grabs my hair and forces my head up.

"You'll live and you'll know, Chris. And you won't tell another single soul. Do you understand?"

I nod.

"Do you understand?"

"Yes," says the voice of some wrecked person. Is it my voice?

The hand lets me go, and I collapse into a pile of mush.

"Leave and never discuss this again."

I stand.

I shake.

"Now," the voice orders.

Jocelyn is there, right in front of me, that sweet angelic face. Beauty like I've never known. A soul larger than life, a soul just trying to make it by.

A soul that loved me.

*I let you down.*

*I let you go.*

*I let you die.*

"Now!"

I glance at Jocelyn one last time then start to walk away.

As I near the edge of the trees I start to turn, but I can't.

I hear the crackling of an inferno behind me.

I see the glare of the smoldering blaze move along the sides of the trees.

I want to turn around, but I can't.

I don't see what's happening. I already know.

The smell of black, hellish smoke reaches my nose, and I double over and throw up what little there is in my stomach.

Then I turn around and see the bonfire.

The flames reach the heavens, as if daring them to do something about it.

97. ...

The shivering doesn't stop.

Even when I'm home, some time much later, and when I'm under my sheets with the door locked and the pillow over my head.

The shivering won't stop.

My body won't stop grieving.

I want to shut off my mind, but it's still somewhere in those dark woods.

It's too far behind to make sense of anything.

My heart is frozen, cracked, chipped, lifeless.

And as for my soul—

That's the thing that went missing the moment I saw what happened to Jocelyn.

I'll never be the same.

Regardless of whether I have one day left or twenty thousand, I'll never be the same.

# 98. My Private Place

The sun comes up.

The skies open up.

The new year arrives.

It's midday and I've asked Mom if I can borrow the car to go into town.

She has no idea, not a clue about the hell I've walked through.

I don't want her to know.

I can't let her know.

They threatened me, and I didn't believe it.

I believe now.

I park alongside the tracks and then walk down them until I reach the old railroad signal.

I walk through woods and get to where the growth subsides.

I see the old barn.

Perhaps I should know better—perhaps I should do something—perhaps I should do nothing. I don't know. All I know is that I'm here and I'm doing this.

Not for answers.

But for myself.

As I walk on the dirt road that leads to the barn, I see a creature standing there as if guarding the building.

It's a wolf.

*It's the same wolf that I saw that day in the woods by the creek.*

It's gray and tall and beautiful.

It stands there, and part of me wants it to attack me.

I wouldn't fight it. Not today. And not tomorrow.

I'd let it slash my throat and my wrists. Almost gladly.

Instead, it stares me down for a moment, then it bolts off into the woods.

I continue down the path, reaching the opening to the barn.

Part of me is afraid of what I'll find.

Then again, I'll never be afraid again.

When you lose something so close and personal, there's nothing left to worry about losing.

I reach the stall and see that the door is shut.

As I look inside, I don't see or hear anything.

I check out the hay, but don't find anything in it.

The little puppy is gone.

I curse, and I wish there was a god above me to hear it. Because it's Him I'm talking to.

Not even the puppy.

Not even this little, tiny creature named Midnight that made Jocelyn happy.

*Why?*

I don't get it.

*Why?*

Then I hear a shuffling sound. There's something behind the wood of the stall I'm standing in.

And I see it.

A little black face. Bold black eyes. A wagging tongue. A flat little nose.

Midnight bolts out of an opening in the wood and rushes toward me, wagging her tail.

I pick her up and hold her in my hands. The dog feels like it weighs two pounds. She's shivering. I know that she's sick—I don't have to be a doctor to tell.

"I'm here, it's okay," I say as I hold her. I sit down in the stall and gently rub Midnight's fur. I feel her body shaking.

That's when I start to cry.

It's the first time all day that I've done so.

Maybe it's just that I wanted to be alone—to be far alone in my own private place.

I weep tears I didn't think I had in me as I think about Jocelyn.

Midnight licks my hands.

I look toward an open window that peers out past the woods into the open sky.

"Why?"

I don't need to address the one I'm talking to. If He's there, He can hear me.

"Why?" is all I ask.

I just want to know.

I want to know why I got so close to saving someone and yet …

And yet.

Midnight looks up at me.

"I'm going to take good care of you, got that? Nothing's going to happen to you. Nothing at all."

I wipe my eyes and look at the four walls surrounding me.

Then I see something at the edge of the stall. Something dark—a book.

It's the Bible that I gave to Jocelyn.

Inside is a letter.

I keep the Bible shut and pick up Midnight, then leave.

I already feel watched.

Now that I know that Midnight is here and alive, I want to take her to get her warm and to get some food in her.

Then I'll look at the Bible and what's inside it.

Maybe.

## 99. HOLD ON

There's a town full of mysteries out there. A town just outside my door.

A town full of evil.

I sit in my bedroom, full of questions, full of fear, feeling alone.

I finally pull out the Bible that I gave Jocelyn. The Bible that my father gave me. I slip open the letter and read it.

It's not dated. It's in her handwriting.

*Dear Chris,*

*If you're reading this letter, it probably means that the worst has happened. That the bad has outshadowed the good. It means that what I thought might happen did.*

*So let me tell you this.*

*I'm not afraid.*

*And I believe, without a doubt, that I'm in a better place. A place where there's only good. A place where I no longer have to fear—or regret—or apologize—or run.*

*I believe in this place, Chris.*

*You gave me this Bible, and it provided answers.*

*You gave me your heart, too, and it provided hope.*

*Hope that someone could love me unconditionally.*

*So I give them both back to you.*

*I give you this book because you not only need answers, Chris, you also need hope.*

*This whole dark world needs hope.*

*Hold on to it.*

*And hold on to the other thing I gave you.*

*Something you've had for a while now.*

*My heart.*

*Take good, special care of yourself.*

*Perhaps Midnight will be a comfort to you like she's been to me.*

*I love you. Thank you for loving me back.*

*I have to believe that love continues. I believe it will. And I believe that I'll be able to watch out for you.*

*Jocelyn*

I fold up the letter and feel like she's right there, talking to me. *Maybe she is.*

I look at the Bible and don't know whether to toss it in the woods or open it up and start reading. I decide to do neither.

I stay there, sitting on the floor next to my bed where a stuffed and happy Midnight is curled up. I stay there for some time, thinking of the letter, thinking what it means.

Wondering what tomorrow will bring.

## ... a little more ...

When a delightful concert comes to an end,

the orchestra might offer an encore.

When a fine meal comes to an end,

it's always nice to savor a bit of dessert.

When a great story comes to an end,

we think you may want to linger.

And so, we offer ...

**AfterWords**—just a little something more after you

have finished a David C. Cook novel.

We invite you to stay awhile in the story.

Thanks for reading!

Turn the page for ...

- **Three Recommended Playlists**
- **Behind the Book: Some Kind of Wonderful**
- **A Snapshot**

# THREE RECOMMENDED PLAYLISTS

SOLITARY PLAYLIST #1:
FOR THE WALKMAN

1. "Oscillate Wildly" by The Smiths
2. "Leave in Silence" by Depeche Mode
3. "Watch Me Bleed" by Tears For Fears
4. "Someone Somewhere in Summertime" by Simple Minds
5. "Invisible Sun" by The Police
6. "Oomingmak" by Cocteau Twins
7. "Please, Please, Please Let Me Get What I Want" by The Smiths
8. "Thieves Like Us (Instrumental version)" by New Order
9. "Just One Kiss" by The Cure
10. "Souvenir" by Orchestral Maneuvers in the Dark
11. "But Not Tonight" by Depeche Mode
12. "Musette and Drums" by Cocteau Twins
13. "There Is a Light That Never Goes Out" by The Smiths

SOLITARY PLAYLIST #2: FOR THE iPOD

1. "Black Mirror" by Arcade Fire
2. "Losing Touch" by The Killers
3. "Houses" by Great Northern

4. "Come Alive" by Foo Fighters

5. "Ghosts" by Ladytron

6. "Until the Night Is Over" by M83

7. "Hearts on Fire" by Cut Copy

8. "Theft, and Wandering Around Lost" by Cocteau Twins

9. "Highway of Endless Dreams" by M83

10. "If You Were Here" by Cary Brothers

11. "Wait for Me" by Moby

12. "Beautiful" by Ruth Ann

13. "Strangers In The Wind" by Cut Copy

14. "2-1" by Imogen Heap

15. "Alice" by Cocteau Twins


## SOLITARY PLAYLIST #3: FOR THE MOVIE

1. "Be a Good Boy" by Thomas Newman (from the *Little Children* soundtrack)

2. "Twin Peaks Theme" by Angelo Badalamenti

3. "Eli and Oscar" by Johan Söderqvist (from the *Let the Right One In* soundtrack)

4. "Any Other Name" by Thomas Newman (from the *American Beauty* soundtrack)

5. "Oscar In Love" by Johan Söderqvist (from the *Let The Right One In* soundtrack)

6. "Cool at Heart" by Tangerine Dream (from the *Melrose* album)

7. "Bruise" by Thomas Newman (from the *Flesh and Bone* soundtrack)

8. "Town of Austere" by Alexander Malter (from the *Fireflies In the Garden* soundtrack)

9.   "The First Goodbye" by David Helpling and Jon Jenkins (from the *Treasure* album)

10. "Night Life in Twin Peaks" by Angelo Badalamenti (from the *Twin Peaks* soundtrack)

11. "Be with You" by James Newton Howard (from *The Happening* soundtrack)

12. "Leaving Hope" by Nine Inch Nails (from *Still* album)

13. "The Letter That Never Came" by Thomas Newman (from *Lemony Snicket's A Series of Unfortunate Events* soundtrack)

# BEHIND THE BOOK: SOME KIND OF WONDERFUL

One of the reasons I'm a novelist is because of John Hughes. The director of eighties classics like *Ferris Bueller's Day Off* and *Sixteen Candles* inspired my love of both film and storytelling. It wasn't just that he captured moments of the era I grew up in; it was that he captured the soul of a teenager.

Three movies stand out to me: *The Breakfast Club, Pretty in Pink,* and *Some Kind of Wonderful.*

As someone who attended four different high schools, I felt like I had four completely different high school experiences. I had different personas for each of the schools I went to. At times I was a jock, a rebel, an outcast, or part of the popular clique. All along I saw myself in John Hughes's films. The agony of being a teen, the thrill of falling in love, the angst of saying good-bye, and the utter hilarity of being a teenager.

The music and mood of these films helped define my teenage years. My life could have been a John Hughes film. I wanted to be Blane from *Pretty in Pink,* but really I was Duckie. I spent my fair share of time in detention, yet I wasn't as cool nor did I have one-liners like John Bender. I was always falling in love and making cassette tapes based on that love. I was that kid with the giant posters of musical groups plastered all over his bedroom walls.

John Hughes died on August 6, 2009, when I was still writing *Solitary.* I had already pitched this series as part *Pretty in Pink* and part scary movie. I wanted to detail some of my high school experiences with these books.

I believe the first eighteen years of a person's life define the remaining ones. I was such a naïve kid when I was in high school, but that's the beauty of that time. I didn't know the big, bad world, and in ways, I was fortunate for it.

When I look back at those John Hughes films, there's a certainly amount of naïveté about them. But there's also a lot of heart. That's what teen movies lack today: that passionate, beating heart.

This series is a nod to those years, and to one of the men who helped shape them.

This ninth grader didn't do anything noteworthy except for one thing: writing and finishing his first novel. Titled *The Adventurer*, it was written in pencil on notebook pages. While he never tried to get it published, the author realized that if he could do this once, he could do it again.

For more information on Travis Thrasher,
visit www.TravisThrasher.com.